Moments

Of Favor

DANIEL BERGNER

SIMON & SCHUSTER
NEW YORK LONDON TORONTO SYDNEY TOKYO SINGAPORE

Simon & Schuster
Simon & Schuster Building
Rockefeller Center
1230 Avenue of the Americas
New York, New York 10020

10 9 8 7 6 5 4 3 2 1

Library of Congress Cataloging in Publication Data

Bergner, Daniel.
    Moments of favor / Daniel Bergner.
        p. cm.
    I. Title.
    PS3552.E719345M6   1991
    813'.54—dc20   90-22311
                                                                  CIP

ISBN 0-671-70457-5

FOR NANCY

ACKNOWLEDGMENTS

Many thanks are due my agent, Suzanne Gluck, my editor, Trish Lande, and my friends Bill Hogeland, Cynthia Kadohata, and Robert Riger for their help in seeing this book through. I would also like to thank two great teachers, Stephen Koch and Verlin Cassill. And I would like to express, for my parents, immeasurable gratitude.

One

THAT WAS THE SUMMER THE CITY FILLED WITH RELIGIOUS RECRUIT-
ers. Or so it seemed to Peter. Possibly they had been there all
along, but suddenly he was aware of the gray-suited mission-
aries on the corner, handing out their hopeful, colorless
leaflets, and of the preacher down by the record store he
sometimes went to. "You got to activate your faith," the man
warned through his microphone and little amplifier set up on
the island park in the middle of the avenue. "You got to bring
it out from the nooks and crannies. You got to drag it down
from the attic, you got to haul it up from the basement, and
don't tell me you don't have no attic or no basement, that I
don't know you city folks, I *do*, you know what I'm saying, you
got to carry it out from wherever you hide it, and dust it off
and polish it up and *oil* it. . . ."

Peter could hardly have told you what the preacher looked
like. He was wary of staring in that direction. Even his glances

were quick and cautious. But he heard the man's words over and over that summer, and found himself repeating them in his head—"You got to activate your faith. You got to activate your faith"—thoughtlessly, nonsensically, laughably, he realized, especially since he had no particular religious background or feeling to put back into use.

And then there were the chanters, not necessarily religious in the technical sense of the term, though they might as well have been. They—thirty, forty of them—were in the schoolyard at dusk; another, smaller group went through their rituals in Riverside Park at noon. They wore white tennis shorts and white T-shirts, and they did jumping jacks and jogged in place and clapped their hands in intricate rhythms, all the time barking out foreign-sounding syllables. It was like a blend of Marine Corps boot camp and Zen center meditation session. "Come join us," one of the leaders said to Peter, rolling a flyer and slipping it through the chain-link fence, though Peter was only one of a dozen people who'd stopped to watch. "Chant for Well-Being!" he read, as he walked away.

He heard, too, the team of radical black evangelists on Broadway in the theater district. "The Bible speaks of the triangle of white evil, and these are its points: America, Europe, and Australia! It's an ugly, misshaped triangle! It's stretched out mean and weak! And it's time to break that triangle's spell!" Perhaps a hundred blacks and seven whites blocked the busy corner to listen, and steadily people drifted off and were replaced, so that within fifteen minutes the audience of a hundred and seven was almost completely new, and Peter, glancing around him, stepped away from the crowd and down off the curb, as if he hadn't been transfixed by the sermon's energy (to the point that its words could have been perfect gibberish), as if he'd only been waiting for a break in the cars or for the crossing light to change.

And he noticed that the Hare Krishnas were in revival, that

10

they were parked around the city in specially designed trucks. The trucks opened into concert stages. The Krishnas had given up parading through Central Park playing tam-tams and tambourines; they'd gone into retreat and reemerged with soft rock. They had synthesizers and drum machines and electric guitars, and the vocalists sang to mellow, modernized versions of the Krishna jingle.

And the Jehovah's Witnesses were coming to Peter's door.

And one morning, when the alarm on his clock radio went off, he heard Al Green telling the story of his second birth.

But it wasn't until early October, in that year toward the middle of the 1980s, that Peter had any prolonged, personal contact with the recruiters. It happened on Fourteenth Street. A woman stopped him.

"Excuse me," she said, and, unhurried, "Can I ask you one question?"

She looked like Carly Simon. For a moment he thought she *was* Carly Simon. The moment quickly passed. But he preserved the dim residue of the idea, a faint fanciful notion that she had heard him at the Tillman or on tape, and that she would take him under her wing, launching, or re-launching, his career. Never mind the problem of her recognizing him two and a half years after the concert, or the *impossibility* of it if she'd only heard one of his demos. He stepped toward her.

"The only thing is," she explained apologetically, "you have to shut your eyes."

Clearly, she wasn't the singer, and certainly it wasn't smart to stand with his eyes closed on Fourteenth Street. Nevertheless, he did.

"Okay," she said. "What do you hear?"

"I don't know."

"Listen."

"That radio."

"You don't hear the ocean?"

"The *ocean?*" He opened his eyes. One of her large front teeth was stained purple along its bottom edge, as if she had been bruised there.

"I thought I heard the ocean."

"I don't know." He tried to hear it, to glean the hoarse whisper of the surf beneath the radio's blaring, or to find it in other noises. The loud sigh of a bus did sound something like it.

"Well." She smiled with the stained front tooth. She wasn't Carly Simon, but she was just as beautiful. "Anyway," she said, "I want to invite you somewhere."

"Where?"

"To a meeting."

"What kind of meeting?"

"A meeting of very special, interesting people."

"I see."

"It's just a discussion group."

"What do you discuss?"

"Important things. History. Religion."

"What kind of religion?"

"An old religion."

"How old?"

"Very," she said.

He thanked her and told her he was busy. He started away. But what he wanted more than anything was to go with her, to be escorted by the beautiful woman into the rigors of whatever faith she adhered to. The desire dissipated fast. He was rational, well-educated, intelligent. He laughed silently at his own longing. Still, as he rode the subway home, he stared at the advertisements and saw calls to salvation. Beauty schools, business schools, computer schools, even the cigarette and liquor ads were promises of rebirth. He wished he was more susceptible, that he was blind enough to believe a little in the metamorphic powers of a particular brand of scotch.

Off the subway at Ninety-sixth Street, he walked up the station stairs, up Broadway, and turned west. Through the wrought-iron gate, and inside his garden floor apartment, he went, by habit, straight to the phone machine. The tiny flashing light never failed to stir hope. He pressed the playback button. There was a hang-up, and a brief, somewhat timid hello from his father. "Just checking in, pal," his father said.

These were followed by his old friend Glickstein. "Yo, dude. It's Derek. Long time. I know it's my fault. I haven't been in touch. I'm sorry. I've just been incredibly busy. Anyway, Michael's having a party tonight, a cocktail party for his birthday, and, uh, the godfather's going to be there. I told Michael to put you on the guest list. So put on your high-heeled sneakers—seven o'clock, the Helmsford—and I will see you *ce soir*. *Adiós,* dude."

And then the machine went back to listening.

Two

THE HELMSFORD IS ONE OF THE GREAT OLD CASTLES ON CENTRAL Park West, but that night, at Michael's party, there were plenty of complaints about the setting. The criticisms began with the building in general and got as particular as the wallpaper in the apartment's front bathroom. In between were the lobby, which was said to be surprisingly small; the elevator, which had gorgeous cherry paneling but no chandelier or velvet-cushioned bench, and no operator; the living-room ceiling, which was not quite as high as certain ceilings certain guests had seen, and not as ornately sculpted; and the placement of that Turner, which was lost on that wall. The furniture, too, was poorly received. There was skepticism and disapproval. It was suggested that two too many Louis Seize chairs crowded the living room, and that the room was too bare, that the couches were insufficiently grand, and that they should have been more demure, that the rug should have been less elaborately patterned, and that it was strangely plain. And the food, for a cocktail party, was deemed excessive.

All these observations were made quietly, within clusters. Peter heard them as he drifted from acquaintance to acquaintance, from the periphery of one conversation to the mute circumference of another, and he *over*heard them as well, when he ran out of acquaintances to stand near, and posed, as nonchalantly as possible, by himself. At first, he was heartened by the critiques. At least these people had eyes. At least they hadn't forsaken every ounce of judgment. At least they were letting themselves be disappointed, not deciding everything was perfect, not insisting on their fantasies. But then he realized he'd given them too much credit. Their criticisms were like nervous ticks, unwilled efforts to rid themselves of tension, to keep themselves calm in Michael Marr's presence.

He, Peter, was willing to be impressed by the apartment, to admit its flaws were few and even fabricated by Michael's guests, to admire the sheer size of the front rooms and their storybook view, because he, Peter, was not in awe of Michael himself.

Oh, he scorned the others, smirked inwardly at their fault-finding, remembered the morning almost three years ago when Michael had arrived at Palmer. He'd transferred from Yale in the middle of his junior year. Peter had been a senior, his building two doors down from where Michael would be living. For months Palmer's students had been in a flush of anticipation over Michael's coming, but that morning it was mostly locals from the surrounding New England city who crowded in with the journalists, waiting for Michael to show; the students, hopeful, ambitious, were discreet. Not that they'd always been so subtle. The previous Sunday the local paper had run a special insert on the history of the Marrs, and that was the one Sunday students bought the *Courier* in addition to the *Globe* or the *Times*. The insert didn't have anything everyone didn't already know, but everyone read eagerly, rapturously, anyway—about the grandfather, the wealthy inventor and manufacturer; and of course about Michael's father, Walter Norman Marr, the leader of pure promise, the perpetual President-elect, dead two weeks before his inauguration; and about Michael, his childhood, his adolescence, his young adulthood. There was the story of the grandfather's first lucrative invention, talons, the tongue-and-grooves that fasten the waists of men's pants, and the old, accompanying joke about Walter Marr's philandering while in Congress and later as Governor of New York and right through his campaign for President—he hadn't been able to keep his pants on. And there were the usual references to political opportunism, to tactics that were less than ethical and deals that were clearly illegal. Yet the writing was reverent. Even the damning and unflattering details seemed to add to the general glow. It was as if the glorious memory of Walter Norman Marr—handsome and clear-voiced, deeply caring and at the same time vigorously pragmatic, a great advocate of social justice and an aggressive patriot—were all the more wonderful for defying the evidence of abuses and flaws.

A month before that Sunday insert in the *Courier, Life's* cover story had been on the twentieth anniversary of the President-elect's death. The first picture was of the funeral, at graveside, Michael's face still touched by infancy yet twisted by what might have been sudden understanding, a glimmer of comprehension, a surge of permanent loss; the last showed the son twenty years later, at twenty-one, unveiling a monument to his father.

Now, at the party, Peter heard a woman tell her date, "If you have to stand by yourself, can't you do it like you mean to, like that guy over there?"

That guy over there was Peter, and it was true the woman's date wasn't doing very well. He was extremely handsome, with

16

loose curls of black hair that fell almost to his shoulders, but Peter had wondered if he might actually be tripping. The man had been staring at the ceiling with his head tipped far back, as if gazing at constellations. He'd even spun around a few times, slowly, with his head back like that, as if inspired by the view. Earlier, Peter had noticed him scanning the room like a farcical spy, his chin sweeping deliberately, repeatedly, from shoulder to shoulder. And twice he'd broken into a random, strolling-in-the-park kind of whistle.

But the woman's recommendation came as a surprise to Peter, who didn't feel too suave himself. He was on the verge of sweating, and his chest seemed to have contracted with self-consciousness, putting pressure on his lungs. Glickstein had already veered toward him and away, promising to find him as soon as Michael's godfather came, to get Michael to introduce them, then excusing himself, saying he had to go help their host. So far, Michael had hardly lingered in the party's main rooms. His appearances had been brief and intermittent. For which Peter was greatly thankful.

He was grateful, as well, to the woman who'd pointed him out. Before, he'd suspected his aloof, amused expression was transparent, and growing more see-through by the solitary minute. Now he felt closer to opaque. And his composure, he thought, made sense. It was a matter of simple dignity. He remembered the afternoon at Palmer, the spring of their senior year, when Glickstein had come to his apartment glowing, literally beatific, and trying to downplay the reason: Michael had invited him to Seaver Lake, the Marrs' camp in the Adirondacks.

Glickstein. Glickstein who had sometimes sat in with Peter's band; that is, until he'd "loaned" his saxophone to Michael (he was *supposed* to start giving him lessons), never expecting or wanting it back. *Oh, let me give you my saxophone, in case you ever want to learn to play it.*

Well, Peter reminded himself, he shouldn't be too harsh. Glickstein had had him put on the guest list so he could meet Stephan Zadeh, the head of Continental Records. Which meant, really, that his old friend had believed in him all along. For over a year Peter had figured Glickstein was silently ridiculing him, thinking he should grow up and give up and join the real world. But that, it turned out, wasn't the case. And what did it matter if Glickstein had chased Michael like a lover? What did it matter if he still prided himself on that friendship? Different people needed different things. One human need was no better or worse than another. The important thing was to be generous. And Glickstein was. He's given you back a little faith in yourself, Peter thought, and what greater kindness can there be?

Nevertheless, Peter stood alone at the party, a situation which made it difficult to dwell on human generosity.

"Have you talked to Cynthia lately?" he heard a man ask slyly.

"No," a woman said. "God, I have to call. I'm a little worried about her."

"A *little* worried?" The man started to laugh.

They—the man, who had the jaw for a shaving ad, and the woman, a crinoline-clad version of the Pillsbury doughboy—stood in front of a wall of African masks. Nearby in the chandeliered room (this was the apartment where Michael had grown up, first with his mother and later, when his mother sequestered herself, with his aunt) was a cluster of three men.

"Hey," one of them said. "I just remembered what I had to tell you. I saw Davis's father last week in Petland. He's working in Petland."

In response, another let out an ambiguous groan, face twisting into a gleeful grimace. "This is a guy we went to Deerfield with," he explained to the third man, and said, "Davis must be slightly bummed."

"You would be too," the first one said, "if your father blew your inheritance and wound up in Petland selling guppies."

Peter almost laughed with them. He maintained his detached, faintly entertained expression, a subtle, almost imperceptible curve of his lips and crook of the corners of his eyes, and he kept his free hand, the one not holding his drink, at a certain angle in his pocket. But two things wrecked his pose. First, the guy who'd been acting weirdly, gazing at the ceiling and whistling randomly, began to mimic him. He tilted his head the same way, held his drink the same way, did the same things with his lips, eyes, and unoccupied hand. Peter switched his glass from one hand to the other, a move the guy didn't replicate—not right away. But a minute later Peter saw that he'd made the same switch. It was impossible to tell if the imitation was mocking or hopeful. And it didn't matter. Flustered, Peter forgot he'd recently refilled his glass; bringing it to his lips, he tipped it too early.

And just as he was wiping the bourbon off his chin, Michael walked in from the dining room. He passed within inches of Peter's shoulder, then crossed toward the bar. Feeling tenuously safe at that distance, Peter watched him. There was the short, straight, light brown hair, cut to angle across a corner of his forehead, the pale gray eyes, the sharp nose, the sturdy chin, the looks that were handsome, sure, but, Peter thought, dull, straightforward. And even his clothes—he wore brown bucks, loose, pleated khakis, a tweed jacket, a thin black tie—were just stylish enough. There was nothing to them.

"Have you ever looked at his eyes?" Peter recalled asking Glickstein at Palmer, before Glickstein had vanished into Michael's coterie. "They look dazed. Not drug-dazed. Just unsure. And why shouldn't he be? He's spent his whole life wondering, what have I done to deserve this? and his whole life hasn't been long enough to figure it out.

"I mean," Peter had nearly screeched, "it's not like everyone's fawning over some great talent. Or some self-promoting fraud. He just happens to be Walter Norman Marr's son!"

But tonight Peter did notice a difference—Michael's eyes were no longer vague with uncontrolled doubt. They were slightly disdainful. Though it was Michael who approached the angular-jawed man and Pillsbury woman, it was he who appeared immediately bored. They went straight to work, trying to engage him. They strained for wit, and when that didn't work they asked him a serious question, something about political advertising. He answered briefly. When they asked another question, he returned it. And as the man gave his opinion, Michael glanced over his own shoulder, excused himself, and walked toward the table of hors d'oeuvres.

It was as if he'd learned something in his senior year at Palmer, or in the year since. His gray eyes weren't worried; his manner was close to rude. At college, Peter had watched Michael surrounded, not knowing what people expected. He'd looked like he was waiting to be told. Tonight he didn't seem to care. He seemed to do what he pleased. And often, in his living room, ensnared by various guests, what he did was barely respond to, or ignore, or slip away from the people he was with.

Yet Peter saw glimmers of panic. It showed fleetingly, like a piece of gray metal glinting in momentary light. It was there and gone in the focus of Michael's eyes, an instantaneous sharpening, and in the tendons of his neck as he turned to look in another direction.

He looked suddenly at Peter. Peter wished he could inject himself into some conversation. Glickstein was over by the library, hovering around one of Michael's birthday presents. It was an electric Halloween toy. Ghosts and goblins flew across a magnetic screen. Peter had already tried to take part in a whimsical discussion about the gift—somehow he'd failed to say the right whimsical things and ended up feeling like a crasher at a children's party, with about as many defenses as a child might have. Worse, he felt inhuman—almost dead, in fact—for thinking that the toy was ridiculous and not even ingenious, and that these people were idiotic for carrying on as if it were one of the Seven Wonders.

He was sweating. His shirt was pasted to his lower back. He went to the bar. He thought for a second about talking to his mimic, who seemed to have given that up, and who was over by the wall of African masks, studying them. The masks had been given to Michael's father when, during his second term in Congress, he'd led his fact-finding mission to study Africa's poverty and rouse interest in aid.

Peter took his drink into the dining room, with the sense—which he knew was deluded—that Michael was watching. He gazed out a window at the view of Central Park. At an hour past dusk, from sixteen stories up, the park looked old and pristine. It had nothing to do with the battle it waged on the ground, asserting its fairy-tale landscape against evidence of the city. From up here, there was no battle. The park was magical. Its trees were purple clouds. The rowboat lake glinted silver. And in the morning the sun would reveal some immaculate kingdom of fresh water and deep forests and secluded fields.

Peter turned from the window.

". . . I assumed you knew," a short man with a large mole between his eyebrows was saying to a woman with a wide, pretty face and bewildered eyes.

"No," she said. "What happened?"

"Do you want the long or the short version?"

"The short and then the long."

The man made his face grave. He peered quickly at the woman, as if trying to guess her reaction. "Justin's dead," he told her.

"What?" she almost screamed. "Are you serious? Oh, my God! What happened?"

"Well." The man paused, releasing his lips to form the beginning of a smile, but at the same time shaking his head. "You knew he went to that camp in India, right?"

"No."

"Well, he did. I'm actually not sure it was in India; it could have been the Far East; but anyway it was some camp he'd read about, and when he came back he went up to his parents' roof to practice what he'd learned. Apparently, at the camp, you get a choice—you can learn to levitate, walk through a wall, or fly. But"—he waited a moment—"I guess the trick didn't work so well at home."

"You mean?" she asked.

"No," he continued, his voice rising. "He barely hurt himself. He cracked a rib, that was it. His parents must have figured out something was wrong, though, because he wound up in the psychiatric ward of some Los Angeles hospital. But I guess the security wasn't exactly tight."

"The windows weren't bolted?" She started to grin.

"He got up to the roof of the building, which was a few stories taller than his parents' house."

"Oh, my God," she gasped, grinning fully.

Hearing this story, Peter imagined himself for a moment in a suicidal plunge toward the park's cloudlike trees. Then, picturing such a fall in more realistic detail, he shuddered.

He thought of Stephan Zadeh, Michael's godfather. The son of a wealthy Turk, thirty years ago Zadeh had built his own record company, trusting only his own ear. In back-road bars, in churches, at pig roasts and fairs, he'd discovered the idols of Peter's idols. One night he'd pulled over to study his map and heard music across an unkempt orchard. There were no houses on the road and no road lights, and the music had no visible source. But he'd taken his flashlight and locked his car and traversed the overgrown orchard—a short, burly Turk looking something like Edward G. Robinson.

Zadeh had been in his thirties then. He was fifty by the time Peter first read about him. He worked more conventionally. Still, as a kid, Peter had imagined scenes of his own discovery—Zadeh driving past the hedges of Peter's family's Westchester house, hearing Peter sing. Even during college, when he'd begun to gig seriously around New England and get bits of local studio work, he'd sometimes conjured scenes in which Zadeh transformed him.

Tonight, this is what he hoped would happen. They would chat—awkwardly, maybe. Then Zadeh would say, "Well, send me a tape." And with a smile that was both self-deprecating and cocky, Peter would reach into the pocket of his black blazer and say, "Well, I have one here."

He wandered through the living room, library, vestibule, deciding he would wait ten more minutes. In the dining room, staring at a painting, he found himself next to Michael. He slipped out onto the terrace. There was Glickstein with Roberto and Annette. Peter knew them from Palmer. Or rather, he'd seen them, watched them, known them the way you know very visible people you've never met, Roberto the son of a Somoza and Annette the daughter of a deputy to the Shah. Black hair, narrow faces, black clothes—the couple stood now at a corner of the railing, looking like a pair of elegant eels. "Do you want to go to P.S. 5 afterward?" Glickstein asked them. Peter ducked back inside.

Again, he tried his nonchalant lean, his aloof expression. But he felt his lips shiver faintly and saw that the mouth of his double looked about as composed as a stroke victim's. Michael turned abruptly from another snare of guests, and Peter, seeing that his host might pass near him, switched rooms. It was exactly the way it had been at Palmer. There, though they'd lived one building apart, they'd never met or nodded hello. When they'd passed on the street, Peter had made his gaze go blank or averted his eyes. If he'd had time to do it casually, he'd crossed to the other sidewalk. He'd veered away from friends when he saw them chatting with Michael or one of Michael's crowd. He'd avoided Glickstein. One night, walking home from the gym, glancing up and realizing he was on Michael's heels, he'd done a pantomime of forgetfulness and quickly reversed directions. And when, in the dressing mirror of a small basement thrift shop, he'd glimpsed Michael strolling in, he'd swiftly replaced the jacket he was trying on and slipped out the door.

But that was him! Peter glimpsed Zadeh's black hair, his thick shoulders in a dark jacket. And he was leaving. He was in the vestibule, and he was leaving. Somehow Peter had missed him, or he'd stayed only long enough to wish Michael happy birthday.

Peter reached for the door as the butler shut it behind Zadeh. He had to step back, let the butler open it again.

There was a square, marbled hall where the elevator came. "Excuse me," Peter began—and knew, the instant he spoke, that the black hair and dark jacket belonged to some other older man.

Returning inside, Peter asked Glickstein if there was another bathroom. There was a line for the one off the library. "It's off the second bedroom on your right," Glickstein said, pointing down a hallway that was carpeted a vivid purplish blue. Peter wasn't too keen about venturing into the back of the apartment, but, Glickstein having directed him, it would have been ridiculous not to go. The second bedroom was empty. It was carpeted and painted the same shade of blue. The room was unlit except for a bedside lamp, which seemed to disperse the color—a paler, neon version of it—through the air. Though he barely glanced at them, the photographs on the waist-high bureau to his right made Peter certain the room was Michael's.

He was quick. He pissed, conscious of Michael's things—his medicine cabinet, his toothbrush, his comb—around him. He checked his face in the mirror and decided to rinse it. Drying his face, he kept the small towel folded and didn't remove it from the rack.

When he opened the door the blue of the air looked thicker, almost murky. At the near side of the bed, seven or eight figures, mostly men, were arranged in two loose rows. The first, closest to the bed, knelt. Their backs were to him. He turned abruptly. He realized Michael must be in the room, that the others must be there to do his cocaine. The last thing Peter wanted was to be caught, perceived as an intruder on this, what other people considered the height of bestowed honor. Hoping the soft carpet and thick air would let him get out unnoticed, he opened the door to the hallway. But it wasn't the door. It led into a closet. There he was, staring into Michael's closet—a blur of ties, shoes, jackets—certain he was being stared at. He shut the door and tried the next one over, discovering a bright, empty bedroom. The last door to his left must be it, he thought; but it wasn't, and around him he saw half a dozen identical doors, all mounted with identical dressing mirrors, and he wasn't even sure which ones he'd tried.

"Peter" someone said. "Peter."

Like the blue, the voice seemed dispersed throughout the room. Blurred at the edges, it surrounded him like a waking voice. At first, he couldn't place it. But it was Michael, standing away from the foot of the bed, gesturing to him to join the others. Peter began to stand behind them. But Michael indicated the foot of the bed. A frameless rectangular mirror lay face up on the quilt. Kneeling, Peter saw his own reflection and Michael's close above it. Cocaine was tapped from a vial onto the glass, but Peter was hardly aware of the powder being furrowed. The drug was nothing new to him; he'd felt lifted by it and felt next to nothing by it, and at that moment it was barely relevant. For there, in the mirror, was Michael's face, floating above him.

"Well," Peter said, standing after doing two lines, "since I've practically crashed your party and done your cocaine, I guess I should introduce myself." He grinned. "But I guess you know my name already." He waited for Michael to respond, to say "Yes" or "Right" or "I put your face together with the name Glickstein gave me for the guest list." Michael said nothing. He eyed Peter unreadably—condemningly? quizzically?—and Peter, who was nearly six feet, was conscious of gazing uncomfortably upward, though Michael was only an inch or two taller.

"Anyway, I'm Peter Bram," he finished, and put out his hand to shake. Michael took it, still not speaking. The silence expanded. Or probably it lasted two or three seconds and Peter only imagined its expansion, anticipated it, and spoke thoughtlessly, reactively, to cut it off. He heard himself ask in some alien, nearly thuglike, offhanded voice, "You went to Palmer, didn't you?" He winced. He'd meant to say something else, he didn't know what, maybe "I'm a friend of Glickstein's" or "I went to Palmer," not "You went to Palmer, didn't you?" as if it were possible to pretend he didn't know who Michael was. How much idiocy could he pack into one question? He'd been fighting to stay collected; now he wished he would just evaporate.

But Michael didn't seem to consider the question one way or another. Either that or he was dumbfounded by its obvious pretense. "Yeah," he answered tonelessly.

The others started to leave the room, thanking Michael as they went.

"Well," Peter said, more than ready to get out.

"You want to do a few more lines?" Michael asked.

"Mike." A man Peter had wondered about earlier had stepped in from the hallway. Almost all evening the man had been standing in the vestibule, next to a table of Indonesian statuettes, greeting guests and taking their birthday presents (of which there weren't many—no one was sure whether to bring anything, or, if they should, what it should be). And later, the man had begun bidding guests goodbye, saying, "Take care. Glad you could make it." He was huge—six four or five and on the verge of overweight—and while everyone else was dressed casually or stylishly or in an excess of elegance, he wore a business suit and standard red tie. His collar was snug around his stumpy neck, which, Peter had noticed, was lurid with blue-black acne. His face was puffy and clear-skinned. A gold collar pin cinched his throat.

He laid a large hand on Michael's shoulder and reported with a great show of conspiracy, "Emilio wants to know if he should start to clean up the bar, if you want people to start going home."

"Yes," Michael said, pulling back a bit from the immensely serious face.

"Okay. I'll tell him."

As the man left, Michael rolled his eyes slightly.

"Who is that guy, anyway?" Peter asked.

"Paul Becker. At my service."

"Your maître d'?"

"Self-appointed. Maître d'. Valet. You name it."

"Where do you know him from?"

"Well, he went to Yale. He played football there. But I didn't know him until the beginning of this summer. He showed up at some dinner where I wrecked these pants. Or not these—another pair like them. The next morning he calls, asking for my waist size and inseam. I barely remembered him. He had to explain who he was. And he's taking my measurements!" Michael laughed—nervously, it seemed to Peter—and shook his head with careless incredulity. But at the same time Peter caught real worry in his eyes. "Anyway, that night he's at the door. With these! What am I supposed to do? I tried to pay for them. He said they were on sale. Then he said he'd forgotten the price. Since then he's showed up with all kinds of shit. Shirts, ties; a linen jacket for chrissakes! It's unbelievable. I mean, he can't afford it. He works in some Citibank. He's an assistant branch manager or something. I told him, 'Becker, look . . .' But what am I supposed to do? I mean, there's a limit to how much I'm going to protest."

He laughed again, and when Peter joined him, the worry in his eyes seemed to diminish. It wasn't concern for Becker, Peter decided; it was uncertainty about himself. Instead of boredom and scorn, which had shown in his gaze all evening, now there was a question, an anxious need. *How do you see me?* The focus of his eyes was slightly askance and very intent, as if he were trying to peer behind Peter's retinas.

"It must be kind of hard," Peter said, feigning a sort of naivety and rebuking himself for it, for wanting to draw Michael out.

"What?"

"I don't know. Having people like that."

"It is," Michael said plainly, and though his face didn't dissolve with self-pity, there wasn't any humor in it, either; there was no tilt to his words. Which surprised Peter— the confession was too sudden and strong. And the lack of irony gave him the sense (or confirmed his assumption) that Michael wasn't particularly bright. "I wouldn't mistake any of these people for my friends," Michael added.

"Yeah," Peter said, smiling, as if sympathetically, acutely aware that they were alone in the room, that all the other guests were outside, that he was in this envied position. "Well, what about Glickstein?" he couldn't resist asking.

"Glickstein?"

"Not friends?"

"Annette calls him the *Times*'s Neediest Case."

They laughed together.

"I mean, I don't mean to get down on him," Michael said, "if he's a friend of yours."

"No. No. Actually . . . well, we pretty much started drifting apart when he started kowtowing after you."

Peter smiled again—sincerely this time, as if there really were a deep understanding between them—and quickly checked Michael's eyes for some reaction. He saw none, and felt his small confession had been a terrible mistake.

Then a woman, alarmingly beautiful and overdressed, burst into the room. She wore a floor-length red gown which rustled loudly and had a resplendent sheen, and her long blond hair was done in an elaborate tousle of curls, the way Farrah Fawcett would have worn it years before. But it was hard to laugh, even when she walked briskly toward them, planted herself in front of Michael, paused, seemed to have forgotten what she'd planned to say, and blurted finally, "Hi." It was hard to laugh, because her breasts and narrow hips were so tightly sheathed by the crinkling red satin.

"Peter," Michael said, "this is Terry."

But she couldn't be distracted. She asked Michael what he'd gotten for his birthday, and he began to tell her (two ties, a book, some joke toys . . .).

"Oh, you poor baby."

Still it was impossible to laugh.

"Well," Peter said, in a tone that was part sarcastic complicity, and part disinterest, "take care."

And keeping his steps unhurried, he walked out of the blue-lit room and out of the party.

Three

TWO AND A HALF YEARS AGO PETER HAD PLAYED THE TILLMAN, opening for Jackson Browne. It was the first time he'd been in front of a crowd anywhere near that size, and, following his band onto the stage from the portable metal stairs, the sheer depth and height of it, in addition to the surge of its reception (noncommittal as the greeting was for an unknown like Peter), seemed to create involuntary muscles out of the voluntary ones in his legs, arms, hands. He felt as if his body and brain had slipped off close behind him, that he was left with something vague and unreliably autonomous. "Just think of it as all the bars you've played, dragged away by tractor-trailer, and deposited in front of you," Rudy Wells had told him, after he'd told Wells he'd won the Michelob contest, and where and when he'd be performing. Wells, by then sixty years old, was visiting Palmer's music department. At forty he'd made it, more or less, in country music, after twenty years of not making it at all. "Of course," he'd laughed, "you probably haven't played in that many bars."

There were nine thousand people in the Tillman that night, and it was true—if you'd added up all the crowds of fifty and two hundred Peter had played for, it certainly wouldn't have come to that.

But the advice helped, as did the endless rehearsals Peter had insisted on. He opened with a song by Eric Kaz, during which something clicked, cleared; he was in control after all. He had the kind of grainy, gruff voice that often seems on the verge of cracking, that sounds as if it won't be capable of carrying any real intensity, and he used the apparent flatness, the frailty, let sentiment stay partly locked inside these seeming limitations, and then, his raspy voice deepening, stretching, rising, *lasting,* he swallowed the arena of nine thousand as he had rooms of a fraction that size. Not that the crowd was constantly transfixed. They were hearing mostly his own songs. They weren't always won over. But they were with him. And on the ballad he finished with (written for Wyatt, his thirty-seven-year-old bass player, about Wyatt's very brief first marriage) the place was so thoroughly hushed people might not have been breathing.

Afterward, backstage, Jackson Browne asked, "What was that last song?"

(Peter was not a particular fan of Browne's—somehow his music held no miracles within its smartness and self-pity.)

"'Heroines and Heroes'?"

"Yeah," Browne said. "That was poetry."

(Which elevated Browne in Peter's esteem.)

And later, leaving through the lane of barricades meant to shield the headline act, Peter had several requests for autographs and heard, in the twisted vowels of that New England city, an unseen man declare, "That was the best fucking opening band I've ever heard."

Two and a half years ago.

* * *

Peter often laughed at himself. How, at the age of twenty-four, could he imagine himself the center of a story about being over the hill, about a man whose best days were behind him? He'd had a single moment of glory in some minimal sun. He hadn't risen or fallen very far. But at times he did imagine the gig at the Tillman to be the height of his entire life (the future utterly included) so that the memory of it became more cruel joke than reassurance. When had he become so adept at despair? Two and a half years was nothing! And it wasn't as if there hadn't been hints of success. He'd had a contract at an indie label and gigs that were at least decent. And twice Leonard Cohen's publisher had called about his songs, complimenting him, encouraging him. But, he reminded himself mercilessly, the indie label had folded (and he hadn't quite had a contract there anyway; it was still in negotiation; the owner hadn't completely committed himself yet), and getting booked at those bars didn't necessarily mean anything, and compliments were cheap.

He knew he just had to keep at it—write more songs, finish another tape, things would fall into place. He knew he just had to see things realistically. The response of nine thousand people was *not* a joke. The interest from the label was *not* a joke. "Keep On Keeping On," he wrote in big block letters in black magic marker across a plain sheet of paper, remembering an old soul lyric. He taped the paper up on his bedroom wall, and so what if it was like those sayings housewives needle-pointed for their cute little cushions? Maybe a little hackneyed inspiration was what he needed every morning. But right away he yanked down the sign (and scratched off the remnant of tape that clung to the wall). It was just too ridiculous. It was just too depressing.

Weekly, his father called. "You hanging in there, pal?" Dr.

Bram would ask, and Peter would say, "Yeah, I'm hanging in there," though increasingly this wasn't the case. Forgotten, or seemingly irretrievable, was a time when the world hadn't mattered. Before what was outside had put a choke hold on what was inside. Before ego had got mixed in with beauty. Then, at the beginning of that other time, he'd gone to a concert. He was eighteen. He took a date. It was a first date, with a girl he'd liked a long while, but after the concert he refused her offers of dinner, drinks, coffee. He walked her home, not speaking. It had nothing to do with her. It was what he'd heard for the past hour and a half.

The concert was in the lounge of the Ramada Inn, down the hill from Palmer. The musician, a man who would kill himself six months later, had written songs for Bonnie Raitt, Emmylou Harris, Joe Cocker, Waylon Jennings. That's what he was, mostly—a songwriter, not a performer. So few people knew who he was, and he was booked into the Cozy Harbor Lounge at the Ramada, and the Cozy Harbor was almost empty. He had a lot to overcome. It would have been one thing if he'd been playing to twelve people in a place with bare, beer-spilled floors and battered tabletops; instead, he was surrounded by swordfish and captain's wheels mounted on the walls, by murals of whaling boats, and lots of burnished wood.

"Welcome to the Cozy Harbor," he said, deadpan. He knew he had his work cut out for him. He had a broad, flattened, concave-looking face, and practically no lips at all, as if his teeth had been knocked in. He looked like Nick Nolte on a bad day. Or a very bad day. He had that kind of hunched, lumbering durability, and a way of seeming inwardly disgusted with the world and with himself, as if durability were the last thing he'd wish for.

His twelve fans (there were, in addition, a few guests of the

Ramada who came and quickly went) tried to make up for the sparseness of the crowd with ardent clapping. "Man, that sounds worse than silence," he said. "Just let me play."

Then he went further inside himself, deeper than the inward disgust, to the part that had generated his slow, regretful songs. He was not a young man, and if he'd said he was twenty years older than he really was, you wouldn't have doubted it. It was a journey to the small, central place he sang from. He had to fight past bitterness to get there. After he mumbled, "Just let me play" and shut his eyes, you could see bitterness take shape and dissolve on his face. Then he reached the place of beauty.

The beauty was muted, half-spoken as often as sung. Sometimes it was slashing in an implied way, in a repeated cry that was as much sigh as shout. And when he broke into real volume he would take you to a high, desperate place and cut the ground out from under you, and you'd dangle the way he dangled, though separately.

"And this was my one monster hit," he said, introducing his final song. He said this to be funny, and diminished the sadness in the room by starting to play the song the way it had played on the radio, upbeat and positive-thinking, a series of hopeful suggestions for keeping love strong, a list of helpful hints delivered to a follow-the-bouncing-ball kind of tune. Toward the end of the first verse, he stopped, laughed, stayed quiet, began again. This time he played what he'd meant, or, anyway, what he'd grown to mean. It was nearly opposite to what the producers and radio version's singer had come up with, though not quite; opposite would have been sarcasm, and this was soft rue that hopeful suggestions should be so impossible to follow. He ended on an extended note behind which promise achingly receded . . . but the note itself was partial replacement for what was mourned.

"Okay," he said. "You can clap now."

Only a few people did, and they quit almost immediately. It was as if everyone realized that twelve people couldn't create enough applause for what they'd just heard. They kept silent.

"Thanks," he said, hardening again. He stepped off the riser and through some back door.

"So what do you want to do?" Peter's date asked, after they'd sat a minute, not talking, not looking at each other.

But Peter was rigid with appreciation. He didn't want to do anything.

What had happened to that time of pure inspiration? When had the world's terms—success, failure—wedged themselves in? Peter needed to know. Lately he was spending time on his futon, fixated on the view out his window. Since his apartment was on the garden floor, he had a good vantage on people's shoes. And he could become mesmerized, not by the shoes themselves, their styles or colors or states of repair, but by their movement. And not by the little details of their motion, either. He wasn't interested in whether their wearers were pigeon-toed or duck-footed, in whether they minced or bounded. He was simply, sadly, almost indiscriminately engrossed in the movement itself. All those people—in business shoes and orthopedic shoes and chic, Velcro-tied sneakers— were involved in their regular journeys, while he, ensconced in his own suddenly stillborn life, envied their every step.

Or he was listening to a cat that spent its evenings on the fire escape two floors above him. Its high, thin whine resembled an infant's crying; twice, as he was trying to write, Peter had gone out to check the alley alongside his building. He'd had visions of an abandoned baby wailing behind a dumpster. The second time, he'd seen the cat. Still, when the sporadic pleas came he was vaguely fooled; he silenced his guitar, and quit straining for lyrics or parts of melodies, and listened.

And sometimes he wondered if he needed to fail. Not consciously, no, for on the levels of cognizance, desire dominated his life, disciplined him, made him sit every day with his guitar—even now, when the early, easy promises life had made him seemed to be wafting—to dredge for the missing parts of half-finished songs. No, not consciously, for desire kept him working hour after hour and, when his acoustic was back in its case, kept him bargaining with gods he couldn't imagine and only tried to believe in, claiming to these vague powers that he would willingly die at thirty-five, or cut off his left leg, suffer the most arbitrary and severe deprivation, if only his songs would get the responses he felt they deserved. No, not consciously. But he wondered whether secretly, in some seeping way, a need to lose out, to get close but get nothing, were effortlessly overriding all his want and determination.

He remembered a weekend during the winter of his junior year. Mardi Gras. He and two of his band, Wyatt and Andy Phelps, had decided at the last minute to drive the thirty-two hours to New Orleans. They arrived Friday night, and spent three days drunk and stoned and begging for beads, trinkets. Amidst the clamour of high school drill teams, the parades rolled by, the long, colorful floats, two stories high, with their immense, campy sculptures of alligators and African kings and licentious Greek gods, and from them the krewes, in masks and full costumes, threw ten-cent necklaces, plastic cups, rubber snakes, toy tambourines. "Beads!" the crowd pleaded, pressing up to the moving floats, hands waving, reaching, "Beads! Pearls! Cups!" And because the krewes were made mostly of young men, most of the prizes were thrown to pretty girls. Tall, agile men could get their share as well, jumping and snatching things from the air. Peter grabbed a fair number of prizes in this way. But he worried about the others, the homely girls, the people his parents' age. His heart—excessively, perhaps foolishly, he knew—went out to them. It sank the way it would for a left-out child. And truly, this wasn't so different from a game at a children's party, or from the social hopes and maneuverings of twelve- and thirteen-year-olds—everyone was as intensely involved. One middle-aged woman stepped in front of each float, half-kneeling and blowing huge, histrionic kisses up at the krewes, then clasping her hands prayerlike in front of her chest until she was almost run over, screaming, "Please, *please* throw me pearls! Please! Please! Pearls! *Please!*" She was thrown none.

Of course, she was clowning, carried away by the theater of the parade. But mustn't she have felt bereft when krewe after krewe decided they didn't want her as part of their play? Mustn't she have begun to feel that she, for some particular and personal reason, was being spurned? And the older men and homely girls, elated as they were by their own yelling within this happy, energetic mob, mustn't they have remembered gradually their own age and weakness, their own unappealing faces? Wasn't the lesson of this holiday the same as what was taught by life?

When Peter found himself in front of a couple in their fifties, he didn't reach, didn't leap. He hoped the trinkets would fly past him into the hands of the older man, who could present them gallantly to his wife.

His worry came and went, spread through him and faded. Most of the time he shouted with everyone else, leaping, pleading, transported. It wasn't until the last day, Mardi Gras day itself, that Peter lost the spirit of the festival.

In the French Quarter, he and Wyatt and Andy were invited onto a private balcony by an old friend of Wyatt's. The third-floor balcony was barely more than a cornice with a wrought-iron rail, but seven or eight people shouldered onto it, overlooking the square. The parades were over now; the spectators thronged the Quarter for the free-for-all of final revels. From above, empowered merely by this chance invitation, Peter watched them. They kept begging. A balding man holding the small hand of his son yelled, "Throw me something. Throw me something," and waved his arm at Peter's balcony like a marooned sailor trying to signal a search plane. "No way," Andy called, before Peter tossed down three necklaces . . . and something he couldn't quite understand made him regret playing the benefactor to this stranded father.

"Show us your tits," Wyatt yelled down at a pair of slender women.

They lifted their shirts, bowed their backs, shook their breasts toward the balcony. Wyatt awarded them Rex medallions.

"Show us your tits," Wyatt yelled again, though he was, almost ceaselessly, gentle. Older, he didn't go to Palmer like the rest of the band. He was on his second marriage, had two kids, had been able to make this trip only because his family was away for a week seeing relatives. He might look like some kind of bar rat or honky-tonk brawler, with his never-combed reddish hair and the thick, crooked nose that made his child-blue eyes and hopeful smile seem off-center, but he was devoted, kind.

A woman unbuttoned her shirt to her stomach, squeezed her breasts through the V. Wyatt and Andy dropped more medallions, more beads.

It was the tradition. All over the Quarter a woman's half-nudity was the purchasing price of a trinket. It was a ritual of Mardi Gras.

And Peter looked. Of course he looked, gazed, stared, and was turned on by these sudden, sensual revelations in the middle of a city street. But he said to Wyatt, "Don't be an idiot." Wyatt was too enthralled to hear.

"Throw me some pearls!" a woman called up to Peter.

He did, flung her four or five strands, demanding nothing. She looked surprised, disappointed, hurt.

And later, from the far end of the balcony, Peter saw a man in dazed supplication. He reminded Peter exactly of his father. There was the dignity in his height and thick white hair, and the irony in his half-hearted waving toward the balcony, as if he knew this was all silliness and he wasn't really taking part, yet he seemed disoriented as he called, almost inaudibly, "Here . . . here." He smiled faintly, foundering badly between making a real joke of this and actually trying for Wyatt's attention. Peter was out of beads. "Would you just give him something," he said, walking over to his friend. But Wyatt was dangling his pearls over the rail, bartering over a halter top, and, hardly in control of his own hand, Peter snatched the trinkets from his friend, and sent them floating toward the image of his own father's frail authority.

Though Peter could not place why, this kind of memory seemed to reveal the chance of his own failure—or rather, the chance of its necessity. But it was only a chance, and he wasn't about to quit gambling because the odds were unknowable.

"Yeah, I'm hanging in there," he would tell his father, who was, genuinely, on his side. He wanted what Peter wanted. In fact, he was the closest thing Peter had to the encouraging message—"Keep On Keeping On"—he'd torn off his wall. "Good things don't happen overnight" and "Don't be too hard on yourself," Dr. Bram would say, and in his innocent, helpful way would tell his son to get out with friends, take it easy. He would recall his own days in medical school, when Peter's mother had made him take Sundays off from studying. And while Peter couldn't convince himself the situations were similar, he tried to heed his father's advice, to steal out of the isolation he'd grown solidly into. He'd called the drummer he'd worked with until a few months before; they'd shot pool on the Lower East Side. He'd struggled through dinners with high school friends. He'd taken himself to afternoon baseball games. But these simple things, which other people seemed to enjoy so thoroughly, mocked him with their transparent, temporary pleasures.

It was during one of these efforts, though, that he ran into Michael, two weeks after the party.

He, Peter, was on his way to an Einsteins rehearsal. The Einsteins were a wedding-and-bar mitzvah band he'd been singing with. For a while, he'd looked forward to the gigs. Because of them he'd had affairs with two forty-year-old divorcees, and always, at the bar or bas mitzvahs, he attracted thirteen-year-old groupies. The groupie business was a joke. The rest of the band—which ranged in age from twenty-five (the drummer's son) to fifty (the drummer)—kidded him. They called him "Donny," after Donny Osmond, whom Peter resembled only in that he had black hair. Peter didn't mind the nickname. In truth, the giggling and dancing in front of the stage could inspire him during the most predictable covers. He could get elated doing "Celebrate" or "I Love You Just the Way You Are." On the other hand, his susceptibility could make him sick. It was bad enough that he had to play these gigs, that he had to spend his time rehearsing for them, but that he let himself care about them, that he actually worried about the attention of eighth-graders . . . One night, the drunken father of the bas mitzvah girl took Peter's microphone. "My daughter didn't think I would do this," he announced. And as the man started to rap, strutting and rhyming and attempting to moonwalk, Peter lost his following, and—he would always remember this interchange of eyes—a girl with two tiny, endearing moles above her upper lip had caught him glancing at her jealously.

Anyway, he was on his way to rehearsal, which was in the

east Twenties, and instead of taking the Seventh Avenue subway and walking across Twenty-third Street, he'd decided to cross Central Park, because the smell and thin afternoon light of fall was making him nostalgic, and he had the vague notion that he'd like to trample through some unraked leaves. The park did not disappoint him. Miraculous it might be from sixteen stories up; at ground level its besieged, sturdy beauty made Peter want to cry or cry out in tribute. He ended up walking much farther than he'd planned, heading downtown as a pale, thick-rumped quarter horse trotted by on the black soil of the riding path. Peter was no country boy (he'd grown up in Brooklyn Heights and in Larchmont); his sensations as he watched the horse (whose gray flanks seemed speckled with orange, though that might only have been a trick of light and the color of the autumn leaves) had little to do with memory. He didn't long to be in that saddle. He was transported by the animal itself, trotting obliviously—steadily, beautifully, heartbreakingly—through the middle of Manhattan.

At the north end of the rowboat lake, Peter turned—against common caution, for it was now dusk—in the direction of an isolated, narrow trail leading up a hill into a dense patch of trees. He crossed an arching wooden bridge, his arm slightly sore from carrying his guitar. But he didn't mind. This was worth it. The patch of trees was practically a legitimate forest. The overgrowth shut out almost all the remaining daylight, and bushes and saplings grazed his legs and guitar case. The path wound above the lake, hooking behind one knoll and weaving in front of another. To one side was a cliff, steep if not treacherously long. In the near-dark he had to concentrate not to lose his footing. He could scare himself—not with the possibility of falling (though somehow that was part of it), but with the knowledge that he was completely cut off. The rowboat lake was desolate; the joggers at the park's periphery were a long, tree-muffled distance away. Yet the threats he

41

imagined weren't typical—no muggers, no violent, homeless psychotics, none of the traditional urban dangers. No, he was scared the way he'd been at fourteen, walking at night along the forested lane leading to his family's house. He was scared the way anyone, at any age, can spook himself amidst expanses of nature. The fear was diffuse, and at the same time right at his shoulder. It was nothing he could picture. And, as he hiked through the park's secluded woods, Peter conjured it irresistibly, almost pleasurably.

Then he glimpsed someone ahead of him, and the other, more concrete threats came to mind. Was the person approaching? Headed away? Male? Peter told himself to calm down, that the chances of a mugger were minuscule. Still.

But when he saw the face of the man coming toward him, he was confronted by a very different problem. Should he avert his eyes? Act lost in thought? Michael probably wouldn't remember him. Peter could just slip past.

They were four or five yards apart when Michael laughed. "Shit!" he said. "I thought I was about to be robbed and savagely beaten."

Peter started to feint a slow roundhouse to Michael's jaw, a stiff attempt at humor. "I had a moment of doubt there, too."

"What are you up to?"

"Going to rehearsal. By a kind of circuitous route."

"You're a musician?"

"Yeah," Peter said. "Glickstein didn't tell you that?"

"No."

"Oh, well, I mean, actually that's why I was at your party. To do a little self-promotion. He said your godfather was going to be there." He was glad to make his motives clear.

"Glickstein." Michael rolled his eyes and Peter smiled, faintly guilty for this moment of understanding, this repeated exchange at his old friend's expense.

"Anyway."

"Yeah," Michael said, "this is a great part of the park."

"It is." Peter kept his voice toneless.

"If you don't look at the buildings you think you're in some kind of wilderness."

"Yep."

"I mean, have you ever thought about what New York would be like without Central Park?"

"I know," Peter said, and he *had* thought about it, but he really didn't want to stand there celebrating the landscape with Michael Marr. He really didn't want to stand there agreeing about anything with Michael Marr. In fact, he was having some trouble with the standing itself. It was as if his body were improperly balanced. He felt as if he might keel. And making eye contact, easy, indifferent eye contact, with this person all of Palmer College had idolized and who nine-tenths of the country adored—the effort was too difficult, too demeaning, and if he hadn't been trying so hard to be disinterested he'd have felt the beginnings of rage. But he said, "It's amazing to look at a map of Manhattan and see how much of it's taken up by this huge green rectangle. It's almost impossible to imagine filling it in with streets and buildings. It's like it's *physically* hard to imagine. Your body has some kind of reaction against it. The city just . . ." he made an abrupt leveling movement with his hand ". . . continuing." He heard himself gushing like some Friends of the Earth volunteer.

"I know. I've had that thought exactly." Michael's eyes brightened; he smiled; he shook his head at the coincidence.

"Well, I don't want to sound too much like *Small Is Beautiful*, or whatever that book was."

"Yeah." Michael didn't seem to understand.

"Well . . ."

Bending, Michael picked a stone off the path and flung it through the trees. He had a good arm. The stone landed on the lake, its contact with the water barely audible.

"Anyway," Peter said.

"You want to get some dinner?"

Peter was startled. He'd been about to leave. And he'd just told Michael he had a rehearsal. "Well," he said, "why not? My rehearsal's with this bar mitzvah band I play with to make money, and there's only so many times I can sing that shit. So maybe I should just save myself for the actual events."

"There's a trail down there that's shorter," Michael said, and led them out of the park.

They walked awhile in silence, as if the commitment to have dinner together had unnerved them both. Peter couldn't think of any innocuous questions—all the commonplace details of Michael's life, past and present, were public knowledge. More and more over the last couple of years, there had been countless articles and photographs in magazines from *Newsweek* to *People* to *Town & Country*. Even after Palmer it had been impossible for Peter to ignore the chronicle of Michael's existence. There were the anecdotes from people like Glickstein (worked, with inevitable craft, into unrelated conversations), and the accounts in the periodicals (true, Peter's scorn sometimes urged him to reach for whatever magazine had Michael on its cover). And there was his proud and innocent grandmother, who kept a scrapbook of stories about Michael, with whom her grandson had gone to school.

"So who was that blonde?" Peter asked finally. He had the sensation of being watched, though they were still alone, not yet out on the park's main road. He tried to dismiss the feeling. It was ridiculous, he knew, this fantasy of disembodied attention, paid him because he was walking with Michael Marr.

"Who?"

"The blond woman. You know. Farrah."

"Oh. Terry. Yeah, well. That was not one of my prouder moments."

"She didn't give you much choice."

"No. And I mean, she *is* serious. Fucking is like an athletic event for her. I mean, that chick screwed my lights out."

For reasons running from feminism to jealousy, Peter was silenced by this report. "Sounds pleasant," he managed. There were about twenty speechless steps. "Do you ever hear from Carey Esser?"

"No," Michael said.

"Is she living in the city?"

"I don't know."

"She was a pretty good friend of mine at Palmer. That's why I was wondering."

"Strange lady."

Strange lady? Peter winced. In truth, he and Carey—bony, flirtatious, short-lipped Carey; smart, sly, introspective Carey, with whom he'd traded all kinds of stories—had been something more than friends, though timidity and timing had kept them from being lovers. Peter let the subject drop.

And he was wishing he was on his way to singing some Top Forty ballad, backed by the harmonies of the drummer's hapless son, when Michael said, "You didn't think too much of me."

"What?"

"I said," Michael repeated, his voice low and controlled, with an undertone of regret or a stoic kind of shame, "you didn't think too much of me. At Palmer."

Never had Peter felt Michael's presence so intensely—not in the moments at college when he'd narrowly evaded him, or in the minutes of kneeling and talking at the party, or as they'd stood on the overgrown path. They'd come out onto Central Park West and were walking with the park's low, medieval-looking wall to their left and the Museum of Natural History across the street. The sidewalk was wide and uncrowded. They were not particularly close together as they walked. Yet

Michael's face—the pale gray eyes, the sharp nose, the bit of light brown hair angling across a corner of his forehead—seemed, as Michael's gaze trapped his, extremely near. The face almost blurred in Peter's vision. He sensed that Michael was making some huge, tentative offering. Fleetingly he recalled an old girlfriend, a woman who'd been desperately in love and who'd wanted, constantly, the reassurance of full, protracted kisses. There was nothing sexual in Michael's expression, and nothing really loving. But there was, for an instant, that kind of submission.

"Who told you that?" Peter asked, smiling, half-laughing, diminishing Michael's statement without denying it.

"No one," Michael said calmly. "But you didn't."

"No, that really isn't right. No. That wasn't it. It was that I didn't think too much of everyone else. I still don't. All the fawning. Whatever."

"Neither do I." Again, there was the anxious concentration in Michael's eyes, the questioning, the attempt to peer behind Peter's retinas, as if to ask, Is that true? Is what I just said true? "I mean, it's *boring,* for chrissakes!" he added. "It's just fucking boring. I mean, I'll give you an example. Waking up with that chick after the party, I didn't even want to go for it another time. I was just like, Get out of here, quit tonguing my ear. I would have rather had a fucking fly buzzing around in there."

Listening, Peter was overwashed by a wave of excitement and tugged by an undertow of distrust. The wave was for the realization that Michael Marr seemed truly to need him, that Michael Marr was latching onto him, and for the belief that Michael did indeed hate the way the world surrounded him, swarmed him, that he really did wish to escape it. The undertow was for the rattle of overemphasis in Michael's voice.

They were crossing the street toward Michael's building. They entered the small lobby that was a cross between classical and Louis Quatorze. There were four simple pillars and one small fountain, and there were love seats in red velvet and mirrors with lavish frames. There was an assumption in the rich, cramped randomness of the room. The doorman said hello to Michael and glanced at Peter, who couldn't help feeling studied, to be recognized in the future.

"Do you want the full tour?" Michael asked, upstairs.

"So I won't get lost?"

"Yes," Michael laughed, and led Peter through the apartment.

At dinner—in a Japanese restaurant, in a booth of black plexiglass—they talked about Michael's aunt, his mother's sister. Sylvia, the aunt, had raised Michael from when he was seven, five years after his father's election, five years after his father's death, and five years after the inauguration of Walter Marr's running mate, who had ushered in an era of increasing nostalgia, an era in which even the most curmudgeonly analysts and critical biographers celebrated the glory of what might have been. A year before Sylvia's arrival at the Helmsford, Michael's mother had begun to dissociate herself from her husband's memory. She'd gone off on some archeological dig in Sumatra, and, basically, she'd never come back. Goodbye, Natalie Marr. Goodbye, wished-for first lady to the longed- and mourned-for first man! Goodbye, queen to the wonderful kingdom that might have been!

She'd married the archeologist, Marcus Oberman, who'd directed the dig, and settled for the next few years on Timor, another, still more remote Malaysian island. Since then she'd lived in Rwanda and in the Amazon basin of Brazil. And the U.S. press and public had let her go. That is, of course, they *had* to let her go; there was no law against isolation that was rigorous and unroyal, or against staying permanently away; but, psychologically, they gave her up with surreal ease. There was no genuine desire for her return. There was no fervent speculation about what her life was like now. Only the most tactless, scoffed-at rags sent photographers to track her down, and those pictures of her (looking haggard and intent, and later decrepit, her high forehead having collapsed into wrinkles, the bone structure itself seemingly shrunken) were treated with even less credulity than the horrors that always filled those tabloids, the disappearances over the Bermuda Triangle and the men with transparent skin. In the better magazines, though, her current life was referred to briefly (without photos) in writing that was vague and full of sympathy. "Wherever she travels," *Life* had offered, "the nation's hearts are with her, and we wish her well." Natalie Marr was preserved in endless condolences.

"So is she happy?" Peter risked asking, that night at dinner, and Michael, who visited his mother about once a year, said she was.

"I mean, she's got no regrets," he said. "But I think her husband's been sort of a serious asshole. I mean, I think he's been exactly like my dad. Not exactly faithful. And the last time I was there, she said, 'You know, I could forgive your father, but I can't forgive myself for all the things Marcus has done.' It's seriously depressing."

"Yeah," Peter said quietly, touched, in spite of himself, to be given this inside knowledge of the Marr family, and moved by its sadness. "That is."

But mostly Michael told Peter about his aunt, whom everyone adored (for rescuing Michael from motherlessness) and envied. Even Frigid's punk song held a bit of tribute within its mocking:

> *I want to be Sylvia*
> *I want to wear hats with low brims*
> *I'd die to be seen in her*
> *Black scarves like second skins*

Michael, though, was less than loving. He talked about how, when his aunt had first moved in, she'd insisted on taking him to school, though he'd been walking himself for several months. She'd started by asking, "Can I walk with you to school today?" and he'd said, "No." "Don't you want my company?" she'd asked, and he'd said, "No." She'd gone with him anyway. He'd just let her walk along next to him. He said it was one of his earliest memories, ignoring her over those few blocks. She'd chattered, and he'd said nothing. Until she'd given up on talking and, later, on the walks themselves. But before that, she'd got what she wanted. During her first weeks at the Helmsford, photographers had covered the place constantly to document the change in Michael's life. The morning walks were, for her, a photo opportunity. She was the new mother. Or, better yet, the new mother beleaguered by lack of privacy. She took to wearing sunglasses regardless of the weather. And one morning, Michael said, she put on a new pair—wraparounds—and when they stepped out of the lobby a photographer called out, "Miss Blanton, I don't think those glasses are right for your face." "Why?" she asked, pulling them off, before she realized the photographer was snapping away.

"I can still remember the look on her face," Michael said, laughing. "It was like Scarlett in that scene in *Gone With the Wind*. Where she opens her eyes after Rhett doesn't kiss her."

And the next morning, Sylvia not only had another new pair of sunglasses (just in case the wraparounds really had been unflattering), she had her head and half her face ensconced in a trailing black scarf. Such was the beginning of her covert glamour.

Michael finished this story as the waitress delivered their check. So he really did grow up without parents, Peter thought, as if knowing it for the first time. His father dead; his mother fleeing and unhappy; his aunt vain and impossible to trust, no substitute at all. And again, Peter felt an inner flush of sympathy.

Michael was reaching into his pockets. He patted them a second and third time. He apologized. He'd forgotten his wallet.

"Don't worry about it," Peter said, feeling warmly paternal as he paid for the meal.

On their way out, Michael invited Peter to P.S. 5. Peter hesitated, accepted. They went first to Peter's apartment, where he dropped off his guitar and changed into a white T-shirt and his loose-fitting, three-buttoned thrift shop black blazer. (This was half of what he sometimes wore when he played in bars. The rest was black jeans and black wingtips. He liked the hint of punkish severity. He liked the contrast to his music. After one of his first gigs in the city, in a small Houston Street bar called the Crescent Lounge, a woman had told him that when she'd seen him come out on stage she hadn't expected his songs to be so emotional. He liked to imagine himself like that—looking stark and tight-lipped, and emerging suddenly as vulnerable in a powerful kind of way.)

Peter had been dancing a few times at other clubs; he'd never been to P.S. 5. The club was named for the public school that had once occupied its building. When the city had decided to close the school there were community protests, but the structure was sold to two festive and wealthy design school dropouts. This history added to the club's allure. Other places mailed out free passes (or even gave them away in stores), for the club scene in general was heading gradually out of vogue; but at P.S. 5 everyone paid (with a few exceptions, including Michael and his guests). And the crowd outside was vast and desperate. They tried open supplications or detached telepathies, hoping to be picked by the impassive doormen. And tonight, because the club's decor had just received its monthly transformation, they were electric with need.

Ducking out of a taxi, Michael led Peter toward the side of the entrance. Swiftly, almost imperceptibly, one of the doormen caught Michael's eye. The crowd seemed to see this, to understand, without turning around, that someone would be admitted and that it wouldn't be them, because as the doorman unhitched the red rope no one made a move forward. Instead, people edged apart along the line of the doorman's glance. Meanwhile, Michael had gestured for Peter to go in front of him.

So, feeling warmly protected, not paternal now, Peter sidled through.

Four

THE CLUB'S DECOR, IT TURNED OUT, HAD AN UNDERWATER MOTIF. Along the sides of the wide, downward-sloping entry hall, with its purple lighting, were a series of display cases, large as department store windows. They were huge versions of household aquariums. The fish, the fake shipwrecks and flora, the bubbles from the filters were all oversized. There was a diver in each case, in full scuba gear; they might have been mannequins, suspended by invisible wire, except for the shifting of eyes behind a mask and the momentary paddling of fins.

The main rooms were decorated with playful, childlike sculptures. Distorted sharks' heads loomed from the walls. Impossibly colored starfish clung to the backs of chairs. A school of silver sea horses dangled above a bar.

It was beside one of these sculptures that a woman, who introduced herself as Lee, came on, at first, to Michael. She was blond, with a severe, geometrical shape. If the shoulder

52

pads she wore under her paisley jacket had projected out any farther they would have qualified as wings; as it was, they jutted like cornices, making the upper part of her sleeves look inhumanly empty. Her silk shirt was a glossy blue. It was the color of the inside of a geode, and under it her breasts, which were not small, might have been formations of geodelike crystals.

Below the jacket and shirt, she had on a short, black leather skirt and black high heels. Her stockings were more or less transparent. So her legs were on display from the middle of her thighs, but somehow—maybe because they were framed by black, or maybe because of the stiffness of the leather or the harsh rise of the heels, or maybe because the rest of her outfit was so rigidly angular—somehow even her legs seemed unnatural, slightly less than alive.

Peter didn't take all this in right away. It had its effect on him later. His first thought was simply, enviously, this: that yet another pretty woman had edged in to try her luck.

"Do you mind if I share this with you?" she asked Michael. "Whatever it is."

What she meant was a shapeless mass of smooth, iridescent red plastic, four or five feet high, with a dozen irregular protrusions like giant thumbs. Michael leaned against one of these growths, Peter stood next to him, and Lee positioned herself on Michael's other side.

"I think it's supposed to be coral," Peter said, stepping away from the amorphous red object into Lee's line of vision. But either she couldn't hear him over the music, or she couldn't be bothered to respond. She glanced at him and then leaned toward Michael, her lips moving close to his ear. Standing there in front of them, Peter felt like a hideous fish. He was inclined to wriggle back against the plastic coral, but this would involve a further loss of dignity. He stayed where he was, feigning interest in the distant sea horses.

Meanwhile, Lee had pulled away from Michael's ear, and Peter could hear her questioning Michael, asking, "You went to Yale for a while, didn't you?" and "Do you know Mimi Adams?" and "Do you know Colin Davis?" and "How about Katrina Kennedy?" and "Oh, do you have a house on Nantucket?" and "Which part of the island?" and "Oh, do you know the Davisons? Or the Applefords?" and "Do you ever go windsurfing there?" Of course, she knew the answers, and every time he nodded or said "Sure" she was ready with a response. She'd spent a summer at Yale and had lived at his college, and Mimi Adams had been one of her closest friends in high school, and Colin Davis had gone out with her sister, and Katrina Kennedy she'd known since kindergarten, and she loved Nantucket, especially that part of the island, and the Davisons and the Applefords were like second families to her, and she was "addicted" to windsurfing—she was a "windsurfing junkie."

Listening, Peter found himself thinking ahead—to sharing a cab home with Michael. (Temporarily, he forgot that Michael would probably be taking a cab home with someone else.) He imagined them laughing, briefly, about this woman on the coral; he imagined them recounting, for a minute, her imbecilic rap; but soon the conversation would shift; fluidly they would shed their ridicule and their talk would deepen; it would become self-reflective, self-revealing. What they would say remained vague in Peter's mind. Perhaps Michael would lament the worthlessness of everyone's affection, and the lament would be soft-spoken and sincere, with no hint of hollow emphasis, no tinge of dishonesty. And maybe Peter's reply would be pure empathy. But in this imagined descent into serious talk the specifics were unclear; it was the feeling of the conversation that Peter knew perfectly in advance. It was being the only person Michael could say these things to. It was being the only person he could communicate with. It was riding uptown with Michael, distinct from the adoring world. It was Michael's choosing him for real friendship. It was the sweet, blood-slowing envelopment that came with that choice.

Then another woman, who'd gone off to get drinks before Lee's arrival, returned with beers for Peter and Michael and a glass of wine for herself. She was Asian. She wore a white carnation in her thick black hair, and she had on a plain black jumpsuit. Something about her struck Peter as skeptical and intelligent. Drawn to her, he wanted to warn her away from chasing Michael. He watched Michael's seductive ambivalence toward both women. You're too smart for this, he wanted to tell her, as the three of them—Michael, Lee, and the Asian woman—chatted, making comments about the club's weird furniture.

"What is *this*?" the Asian woman asked, pointing with her foot at the bumpy red mass.

"I think it's supposed to be coral." But it was as if Peter alone were truly underwater and no sound came out of his throat. Michael stared, luringly impassive, at the Asian woman, and Lee said, "It's an unidentified species," and the three of them laughed.

Then Michael took a long sip of beer, and there was a long silence as the women watched him swallow and watched the beer settle back in the bottle as he tipped it away from his mouth. They checked around them for topics of conversation—people in showy outfits and other odd, primitively sculpted sea things—and once, when the second woman pointed out a gray minidress with a wide neckline made to look like a shark's mouth, Lee said, "Oh, I know her. I better go say hello. The last time I saw her at a party she thought I was ignoring her and she literally threw a fit. She's probably standing over there fuming, waiting for me to go over. She's probably about to storm over here and try to attack me with her neckline. I better go say hello." Lee didn't budge, and her eyes returned quickly to the beer bottle. Both women glanced constantly at it. They followed it up to Michael's lips and eyed his Adam's apple as he swallowed, and they peered into the tinted bottle again as he held it upright. And Lee's face, which was strong-featured and smooth-skinned, looked strained. Her cheeks seemed brittle. Meanwhile, Michael's expression had become more detached, his eyes more indifferent. He looked almost completely bored, and Peter thought, This is exactly what they want. Boredom to order. With just a hint of lust distilled. All according to their expectations.

As soon as Michael was down to one swig, the Asian woman asked him to dance. Lee was in the midst of a monologue about someone else she should really say hello to. This one was a guy in stylishly voluminous pants. "He wanted to get back together," she was saying. "But how could I? He looks like a dandelion after a hurricane. He must hate me, because when he showed up at my door I practically screamed. I had to put my hand over my mouth. I didn't mean to be cruel, but his hair had done a disappearing act."

Everyone laughed, but because she'd been talking Lee had missed her chance. Michael finished his beer and followed the other woman to the dance floor. Peter turned, staring at nothing, offering Lee a chance to vanish.

"So where do you know Michael from?" she asked.

"College." It seemed easier than explaining that though he'd gone to school with Michael he'd only met him two weeks ago.

"At Yale?"

"No. Palmer."

"Oh, do you know Roberto Herrera? Or Annette al-Sharah?"

"Sure." Another adjustment of truth. It was out before he could consider it. He pictured Roberto and Annette against the balcony railing at Michael's party.

"She's *such* an incredible person," Lee said.

"I know."

"Has she ever told you about how her family escaped when Khomeini took over?"

Peter nodded, laughing to himself.

"She says she still has nightmares about it. Which I'm sure is why she seems so distant. People think she's stuck-up, but really she's just wary. She's afraid of people. I would be, too, if I'd been through all that."

"Definitely."

"She's really the warmest person once she lets her guard down."

"She's a great friend," Peter said.

"She is."

"Once she trusts you," he said, "she can be one of the most generous people I know."

Meeting his, Lee's eyes, which were gray-blue, seemed to shiver slightly with interest.

"Should we get a drink?" he asked.

"Let's dance," she said. "I love this song."

Peter listened. He knew the song. He hated it. Not an instrument was actually played on it. The whole thing was a barrage of computerized emissions. It sounded like a war zone or an air traffic-control tower. The percussion was like machine-gun fire, the melody an insistent four-note bleeping from a radar. The lyrics consisted of one word, which was spoken and echoed and overdubbed. The word was "emotion," and because there wasn't a trace of it in the song, Peter began to imagine that he, too, was devoid of feelings. This happened as he and Lee started to dance. Suddenly he sensed himself hypnotically attractive, invulnerable. He was a kind of bionic lover, who could please any woman he slept with. And he danced to fit this impermeable prowess. He kept his eyes expressionless, his lips slightly pursed and smileless. He slinked his shoulders from side to side.

Over the next hour, the artillery was fired to different rhythms, the radar chirped to varying minimalist melodies. The lyrics, too, went through small transformations. "Emotion" gave way to "situation," then to "ecstasy." Peter could send all the right signals down all the right wires. He looked across at Lee, took in her outfit, her hard, somewhat inhuman beauty, and envisioned the glitchless interaction of their lovemaking.

"I think you should come home with me," he stated matter-of-factly, after they'd had a drink. He could hardly believe the evenness of his tone.

"Do you think so?" Her voice was equally flat and undaunted.

"I do."

"Well," she said, laughing quickly, raspily, "should you tell your friend you're leaving?"

He glanced over his shoulder as if Michael would be right there. "No." He shrugged. "I'll never find him. I'll talk to him tomorrow."

Their cab took the West Side Highway, passing the gay bars and the pair of battleships and climbing the ramp into the soft stitching of yellow lights.

"So what do you do?" Lee asked.

"I'm a musician." Lately, this statement made him feel tenuously put together, as if, as he spoke, he had to keep his face from decomposing, or cracking and flying apart in shards. The statement seemed, for a moment, no more accurate than saying he'd known Michael at Palmer, or that Annette was one of his closest friends. No, he had to remind himself, it *is* true. And it's about all that is.

"What kind?"

"I write songs." He smiled slightly, investing his reticence with a touch of superiority. "And I sing them."

"Professionally?"

"Professionally."

He considered stopping there. He sensed her impression. He was something of a star, playing it close to the vest. But he added, "I opened for Jackson Browne a while ago. And that, thus far, has been the pinnacle of my career."

"Oh."

He regretted the elaboration. Most people, no matter how self-deprecating he got, were impressed by the Jackson Browne gig. But Lee seemed to hear only his self-doubt. She seemed disappointed or, at best, bewildered.

"And you?" he asked.

"What?"

"What do you do for a living?"

"I work for Phil Orestes."

"Who is?"

"Phil Orestes? Oh, well, *New York* is doing an article on him next week. He just won three Clios. He did the Endymion campaign. The one of the shepherd under the full moon?"

"Oh, right," Peter said. "That *is* a beautiful ad."

"Oh, he's brilliant. Impossible to work for. But brilliant. He had the agency pull two all-nighters last week. It's just me, and three other people, and Phil. He has this inner, glassed-in office, and we could see him pacing around in there all night. And you just knew it was going to be him who came up with the concept. We're his sounding boards. It's incredibly annoying. He has Theresa, who's thirty-four, and who was a copywriter at Ogilvy, fetch his coffee. He can be an incredible asshole. Half the time we're his secretaries, because he says he doesn't *believe* in secretaries. But he really is brilliant. So it's great training for me."

Peter had a thing about the word "brilliant." He felt it should be used sparingly, and from his college friends he heard it all the time. People were brilliant for getting into good business schools, brilliant for buying certain stocks, brilliant for the way they designed display windows or represented books; they were even brilliant for the speed with which they solved the Sunday crossword. No, Peter thought, no. There were artists and thinkers and inventors who could be called brilliant. But the creator of a cologne's ad campaign, for example, could not.

Nevertheless, he felt a surge of affection for Lee as she rattled on about her boss. He wanted to tell her to quit. He wanted to build her self-esteem. He wanted to convince her she wasn't working for a crazy genius—she was working for an abusive fraud. I'm sure there are plenty of good agencies that could train you, he was about to say, when the taxi turned onto his block. He stayed silent.

He paid the driver, and he and Lee stepped down to the gate and into his apartment. In his living room he made drinks and sat next to her on the couch.

"So have you seen Annette lately?" It was the last subject he wanted to reopen, but his brain was refusing to come up with alternatives.

"Oh." Lee smiled. "No. I mean, a few weeks ago. Have you?"

"I saw her the weekend before last at this party. At Michael's."

"He had a party?"

"Yeah."

"How was it?"

"Good," Peter said, nonchalantly. "Jammed. I don't even think half the people there were invited, and most of the ones who were might as well be strangers to him. But people'll do anything to get near Michael Marr." He rolled his eyes.

"Uchh." Lee shuddered.

"Yeah."

There was a pause.

"Anyway," he said, and though her gray-blue irises were unreadable, and the foot or two of couch between them made his gesture even more precarious, he leaned in to kiss her.

This was how: softly, with mouth open and tongue withheld. Which wasn't exactly as he'd foreseen it. Nor was the spirit behind it quite right. What he'd had in mind was dead-certain delivery, and instead he offered a question, replete with memories, going back unconsciously, in spite of the club's music which kept up its automaton pulse in his head, to parked cars, to parties with parents away, to camp, the fade-out of the last song at the end-of-August dance, some Chi-Lites ballad, a grazing of lips.

Lee, on the other hand, was programmed perfectly—the placement of her hand, the trick she performed of tongue-tracing the perimeter of his lips.

"Anyway," he said again, when they separated. *Anyway.*

He tilted back in. He kissed her mouth, her neck. He listened for her breathing. He touched, held, licked her breasts through her blue shirt. He unfastened buttons, licking, listening, listening.

"So," he said. "So should we adjourn to the other room?"

And then this image, though he'd had plenty of fine sex in his life, this, because her breathing was hardly affected by his ministrations, because she was somewhat dry, because entrance itself wasn't easy and some reangling was required: led by her hand, he imagined himself a child—blue corduroy short pants, matching blue suspenders. He had downy hair.

Once in, he attempted several maneuvers. Lee remained impassive. Self-possessed, she did one thing and another with her tongue, her fingers, her hips, deft, dizzying things, while, next to them on the bed, Michael too made love to her. *That,*

Peter could see, was a different story. No problems there. She sighed and moaned, bowing her back until she practically levitated—it was a regular porn movie over there. An X-rated extravaganza. Erotica epitomized. Michael drove her wild with his princely prick.

And afterward, Peter lay on his back next to her, silent with his eyes focused up at the ceiling, deferent to their privacy, waiting for them to finish.

#

IN ADDITION TO GIGGING WITH THE EINSTEINS, PETER SUPPORTED himself by teaching guitar. Through a nearby private school, and then by word of mouth, he'd had no trouble attracting pupils. The older kids were in awe. They'd come to hear him in bars, and the one or two truly hopeful musicians considered him their first real mentor. At the Lone Star he'd beckoned one out of the audience, to play guitar on two covers and harmonize above Peter on one of Peter's own songs:

> So you trade yourself in
> A new lover again
> Babe, if there's a truth inside
> It stays untried . . .

The younger kids, too, were enamored. Peter had a simple recording system rigged in his living room; he told the students that when they'd learned a song they could go "into the studio." In "session," the kids strummed chords and sang while Peter added guitar lines and harmonies, and afterward, the students, whose requests for songs ranged from Lynyrd Skynyrd to old anti-war anthems, walked home along the streets of the Upper West Side, or rode home on crowded rush-hour subways, quietly ecstatic, listening to themselves on their Walkmen.

But there was also Kevin Briscoe. At thirteen, he was five feet ten and beefy, with a squarish face and bristles of marine-cut blond hair, and a large, rose-colored birthmark covering his left cheek. It was a huge splotch, like a wild overapplication of Maybelline blush. Early on, Kevin had asked to learn "Alison," and every week after that, wearing the camouflage jacket he never took off, he'd gone over the song in Peter's presence. He'd strummed doggedly and refused to sing, his face all torpid belligerence. Every so often, Peter ventured a personal question. The boy was not conversational.

When Kevin finally began to mutter the lyrics, it came as a relief to Peter, though as Kevin's voice gained volume it was either phlegmatic or full of murderous emotion. He sang, "Sometimes I wish that I could stop you from talking, when I hear the silly things that you say" and "I think somebody better put out the big light" with such vindictive intensity that the first time he heard it, Peter lurched back in his folding chair. And on "My aim is true," the boy's pale, freckled forehead seemed on the verge of translucence.

"I'm telling you," Peter told Sifkin, the drummer he'd been working with, "any day now, this kid could be on the cover of the *Post*."

But lately Kevin seemed to have quit snarling on every line alluding to violence. Lately he seemed to invest a little feeling in the rest of the lyrics. And this afternoon—the day after Peter's night at P.S. 5, the day after his night with Lee—it was as if the song were entirely new. So Peter said warily, "Maybe we should put this on tape."

"What for?" Kevin sneered. "So I can stick it in my Walkman and walk around listening to myself?"

"No," Peter assured him. "Just so you can hear what you sound like."

"I know what I sound like."

"And how's that?"

"Like shit."

The pronouncement was so flat and tersely pathetic that Peter felt himself about to burst into laughter. To stop himself, he stood and spun around.

"Kevin," he said, facing the boy again, "you do not sound like shit. Once upon a time—two months ago, one month ago, two *weeks* ago—you might have sounded like shit, but now I'm beginning to think you sound pretty damn good. In fact, I'm beginning to think I like the way you sing this song as much as the way Elvis Costello does. I mean, I don't know who you're singing *about,* whether you're singing about some girl at school you're in love with or something, but it seems like you're singing about someone, because it's beginning to sound like your own song."

"My mother," Kevin said.

"What?"

"I'm singing about my mother."

"Your mother," Peter reiterated, as Kevin stood suddenly and went around the long counter that divided Peter's living room from his kitchen. Peter watched. Kevin took a pan from the dish rack and set it on the stove. He jiggled it by the handle as if frying an omelet. "Kevin, darling," he said, in a wistful woman's voice, "there goes a dream." He glanced over his shoulder toward an imaginary door.

Then he abandoned the pan, grabbed a plate from the dish rack, walked out to the small, round table in the corner of

Peter's living room, set the plate down, and said, as if disgusted, "Kevin, darling, last night I met with the greatest disappointment of my life.

"That was a different morning," he added.

Then he stepped behind a chair and placed his hands on the chair's back. "Kevin, darling," he mused, "when you get older I hope you won't give pleasure the way that man does. Because that man is a menace."

The boy, wearing, as ever, his camouflage jacket, picked his guitar off the carpet and sat again in his folding chair. Peter was momentarily shocked—not that such a mother existed, but that such theatrical energy existed in Kevin. He applauded. "That was great," he said. "That was terrific."

Kevin smirked.

"But can I tell you one small thing?"

"What?"

"The only time I've ever talked to your mother, before you started taking lessons, she said, 'Mr. Bram, I'm not a very independent person. But I want Kevin to have something of his own, like an instrument, for whenever he's lonely.'"

"So?"

"I don't know. You tell me."

"So she's a basket case."

"That wasn't the point I was trying to make."

"Spare me."

"All right. Then let's make a tape of your singing."

A while after Kevin went home, Michael called. All afternoon, Peter had been considering calling him. Or rather, he'd been telling himself *not* to consider it. I'm not going to make a major issue out of it, went the rationale. If he wants to hang out, fine. It would be interesting. It would be one of those things you do, just for the experience. Hang out with Michael

Marr. Amusing. But it's not exactly a long-sought goal in your life. It wouldn't make much difference, one way or the other.

Thus he'd kept a certain memory in a corner of his mind. The night before, at dinner, they'd talked a few minutes about playing tennis. "Well, you should give me a call," Michael had said. "We should play sometime. Maybe at the end of this week I can get us a court." And Peter had said, "All right. Yeah. Give me your number." That was it. That was the memory. That and the scribbling of seven digits on the back of a receipt Peter happened to have in his pocket. No woman's number had ever seemed as significant. Maybe because in this case sex couldn't be involved. Maybe because sex couldn't be the reason for nervousness. So there was that much more to cover up—there was the nervousness itself, and there was the hint of sex, in taking down a near-stranger's number, that had to be ignored.

The receipt (from the supermarket: suitably scrappy) had gone into Peter's wallet, and the tension of the moment had dissipated. The moment itself had been forgotten, or at least obscured. But when Peter picked up the phone and heard Michael's voice, it all flooded back. Calm down, you asshole, he said to himself, as he said to Michael, "Hey, mahn," giving his hello a little Rastafarian twist, affectionate but shrugging. And he asked himself, Shouldn't you be busy? and then, What the fuck is your problem? Are you going to say you're shampooing your hair? as he told Michael, "Sure. Yeah. That would be good. Where should I meet you?"

This is insane, he railed, after hanging up. You have no interest in that. You're a healthy fucking heterosexual who gets a hard-on behind half the miniskirts in New York. And your dick is as tiny as a pea right now. So forget it. You're allowed to be nervous. You're playing tennis with America's prince. That's all. And you should try to be a little more sarcastic when you say that. America's prince. Roll your fucking eyes a little.

He took a deep breath. He shook his head, smiling tolerantly, dismissing his silent ranting. He went to the closet to get his gym bag and pair of rackets. He packed his tennis sneakers, socks, his headband, shorts, shirt. He zipped the bag to the grips of the rackets. The tension dissolved again.

But back it came in the locker room of Michael's club. They'd met downstairs in the club's lobby, and, as with the Helmsford's doorman, Peter was very aware of the receptionist's greeting. She'd given a quiet hello to Michael, clearly glad they were on a first-name basis, and she'd introduced herself to Peter, extending a small, cool hand across the counter. Her eyes had held his briefly, warmly. Something had passed between them. She could be interested in second best, her gaze seemed to say. And not the way Lee was. There was something forgiving in the receptionist's eyes, as if she could take second best and treasure it.

Now, though, standing on the black carpet between the black-cushioned bench and the black bank of lockers, Michael pulled off his sweater and unbuttoned his shirt. Peter took care not to glance down from Michael's face as they chatted—small talk about the last time each of them had played tennis. He waited until Michael had turned toward his locker. The shoulders were powerful, carved, but with the kind of definition that seemed given, not worked on. The arms were the same, muscular and unself-conscious, not pumped up.

"I played almost every day last summer," Michael was saying. "But I think it hurt me more than helped me. I started getting impatient and my forehands started heading for the fences."

And the chest, viewed in a separate, quickly swooping gaze as Michael faced him again, was broad and solid, the pecs prominent in a graceful, undeliberate way.

Jealously, admiringly, fleetingly, Peter took in Michael's body. There was no inclination to touch. (Or was there?

68

Peter's mind played tricks on him.) There wasn't the dimmest hint of arousal. (Or was there?) There was only the desire to look.

Peter averted his eyes.

In his boxers, Michael checked a series of open lockers, looking for a hanger. Then he slipped off the boxers and put on his tennis gear. Peter kept his glance high.

They still had a few minutes. They stretched, each pulling his right arm behind his neck, to loosen his shoulders, each propping his heels on the black-cushioned bench and dipping toward his knees, to loosen his legs and back.

But the limbering had little effect as Peter took the court. He had one simple wish, to play very well, and to be much, much better than Michael, which left him as loose as if he'd spent the last five minutes in a freezer.

At the baseline, as he took his racket back, swung through, sent the ball over, he might have been going through these motions for the first time; yet the ball traveled as it should, and as it almost invariably had for Peter over the past eight or ten years. In high school he'd never quite been a star; and at Palmer he'd dangled carelessly for two years at the bottom of the varsity ladder; but he had the strokes, there was no question about that, and when he hit, people often paused to watch. Jittery as he was, and hard as Michael did pound his erratic forehand, he had no trouble keeping his returns smooth and deep. His backswing was nimble on his forehand, efficient on his backhand; his footwork was precise and seemingly minimal; he was always in position, always getting power from his shoulders and hips. It appeared he spent no energy, and didn't have to think at all, though of course this wasn't the case. Keep your backswing short, short, he reminded himself. Get to the ball early. Get your body turned. Keep your shoulder low, shoulder low.

During the longer rallies he grew lost in the rhythm of the

shots and in the cadence of his urgings which became constant and semiconscious and which kept full consciousness at bay. When Michael suggested they play a set, Peter was jolted back into the world. Back came the jitters, the sense that motor control was a temporary gift.

He shouldn't have worried, though. He spun his serves to the corner, drove his ground strokes to the baseline, and Michael couldn't stay in the points for more than a few exchanges. And though Michael's first serve came fast and flat, his second sat submissively and Peter could do with it what he liked. He felt almost sadistic as Michael said, "Nice shot," or commanded himself, "You've got to get your second serve deeper." He felt pleased with himself and practically abusive as he short-hopped a ball and walloped it down the line, far out of Michael's reach.

"Wooo!" someone exclaimed, a second or two after the shot.

Peter looked over his shoulder to the next court. The woman who stood in the doubles alley was short, no, tiny—she couldn't have been taller than five feet, maybe five one. And she wore comical white shorts that were the length of knickers. They had cuffs below the knees. "Will you please come over here and give me a lesson?" she asked or joked or demanded in a semi-Southern accent. There was no nasal in it, just a hint of soft largess on certain vowels.

Peter smiled and continued back toward the baseline.

"I mean it."

He looked again. She hadn't moved. She spoke sharply, deadpan, as if she fully expected him to duck under the netting between the courts and to begin to transform her game.

"Well, I'd be honored," he said. "But I'm in the middle of a set."

"Okay. After you're finished."

"Okay." He laughed, sure she wasn't serious.

But she was, more or less. As soon as he won, she announced, "All right. That's it," and Peter saw that she'd already crossed under to their court.

"Wait a second," he said playfully. "How'd you know that was the last point?"

"Don't try and trick me. It's time for my lesson. Unless you want to play doubles. We have your court starting in fifteen minutes, for an hour."

He realized he'd misinterpreted. His opponent, not his own skill at the game, was the attraction. He glanced at Michael, who shrugged, smiling, seeming as charmed as Peter himself was by the woman's bravado.

"Okay," Peter said.

"Come on, Carol," the woman called, and introduced herself, "I'm Hallie-Gay."

"Excuse me?"

She spelled it. "And this is Carol, soon to be a *Sports Illustrated* swimsuit model."

There was no telling by Hallie-Gay's testimony, but by sight it seemed possible, if not probable, that Carol could model swimsuits. Both Peter and Michael had noticed her earlier. She was tall and slender and tan, with dirty-blond hair and the kind of wholesome face that could seem oblivious to the fact that her nipples were spearing suggestively through her maillot. Right now, though, in her loose white shorts (unlike Hallie-Gay's, they came only to mid-thigh) and blue Lacoste shirt, and with her hair clipped back, she looked like a very pretty, very premature Connecticut housewife.

Bathing beauty or not, she was no match for Hallie-Gay, and Hallie-Gay seemed to know it. Beneath her kooky, knicker-length shorts, it was clear Hallie-Gay was shaped inelegantly, along the lines of a pear. Yet that fact seemed wholly irrelevant. What mattered were her red Pro-Keds doubly laced with red-and-gold laces, her shorts, her T-shirt, which was red with tiny gold stars, and her huge hoop earrings, also red, with gold bars hanging from the hoops. What mattered, too, were her accent, her brashness, her abrupt way of flirting. She seemed half-crazy and probably very smart, and Peter was glad she chose him for a partner, saying, "I better play with you; she can at least hit it over."

But it was obvious what was up. After several of the points she and Peter won, she turned away from the net and did a cabaret girl's bump-bump with her ungainly hips, for Michael's benefit. Michael shook his head, laughing, paying little attention to his beautiful, bland partner.

At the end of their set, Hallie-Gay suggested (or insisted, in her inimitable way) that the four of them go to dinner. They met in the lobby. Now she wore red snakeskin cowboy boots and a yellow shirt with silver, bull-embossed collar studs. Carol still looked like a child bride from Darien.

"What do I do?" Hallie-Gay said, in the restaurant. "I write the 'Faces in the Crowd' column that runs in that minuscule type at the back of *Sports Illustrated*: 'Doug Travis, 47, a K-Mart manager in Weymouth, Idaho, hit a hole in one on the 368-yard ninth hole of the Weymouth Public Links. The same morning, he hit another on the 326-yard seventeenth.' These are the profound events to which I dedicate my life. And let me tell you, the thought of some K-Mart manager whooping it up 'cause he hit a hole in one in who knows where, it can either make you laugh or it can make you want to crawl under your desk and die."

Then she explained about her "sideline." She did voice-overs, or rather, not voice-overs exactly. What she did was scream on the sound tracks of horror movies. Her screams were dubbed in for terrified actresses or added in for terrified crowds. How had she ended up with such employment? She'd been overheard one drunken night by a director. And couldn't the cast members scream for themselves? "Apparently not," she said. "Should I demonstrate my gift?"

"Yes," Peter said, joking, but wishing she *would* let go at the top of her lungs in the middle of the softly lit restaurant.

Michael looked taken; he smiled loosely at Hallie-Gay. Meantime, Carol faded further from the picture. She spoke little. She would, she confirmed, be appearing in the magazine next February, and she commented enthusiastically about the beaches on St. Croix, where her shoot had been held. Listening, Michael's eyes looked so flat and bored they seemed on the verge of rolling.

"Why don't we all get a drink at my apartment?" Michael said after dinner, the invitation directed at Hallie-Gay.

"Well," she said, "I can think of better options, but that one will do."

The four of them took a cab uptown. At the apartment, they had their drinks on the terrace. The low, calm lights of Central Park West seemed entirely remote from the burst of illumination at the center of the city. Hallie-Gay stepped back inside to get herself and Peter more bourbon. A moment later, Carol went in for her jacket. Peter and Michael were left alone on the terrace. Michael came closer.

"Listen, Peter," he said quietly. "I don't want you to think I'm being a jerk. But, uh . . ."

"No, no," Peter told him, with mock gallantry. "Go ahead."

Michael went in. Peter remained leaning, staring, waiting for Carol to return, wondering how he would make small talk with her until they could smoothly leave the apartment and go their separate ways. Yes, I mind, he said silently to Michael, who was not there.

"Hey. I see things worked out the way we both hoped they would."

Peter turned. Hallie-Gay looked up at him from her diminutive height. He smiled. It took a second for things to register fully. Michael had gone off with Miss Connecticut. That was who Michael had wanted all along.

"Well, maybe we should forget these drinks," Hallie-Gay joked into the silence. "I live right over on Amsterdam. We could have a drink there."

"Sure," Peter said.

But something had happened, and continued to happen as they rode the elevator down, her arm through his. Her small mouth, which had seemed animated even when she wasn't speaking, and which, increasingly all evening, he'd been desperate to kiss, now looked simply sticky with red lipstick. And as they started to walk, her short, plump body began to matter a good deal. It was her energy, her eccentricity, her intelligence that were inconsequential.

"You know," Peter said, as they turned onto Amsterdam, "I should probably head home. I have to be up early tomorrow morning."

"Come again, as my father used to say."

He managed to smile at the joke. "I said, I should probably head home."

But she seemed to have understood the first time. As she glanced up at him, her face looked both rigid and shapeless, and all her energy seemed stripped away.

"That's too bad," she said bitterly.

He didn't know what to say. He didn't know what to think. He just felt sick to his stomach. Sick of himself.

"Well," he tried, his voice trailing off.

"Well, goodnight."

Her smile—forced but steady—froze him. He stood still on the sidewalk as she headed away.

Six

But lee remained alluring. Peter saw her again the following weekend, and twice the week after that. They went to dinner, to a movie, to a new club. They danced, flirted, talked guardedly about themselves. They slept together. Making occasional sounds of pleasure, she stayed remote.

One Saturday they wandered into the Frick mansion. They strolled through the lush rooms, through the gilded, petite Boucher Room with its soft, idyllic paintings of children fishing, children shearing sheep, and with its small furniture that reminded Peter of a dollhouse, and through the dining room with the French windows and their heavy, tapestried drapes. In one of the anterooms Peter stayed several minutes in front of a case of enameled plaques. The plaques depicted a range of subjects, but many shared the same rich background color.

"That blue," Peter mumbled, as Lee joined him in front of the case.

"It's beautiful, isn't it?" she said.

For Peter, it was much more than that. The background color made the faces and scenes irrelevant; the midnight blue had a depth that defied the hard, glinting enamel surface; the hue was an element he could feel, almost taste, and he ached for submersion in it.

After circling through the mansion, Peter and Lee came into its Garden Court, an immense stone hall of pillars and plant beds sprouting a tasteful abundance of ficus and palms, and out-of-season lilies and delphiniums. On the three steps down to the level of the fountain, Lee's shoes touched with a faint, flat sound that somehow made her seem to belong—or at least to know how to present herself—within the decorous extravagance of the room.

They sat on one of the cushioned marble benches. The fountain made a steady, soothing noise that seemed to absorb a part of consciousness.

"You know," Lee said, "I want to live a charmed life."

Peter smiled, then smiled more fully because she seemed to mean it.

The fountain continued its quiet gurgling. He looked at her and, though sure he was incapable of it, wanted to trade his ambitions, his way of thinking, of living, for hers. Her way seemed so much easier, as effortless and coaxing as the constant sound of the water.

"A charmed life," he repeated, almost sighing, imagining a seductive impossibility: himself as her.

"Mm—mmm," she said.

They went, as well, to a play based loosely on the life of Gauguin. In the play, the primitive colorist lived in India instead of Tahiti, and instead of giving young girls syphilis, he blinded or murdered them with the help of the Indians' morality. That is, he seduced them, and when their fathers or brothers discovered they had been ruined, their eyes were ritually burned, or, in the worst cases, the girls were stabbed to death. The girls were helpless to resist the painter. And the painter was helpless to stop. He was a sensualist—the girls were his inspiration. But at the end of the play, despairing that he had destroyed so much for the sake of mere art, he killed himself.

Lee thought the play was brilliant. Peter wasn't too sure. On the one hand, he thought it was trite and terribly romantic. It asked an old question: Are great men entitled to depravity? And it celebrated a ridiculous equation: You *have* to be depraved to create great art. On the other hand, it left Peter wishing he were the painter, or the musical equivalent of him.

After talking for a while about the play, they switched to the subject of Lee's job. And the next day, on the phone with Michael, Peter recounted some of their conversation. "You know," he said, "at some level she's really kind of an innocent. I mean, this guy, her boss, is literally swindling her, and she refuses to admit it. The agency's five people altogether. He has four women working for him, and they're supposed to start some kind of profit-sharing plan. The cashiers at McDonald's wouldn't work for what he pays them in salary, but they're supposed to work out this plan. He's promised them about five percent each. *When* they figure out the details. As soon as the agency's in the black, they're going to put it all down on paper. The guy has just won three Clios! Those Endymion ads are all over the place! I mean, I've been to pick her up at the office. It's two rooms—one for him and one for the rest of them. The guy is *in* the black. Not that it matters. The point is, she should just get the agreement in writing. But she's like a little girl. She's in awe of him. You tell her he might never come through, and it's like she hears you, she *agrees* with you, but it doesn't matter. She refuses to let the prospect settle in."

"Yeah," was more or less Michael's only response.

Peter and Lee had also talked about her past. She'd grown up just outside a Vermont town called Linton, in one of the most beautiful areas in New England. The town itself was colonial, she said, but what made it special was its purity: hardly a building on its main street didn't date back to the nineteenth or eighteenth century. Each of the two churches had a great, austere steeple topped by a golden ball, and the post office and town hall was a grand, porticoed structure fronted by classical pillars, and all the stores were owned by local families and were run out of white houses crested with weather vanes. She recalled getting chunks of hard chocolate at one ("just these huge broken pieces, about an inch thick," she said; "they kept them in a barrel"), and at another she'd bought ropes of black licorice that were sold by the yard. But these weren't just tourist-trap candy stores, she stressed. They were small grocery stores that had been there for years, and that happened to sell shards of chocolate or to be run by a man whose wife made licorice in the back.

She spoke, too, about the surrounding countryside—the horses she'd ridden, the maple trees she'd tapped, the bee farm nearby, the cross-country skiing. And what she obscured, by rhapsodizing about the quaint and the bucolic, were certain aspects of her upbringing. About three miles from the center of Linton is the Humes Academy. Peter had heard of Humes, knew it ranked with Andover and Exeter for education, and had heard it far exceeded them for elitism. But he had no reason to know the name of the nearest town, so it wasn't until he asked what her father did that he learned she'd grown up on the academy's campus. Her father, she told Peter, was an English teacher and guidance counselor. What she didn't tell him, however, was that she considered her father barely a rung above the butlers and maids who'd waited on her classmates at home. He'd started out with some half-baked idea of becoming a writer. And he'd ended up a failure and a fool.

"Oh, it was wonderful," she said, and she described the Georgian buildings and endless athletic facilities of the campus. There had been a lake where the crew team had practiced and where her father had taught her to sail. "It was like living at a summer camp. I was spoiled. And later, when I started there in ninth grade, it was like getting a great education in my own backyard."

"It was never awkward?" Peter asked.

"What do you mean?"

"I don't know. Just your father being a teacher."

"Well, maybe just a little." She laughed, and glanced sidelong at Peter, as if she were about to be completely honest in a wry, amusing way. "There *was* this thing about his clothes. In ninth grade, I spent Christmas vacation with my friend Alese in New York. And with another friend. And after seeing their fathers come home in pinstriped suits, I wanted my father to have one. I wanted him to be a banker or a lawyer. I think I even prayed for it once or twice in the school's chapel when I got home." She laughed again. "But I mean that was ninth grade. I was fourteen. I forgot about it after a few weeks."

She hadn't, though. The fact was she'd talked to God about wardrobes and career changes for months, and made more public, practical supplications as well. She wasn't quite tactless enough to hound her father about why, since he'd quit writing, he kept on being a teacher, but she was persistent about his apparel. "Dads," she said, "I think your tweed jackets are looking the worse for wear." Or, "Dads, don't you ever get hot teaching? I mean because of the way they overheat the buildings and wearing heavy tweeds and all." Or once, as they

walked on Newbury Street in Boston, past Jos. Bank Cloth-
iers, "Let's just take a look around, while we're here."

Until at last, for her fifteenth birthday, he decided to
surprise her. He was substituting that week in her American
Poetry seminar. He came into class at the last minute, dressed
impeccably for Wall Street, reciting Thoreau as he crossed
from the door to his small desktop podium:

> *Within the circuit of this plodding life*
> *There enter moments of an azure hue,*
> *Untarnished fair as is the violet*
> *Or anemone, when the spring strews them*
> *By some meandering rivulet, which make*
> *The best philosophy untrue that aims*
> *But to console man for his grievances. . . .*

He wore well-polished black lace-ups, a dark blue pinstriped
three-piece and a sober red tie, and afterward her classmates
wanted to know what he was so dressed up for.

"Is he going for a job interview?" they asked.

"You should tell him to look up my old man," they said. "He
might give him a break."

"Yeah," they said. "You should tell him to look up my old
man."

No, she did not relate this story to Peter, and certainly she
didn't tell him that she had not been well liked. She kept the
knowledge at the perimeter of her memory. As she did with
other episodes.

Always, through her childhood, her father had been toler-
ated by the students. Occasionally kids even came to him for
personal advice. One evening, years before she'd enrolled at
Humes, Lee had watched him comfort a boy in their living
room, the two of them hunched in a sad, secretive conference,
his hand on the boy's shoulder. From the upstairs landing,

she'd peered pridefully between the balusters. But a few months after she started at the academy, the students began smirking openly at him. (Why didn't they like her? Maybe it *was* snobbery. Maybe it was what they said—she was too pushy. It was true she managed to invite herself almost everywhere, changing the pronoun "you," plural, to "we," trying to insert herself at the center where she had been outside the periphery.) In particular, they started pointing out, indiscreetly to each other, and then to her, and then to him in front of her, that he sweated, in droplets, from his earlobes.

The sweat didn't originate anywhere else. It didn't trickle down his temples and then hook backward, or begin beneath his thick hair before leaping somehow from the sides of his head to his ears. In fact, it was hard to imagine him perspiring at all—he had a bold-featured face that would have been handsome if the skin hadn't been so prematurely withered. No, the sweat dripped only from his earlobes, which were like sporadically imperfect faucets. The leaking was unpredictable. It had nothing to do with temperature or exertion. Outside in December, at a Humes football game, the droplets formed steadily. Lee sat two rows behind him on the bleachers, horrified. For fifteen years she hadn't considered this slight defect; now she imagined his earlobes growing icicles.

And soon she glimpsed signs of his strangeness in herself. Next to where her ears were pierced, visible only with the light directly on them, were pinpoints of sweat, one on each lobe. They looked like impossibly small bits of tinsel, or infinitesimal shards of glass. She hoped they might be fine, colorless hairs. But when she pressed a finger against them, the glint disappeared, and returned a moment later. She repeated this test over and over. A few times, the spot of glitter seemed permanently gone (and she accused herself wildly of insanity), but it was a matter of tilting her head at the right angle to the light.

She decided to wait an hour to see if the specks of moisture developed into beads. They didn't. She forced herself to bed, expecting, overnight, beads followed by pearls followed by full-fledged drops, which would fall as she stood up in the morning, and which would be replaced more and more quickly. In the morning, she had to find the glint by squinting her eyes and tipping her head.

Still, she was sure things would worsen. She thought she could grow her short, stylishly cut hair, but wasn't sure it would be long enough before the sweating became noticeable, or even if it would hide everything no matter how long it got. It was by chance that she read about the Stocklin Medical Group, in New York, and it was after frantic deliberations and delays that she called. Because it was long distance, she used a pay phone, the one outside the football stadium. It was dusk, and snowing in small, windswept flakes; regularly she put in change as the operator demanded, while the receptionist on the other end put her on hold, came back on, and put her on hold again.

"I don't know," the receptionist said, between interruptions. "But lots of people come in here in pretty sad shape."

"Well, can't I just talk to one of the doctors? To ask about this specific thing?"

"They're all in surgery. Why don't you make an appointment? The consultation's free of charge."

In town, Lee took what money she had out of her bank account. (She'd planned to spend most of it on a vacation. Some of her classmates were going to Utah to ski, and, as usual, she'd shifted her pronouns and persisted with "we" and talked as if the trip had been her idea in the first place.) She arrived in New York on a clear, crisp January afternoon.

It was the kind of day—windless, bright, and warm when your shoulders and face absorb the midwinter sun—that seems to have escaped from a future or past October. It was the kind of day that puts things in perspective—it can seem criminal to be self-concerned when the weather has changed so magically. And it was the kind of day that, in collaboration with her surroundings as she walked up Fifth Avenue, reminded Lee of an afternoon she'd spent years ago with her father. Her family had been in the city for a weekend, and her mother had gone shopping; her father took her to Central Park to climb the rocks and tour through the children's zoo. The weather had been like this, warm enough to take off her gloves and parka, which she recalled doing because he'd taught her to wedge her fingertips into tiny crevices the way *real* rock climbers did, and when she reached the top he'd tied her red coat to a fallen branch, fashioning a flag of conquest. Later, they'd come to a hill still patched with snow from an earlier storm. A group of older boys were sledding on plastic discs. He'd led her to them and asked, "Any chance of a ride down for my friend here?"

The Stocklin Medical Group was in one of the old pale stone buildings on Fifth Avenue. Lee was early for her appointment. She didn't want to go in at all. She turned into the park and stared out over the fountain and the rowboat lake from the top of the steps. She passed the simple, cleanly curved band shell and the bronze busts of heroes looking highly principled in the January sunlight. On Central Park South she bought a hot pretzel, which she finished eating on one of the park's climbing rocks, after which she headed toward the children's zoo and paid the dime admission. She was the only one inside. It was dreary—the stalls were in disrepair and the animals were torpid—and she felt self-conscious, but she made herself stand in front of the dingy llama, as if to give her memories a chance to change her, as if to give her father a chance to grab her elbow and yank her, hard, back to where she should be.

Leaving, she followed a path between two low hills. On one there was a couple beside a gazebo. The guy had a shaggy black beard and wore a knit Cowichan cap with long earflaps; he struck a steel triangle with no apparent concern for rhythm, almost as an infant might have done. The woman wore a bulky parka and a paisley skirt. She spun with her arms out, her skirt lifting, her rotations in no relationship to the pinging of the triangle. If I was as old as them, Lee thought, with real longing. If I'd grown up then.

Though the office of the Stocklin Medical Group was in a building dating back to the twenties, its interior was leather and glass. In the vestibule, mirrors covered the walls and ceiling. It was dizzying. Her stomach in knots, she approached the reception counter. Behind it were several tall, slender nurses with small, well-defined features. With noses and chins so little, it seemed they should be timid. They weren't. Some hurried to shelves of medicines; others leaned against tables or sat in typing chairs, their backs to their computers.

"Milton's back for more plugs," a long-haired brunette announced.

A nurse with a close-cropped Afro rolled her eyes at this news before greeting Lee, questioning her, and filling out a series of forms.

"And what are you here to see Dr. Stocklin for?"

When Lee related her problem, the nurse paused, grimaced, then noted it on her sheet.

Lee took a seat in the crowded waiting room. At first, she thought she was the youngest person there. There were plenty of slack women and baldish men. But across the room was a boy who couldn't have been older than thirteen. He might have come along with his mother; as it turned out, she had come along with him. "Unfortunately," she explained to a woman next to her, "in the no-chin department he takes after his father."

"Lee Holt?" a nurse called, and she was shown in to the doctor's office.

Stocklin leaned against the front of his heavy oak desk, one muscular thigh slung sideways across the desktop. He had black curly hair tinged with gray, a wide, reddish face, and shoulders which, as he posed with his arms folded, completely filled out his shirtsleeves. Standing behind him, holding a small notepad and pen, was the long-haired brunette, who suddenly did look timid. Stocklin shook Lee's hand, gestured for her to sit below him in a leather chair, and asked what he could do for her.

She said she wasn't sure he could do anything.

"Lee, he assured her, "they call me 'The Doctor of Personal Perfection.'"

She began to explain. As she spoke, Stocklin walked around behind her and took her earlobes in his fingers, one at a time. He bent them gently and brushed them with his thumb. He made quiet, deep-voiced sounds. She imagined what he saw, the tiny glimmer disappearing as he touched it, then reemerging. He tugged and twisted more forcefully, dictating to the nurse a diagnosis and treatment, which she recorded on her notepad. Brushing Lee's earlobes affectionately one last time, he returned to lean against his desk and declared she could forget her worries.

"It's routine," he said. "We take an electric needle, apply heat to the interior of the pore, singe it. The scar tissue forms almost immediately, closes everything off. From the outside, invisible. Inside, a dam. I've never performed the surgery on the earlobe, but believe me, it's simple, and we have all the facilities right here."

Lee wanted to ask Stocklin if he were sure the surgery would work on the earlobe. She had visions of complications which he, apparently, didn't foresee. She thought of infections that would spread to her inner ears. She asked nothing, though. She was more concerned with convincing the doctor to operate that day. Finally he agreed. Under local anesthetic, her worries continued. She thought again of her father, the trifles of wisdom he'd given her as a child on bitterly cold days, when she'd protested against wearing some hated scarf or hat. . . . She was certain her ears would be damaged irreparably; she would lose her hearing entirely. . . . *You live in your own world,* she shouted. I can't do that. I don't even want to do that. And let me tell you one thing, the *real* world is a superficial place.

She would be deaf.

But things went as smoothly as Stocklin had promised. The electrically heated needle was inserted. Her pores were soldered shut.

Seven

AROUND THANKSGIVING, PETER ADMINISTERED TO HIMSELF A TEST. Straight, Bi, or Gay? the exam might have been called, and, deep down, he knew the answer in advance. Jacking off, to the image of an old high school girlfriend, he forced himself to switch images, substituting Michael's ass for the girl's. Suddenly he felt a good deal further from ejaculation. Then he imagined Michael behind him, pumping *his* ass—this didn't detract from Peter's excitement; in fact, it added somewhat to it; but it was more the conjured *feeling*—of having his asshole reamed—than the prospect of a male body behind him, that turned him on. Indeed, he found it difficult to picture the body at all. Finally, he tried to imagine kissing Michael's mouth. Tongue, lips. Steely-tasting saliva welled from the insides of his cheeks. He felt as if he were starting to gag.

Peter repeated various portions of the test several times, to be as sure as he could that his aversion wasn't shock or fear. Always, he got similar results. No, there was no hint of lust for

Michael. But their friendship could certainly seem like a romance.

One evening, Glickstein stopped by Peter's apartment on his way home from work (he was a bond broker at Salomon Brothers). Except for the party, Peter hadn't seen his old friend in months. He figured Glickstein had heard he'd been hanging out with Michael. But he didn't really mind the reason for his old friend's visit. Because like anyone romantically involved, what Peter wanted to talk about was the object of his interest.

"Yo, homes. What it is, dude," Glickstein said loudly, as Peter let him in.

One of the reasons Peter always had a soft spot for Glickstein was the mutability of his speech. At Michael's party, and elsewhere in the world, he was all decorum. He spoke plain, grammatical, well-educated English, with a few preppy phrases thrown in. All that distinguished his style of speaking from that of a hundred other Palmer graduates was a faint yet constant betrayal of need.

But alone with Peter, Glickstein's voice gained volume, and there were barrages of slang. The lexicon ranged from beatnik to black contemporary. "Cat" and "home boy" became staples of his vocabulary. He used adjectives like "bodacious" and expressions like "it's the joint." He was a walking, talking dictionary of current and antiquated hip. And this hadn't always been the case. Now it was like he impersonated some hyperbolic, misguided stereotype of cool. It was like a nervous tic. Often the phrases came in spurts that seemed uncontrollable. It was as if he were aiming for an idea of his pre-business, semi-musical past, and couldn't help ludicrously misfiring.

"So has Michael hooked you up with the *chef*?" Glickstein asked.

"What chef?"

"The chief. The cat that's going to put green in your jeans."

"Derek, what are you talking about?" Peter knew.

"His godfather, man. Zadeh."

"No, Derek."

"Well, have you asked him?"

"No. Actually."

"Yeah, man, I know how it is." Glickstein seemed to be calming, slowing toward more normal discourse. "It's hard to ask him to do things like that."

"You're right. It is. Not that I haven't made some pretty strong hints."

"He'll do it for you. He's a good man. You just have to earn his trust. He's got so many people coming after him, it's hard for him to know who to r-e-s-p-e-c-t."

"Yeah, well, I'll get him to do it."

"So you talked to him at his party?"

"For a minute."

"Nothing heavy?"

"I ran into him again about a month ago, though. It's actually kind of hard not to like him."

"He's a good man."

"I mean, it's fairly amazing how he can be so unsure of himself. He's like a character in *The Wizard of Oz,* except instead of wanting a heart or a brain or whatever, he wants an identity."

"I know what you mean," Glickstein said.

"Really, sometimes I feel like the Wizard when I'm talking to him, and he's saying, 'Give me an identity. Tell me who I am.' And I'm the fraud. Because I can't give it to him."

"I know what you mean."

"It's like the other day we were talking about why he transferred out of Yale. And I guess he just wasn't doing very well there. I guess they actually asked him to take a semester off. Which means he must have been doing pretty badly, since the last thing they'd want is to tamper with the Marr-Yale tradition. And I mean, he'll freely admit that he's no high-flyer. I mean, he's got a sense of humor about it. He said to me, 'Peter, look, I'm no fucking Newton.' But when he started talking about how he hadn't *wanted* to do well, how he hadn't wanted to live up to everyone's expectations, how he'd hated the fact that his father and his grandfather had gone there, it was like he wasn't sure *what* he'd wanted, whether he'd hated going to the family college or not. I don't know. Obviously no one can say anything about themselves that's completely true. No one knows what they really want. But when he said, 'Sometimes I think subconsciously I want to fail,' it was beyond bullshit. He's not like some con artist who half believes his own lies. Or who doesn't care. There wouldn't be any question in a con artist's eyes. You look for it, and it isn't there. But in Michael's eyes what you look for is a speck of certainty."

"Damn, dude," Glickstein put in. "Maybe you should be his biographer."

"Derek, if the magic genie gave me three wishes, that wouldn't be one of them."

"Have you ever got him talking about his father?"

"He says he used to throw darts at a picture of him."

"What?"

"That's what he says. In his room at Saint Paul's. He taped a *Life* magazine cover of his father to the cork board and threw darts at it."

"*Ho*, Michael."

"But this is another example. He talks about resenting his father. He talks about the burden of living under that legacy. And he tells me about the dart board. But the look in his eyes is so completely doubtful, it's like 'Peter, tell me, *did* I make a dart board out of my father's face?'"

"And it's the same on the flip side," Peter went on. "He told me he's read almost every book that's ever been written about his father. And it could easily be true. I've seen the books.

They're all lined up on a shelf in one of the extra bedrooms. But when he told me he'd read them, it was like his eyes were made of a thousand translucent layers, and he was begging me to peel them off, one by one by one, and to peel off layers of his brain, until I came to the fact. Then I could tell him, 'Yes, Michael, you've read them' or 'No, Michael, you haven't.'"

"Well, did you ask him anything about the books?"

"Sure. And he gave me the standard answers. Rolands' is the best, the fairest, but Collery's is the most sensitive about his father's character. The same things he's heard half his life. I'm not saying he hasn't read them. Just that you get this eerie sensation. That he doesn't know if he has."

They fell quiet.

"I don't know," Peter said. "The truth is it's flattering to be needed. Because he needs someone different than all the people who are down on their knees in front of him. He wants to get away from that. He can't stand it. Not that it doesn't have its advantages. Obviously it's hard to give up. But his heart's in the right place. He knows who's real and who's not. And I guess he thinks I can help him. He lets me see another side of him. With everyone else his eyes are about as human as gray-painted walls. He gives them the cool *they* want. That's what's so sad. But with me, well, he lets go of that. I don't know. He shows this desperation."

"I know what you mean," Glickstein said.

No you don't, Peter was on the verge of answering.

Michael was his. Or he—and he only—was Michael's.

"So what does he tell you he's going to do?" Glickstein asked.

"About what?"

"I don't know. Whatever. Is he heading into politics?"

"Well," Peter began, but he cut himself off. He'd have rather kept on analyzing, confiding, but now the stakes seemed too high. He said they hadn't talked about it.

He didn't tell Glickstein about the night he and Michael had gone bike riding. Around dusk, Peter, feeling more comfortable with Michael, had stopped by the Helmsford on his bike, impromptu. They'd had a few beers and ended up clipping the wheels onto Michael's stored ten-speed, wrestling the bikes into the elevator, wheeling them—derailleurs tick-tick-ticking—past the doorman, and heading down Broadway in the city's traffic-filled dark.

At first, they were cautious. Taxis sped past six inches from their legs, and they yelled nervously, happily, to each other that neither of their bikes had reflectors, and that they were stupid for not at least wearing something bright. Peter had on his leather jacket, and Michael a ski sweater and tan down vest. About the only light-catching thing was Michael's yellow bike hat. Its visor was turned down, perhaps, Peter thought, because he didn't feel like being recognized. On the other hand, the hat wasn't exactly discreet. On the yellow background was a green jungle print, like the patterns on Hawaiian shirts.

In Times Square, limousines were double-parked, cabs swerved defiantly across lanes to pick up fares, and the regular drivers dealt in panicked, aggressive ways with the mayhem. And by now Peter and Michael were threading between the maniac vehicles, like minor maniacs themselves. They forgot they were on bicycles, or rather, they forgot certain essential differences between bicycles and cars. It felt great to be in fast, careless contact with the nighttime November air.

They zipped between taxis and buses, slid between buses and parked cars, swooped through oncoming traffic at red lights, and accelerated far beyond the traffic behind them. They turned onto a side street and flew past the warehouses, veering, keeling, around potholes, and slaloming needlessly around nothing at all. They yelled like kids or cowboys.

Heading downtown again they took up a full lane and, side

by side, got up as much speed as they could. They were fairly matched. They reached the speed where their pedals seemed to spin without them. And their bikes were good. The speed was considerable. But they didn't quite hold it. They both had the same impulse—to touch their brakes slightly. The instinct hit just as they lost all sense of safety, just as their heads seemed indistinct from the wind shooting past.

A few blocks farther on, they stopped at a bar Peter knew. Leisurely, on the sidewalk, they took off their gloves, locked their bikes, stood a moment to let themselves cool down. Inside, they bought beers and talked about the riding. They laughed about the moment they'd both pulled back.

Then, with a semi-despondent sigh and a sip of beer for a segue, Michael said that people had been talking to him about running for Roy Kramer's congressional seat.

There was one other person besides Glickstein whom Peter had spoken to about his new friendship, and that was his father. They had sat in the study of the family house, Dr. Bram in his autumn gardening clothes: brown ski pants and a white mesh undershirt, the kind that looks like a chicken-wire fence. The cloth of the shirt covered about one-eighth of his torso, but somehow the shape of the holes was designed to keep body heat in, and Dr. Bram insisted he could wear only this as he planted bulbs in forty-degree weather. He loved the fact that science could create such a garment, and he loved the freedom given him by the stretch pants and near-nudity of his upper body; "It lets me commune with my garden," he said, mocking the word, "commune," but meaning it just the same.

And certainly he didn't care that his legs looked thin as saplings wrapped in burlap, or that the moles on his stomach and chest peered through the gaps in the shirt like bright red pupils. Or perhaps he was just oblivious, or even vain, pleased he was in good enough shape to wear the revealing outfit, skinniness or no skinniness, moles or no moles. And clearly he was proud to have discovered the ideal gardening suit. In any case, he wore it into town, if it was what he happened to have on, and he'd worn it in the city, helping Peter move—which had made Peter wince. The outfit made him wince even now, in the privacy of the study, though it evoked in him, too, a flood of protectiveness, as if his father were held delicately together by an ingenuous sense of pride, a naive independence.

Whenever Peter came to visit, they greeted each other with a hug, a full, sturdy embrace, and usually Peter kissed his father on the cheek, and Dr. Bram clapped his son several times on the back, often with surprising force—for he was not a rough 'n' tumble man—often hard enough to rattle Peter or sting the flesh between his shoulder blades, awkwardly, affectionately hard. Today they had said hello in this way, and now sat facing each other, wishing their feeble, constantly prodded conversation could become fluid, could match their deep regard for each other.

Odd as his weekend attire was, Dr. Bram was not wildly eccentric. He wore plain jackets and ties to the medical complex where he saw his patients, and he commanded, in his own quiet way, a great deal of respect. His patients could not disobey him without a surge of guilt; his reticence, combined with sober brown eyes widened for emphasis, made something moral out of his prescriptions and admonitions to rest, as if to be reckless with your health was simply, ethically wrong. And Peter knew his father's bedside manner, knew it from times he'd been sick and times that had nothing to do with the physical, when he'd treated himself or other people badly. He understood by now that his father's reticence was as much shyness as confidence, that the imperiously widened eyes were a cover for frail authority. It didn't matter. In fact, the fragility meant only that Dr. Bram could infiltrate Peter's conscience more and more thoroughly. Peter couldn't stand what he saw as his father's weakness, and he hated to think about confronting him openly, for fear the vulnerability would become acute, that at the slightest opposition his father would crumble.

In the study, as Peter looked past his father's shoulder, there was the reminder of one of Dr. Bram's moments of glory. It was propped on the sill of the deep window, a framed letter from Walter Norman Marr, from when he'd been Governor of New York. It wasn't a form letter. It was long and had words X-ed out and had obviously been typed by the Governor himself. As a child, when Peter had asked about the framed letter, his father had grunted modestly; his mother would tell the story. When Dr. Bram had been a resident at Harlem Hospital, he'd written Marr about the conditions there. "'It wouldn't be going too far to say,'" Mrs. Bram would recite parts of her husband's letter, "'that the lack of staffing and equipment in this emergency room is a subtle style of lynching.'"

And there the framed reply sat, like a trophy. Growing up, Peter had shown it off to friends. The whole family had been so proud of his father's powerful sincerity, and proud that Walter Norman Marr had been moved to respond.

It was a relic of a different time, Peter knew. Back then Dr. Bram had been politically active, no fanatic, but he'd marched, demonstrated, sent other letters, gotten himself an FBI file, however brief. Now his involvement had shifted, deepened, quieted. He shared in the administration of a city hospital in Yonkers, a job he approached with calm resignation, and which he hoped sometimes to be replaced in, because, he said, "It's just too depressing."

But the sensibilities of the past still held, and in the struggle to keep conversation going Peter figured he could liven things up and please his father by mentioning his new friendship with Michael. Only as he began to speak did he realize that his father wouldn't be impressed at all, but by then it was too late.

"So," Peter said, "I finally met America's beloved son."

"Who's that?"

"Michael. Michael Marr."

"Oh."

"We've actually been hanging out some."

Silence.

"He had a party at the famous apartment. At the Helmsford. That's where I ended up meeting him."

Silence.

"He's actually thinking about running for Congress the term after next. For Roy Kramer's seat."

"Mmm."

Dr. Bram held his son's eyes, asking nothing, interested in no details, using the old bedside manner, letting his disapproval weigh in with silence, and Peter, trapped and angry, thought of his father's simplicity, his doctor's way of looking at the world, as if the right thing to do were always plain, as if there *were* right choices, right ways of living your life; it was practically moronic, he thought; but he wasn't about to apprise his father on this point, maybe because he believed in his father's judgment after all, and definitely because he couldn't bear the prospect of tearing him down, which he was sure the merest disagreement would do, turning the reticence into pure wilted wordlessness, and the steady, widened eyes into uncertain brown discs. . . .

It was the same over the coming months. Twice, circumstances would have dictated that Michael meet Dr. Bram, and both times Peter arranged it so that no introduction took place. He could imagine his father transformed suddenly in Michael's presence, grinning as they shook hands, straining to engage him, even mentioning the letter from Walter Norman

Marr. And Peter wanted to spare his father this involuntary reaction, this virtual decomposing. . . .

Yet with all Peter's worry about his father's resilience, Dr. Bram's tacit disapproval got to him. So, in the study, after blurting out that the last bit of information, about Michael's running for Congress, was confidential, Peter changed the subject. And over the following months he avoided speaking to his father more and more, and when they did talk he let their awkward affection wither; he stiff-armed his father, withholding the changing details of his life.

Eight

THE ACTUAL ELECTION WAS STILL THREE YEARS AWAY. KRAMER planned to run next year, then retire after serving one last term. But the people from the Democratic National Committee, and Kramer himself, who talked to Michael, hoped he'd become a clear candidate early on, if not an officially declared one. Not long after Kramer announced his retirement, a year or a year and a half from now, say, they hoped to begin building anticipation of Michael's candidacy. Ideally, they would keep everyone else—or at least anyone who might put up formidable opposition—out of the race. Michael would run basically unopposed. Because there was no sense diminishing his debut with a serious fight. And there was no reason to risk defeat, however slight the chance of that might be. Once he'd been elected, and once he was a member of the House, the question of background and qualifications would no longer be a potential pitfall. That hole would be filled in with a bona fide political record.

Kramer and the DNC people were fairly subtle. And they were respectful. In fact, they were prone to the same surge of awe that affected everyone in Michael's presence. So they didn't spell out their rationale. Mostly they told him what a great Congressman he'd be, and how much the party and the country needed him. But in their effort to convince him, and to convince him early, they laid out bits of their plans and reasons. And it wasn't hard for Michael to get the picture from the pieces.

He told Peter he was undecided. He said he was leaning toward telling them no. All his life he'd vowed he would never go into politics. But in the meantime he'd agreed to let them get him a job with the city's Housing Authority, and set up a few publicity things.

Shortly after Michael began work at the Authority, Peter and Lee, at Lee's insistence, threw a dinner to celebrate his new job. It was a week before Christmas, and that day there was a concert at Kevin Briscoe's school. Peter went. For the past month, Kevin had been practicing a new song.

"As long as you won't be singing it about your mother," Peter had joked when Kevin had asked to learn it.

"You're sick," Kevin had said.

He'd borrowed an electric guitar and had Peter teach him a screaming five-note riff, and he'd found two other kids, a drummer and another guitar player, to perform with him. And he'd invited Peter. Invited him repeatedly. So Peter stood at the back of the school's gym, beside the bleachers filled with seventh- and eighth-graders, and behind the three rows of metal chairs for parents who'd been able to take off from work. Idly, as he waited for the concert to start, he scanned the crowns of the women's heads, wondering which was Kevin's mother. The blonde with the girl's bow in her hair? The one who seemed to be balding? He felt a sudden proprietary pull, a real sense of rivalry, as if it were he who was responsible for Kevin's life, or at least all that was good in it.

99

The concert began with a choir, followed by two piano recitals and a barbershop quartet. Kevin was the headliner. Not that he was necessarily the most polished musician, Peter realized. More likely, it was that it would be easier to dismiss the kids than calm them down after Kevin's high volume.

It took a while for Kevin and his band to set up. Something was amiss with the standing mike. The anticipation of the kids on the bleachers edged toward pure distraction. "Testing. Testing," Kevin said, but nothing came through the speakers, and glancing over his shoulder Peter saw a boy puff out his cheeks and slit his eyes to mimic Kevin's meaty face. "Testing. Testing," the boy mocked, and Peter nearly walked up front to help with the cables. Or to demand everyone's patience.

A great cheer went up when the problem was solved. Kevin's face hid any sign of relief. He wore his camouflage jacket. "All right," he said shyly, quietly, almost inaudibly, into the racket. The kids were stomping their feet now. "I want to dedicate this song to my guitar teacher."

The kids hushed a bit, not in response to what he'd said, but in expectation. Peter's neck flushed with an uneasy gratitude. His face heated as quickly as if a switch had been flipped on.

Kevin hit his opening run of chords. His band kicked in behind him. "Can't you see," he half-spoke, half-sang, "oh, can't you see, what that woman, Lord, been doin' to me." Thick- and stolid-bodied as ever, he wailed through his riff seven consecutive times. The kids went crazy. And tears of happiness—for Kevin's happiness—welled in Peter's eyes.

"It was fairly touching," he said, a few hours later, as he aligned the sections of the folding table.

Lee stood in the kitchen area of the small downtown loft she shared with a college friend. Lee was trimming leeks. Her head was ducked. She kept sweeping her blond hair away from her eyes, catching the drapelike locks in the curve between her forefinger and thumb. Peter had seen the gesture probably five hundred times in the two months they'd been going out, and he'd joked with her about its preconceived quality, about having her hair cut the way she did just so it would have to be dragged dramatically back. Laughing, she'd admitted that this might be true. The gesture entranced him just the same.

She glanced up from the cutting board. "Do you think we should move the table back a little? So it's not right on top of people when they walk in the door?"

The dinner had been Lee's idea. Peter had tried to dissuade her. He'd said the last thing Michael wanted was another social event in his honor. But she'd said the party would be small, only for close friends. She'd called Michael to discuss a guest list, and apparently he'd complied.

"I don't know," Peter told her. "But anyway, I couldn't help feeling my usual teacherly nausea. Like I was lapping up the thanks for something I didn't do. Or, no—like I shouldn't care about the thanks in the first place."

"What do you mean?" She walked around the counter, sidestepped the table, and went to see how her apartment would look to the guests as they entered.

"Just that some thirteen-year-old dedicating a song to me shouldn't send chills up my spine."

She opened the front door and shut it behind her. "No," she declared, reappearing. "We have to move it. People'll think they're being attacked by the place settings."

Amazing, truly amazing, he thought. He figured he didn't want to be having this discussion anyway.

He pulled one part of the table, then the other. "Okay?" he asked.

"A little more."

"Okay?"

"That's less horrible." She returned to the leeks. "So are you planning to teach for another year?"

"What are you talking about?"

"Teaching, remember?"

"What about it?"

"I just asked how long you're planning on doing it."

"Forever, Lee." She gave no response to his sarcasm. "What kind of question is that?"

"I thought that's what we were talking about."

"What are you trying to say?"

"Nothing, Peter." This in a singsongy voice.

"'Nothing, Peter,'" he mimed. "No, Lee."

"Peter, you brought up the subject."

"No. What I brought up was something else."

"Okay," she sighed. She looked up from the counter. "What?"

"Nothing. I just wish this place was laid out differently."

When the guests started to arrive, Peter, dealing with the watercress soup, watched Lee open the door, exchange hellos and how-*are*-yous and your-dress-is-too-beautiful-I-can't-let-you-ins, and administer and receive little kisses to the cheek. She was theatrical and affected and, Peter thought, self-mocking. She seemed to make a joke of her role while she played it, to make satire out of the rituals of greeting. There was a fine line between that and sincerity, but Peter decided she was on the side of satire.

Roberto and Annette came third or fourth in the series of guests; when Peter heard Lee shriek their names he searched the refrigerator for an unneeded ingredient, peered into the oven at a nonexistent dish. He hoped Roberto and Annette would shift past Lee without seeing him and introducing themselves, without making it clear he'd never met them before in his life. He peeled excess carrots for the crudités.

"Peter!" he heard a woman cry, in something close to a British accent.

It was Annette, with Roberto at her side. Roberto's hand was out to shake; she leaned over the counter for a kiss.

"You are the chef," Roberto said, smiling, making an offer of manly commiseration. He had a long bladelike nose that would have been homely on any other face; on his it was exotic, daunting. She seemed to inhabit her hair, a profusion of black curls.

Peter smiled in reply.

Next came Paul Becker, the linebacker with the skin disease, the valet. He brought six bottles of champagne. Only a few days before, over the phone, Michael had said to Peter, "I guess you'd better invite him." And in fact, during that conversation, though he'd been appreciative of Lee's intentions, Michael had had the same shrugging, cynical attitude about the party itself.

Then Michael arrived. Though Peter was still in the kitchen, though his back was turned and he was trying to find room in the refrigerator for the champagne, though for a moment he heard no voices at the door, neither Lee's greeting nor the guest's response, he knew. He pictured him dressed—in what? His black sweater, the sleeves pushed up on his forearms? His white shirt with the pleated front? Whatever, it would be casual and somewhat shapeless, but somehow wouldn't hide the structure of his body, the long, well-defined muscles to which Michael himself seemed gracefully oblivious.

Peter turned. Michael wore pleated khakis and a simple striped shirt. Classic preppy. No one else could have made Polowear look practically exotic, Peter thought, as Michael chatted with Lee. And maybe it isn't just a trick people play on themselves. Maybe there really is something there. Something he has. Something innate or learned.

So Peter let himself stare. For a moment, he consciously united himself with everyone he scorned—the worshippers, the devotees, the selfless people who felt exalted by association.

Then he snapped out of it. He converted Michael back into an equal.

"Come get a drink," Lee said, as Michael stepped over to the counter to shake Peter's hand. They didn't exactly shake. The alteration had evolved on the tennis court. They'd played several times since October, and after their sets (which were still lopsided, faintly sadistic affairs), what they did was a toned-down version of the high-five, a basketball player's palm slap. The quick ritual could have a physical effect on Peter like the feeling he got at the heightened moments of a great concert (in a place small enough so he could see the faces on stage and hear each note)—the sensation like a vague electrical current spreading across his back and rising from the base of his skull. There could be an instant, too, during the semi-high-five, when he felt his vision was about to blur.

"Hey, Peter," Michael said.

"Hey."

Michael continued on into the living room, and Peter could hear the other guests greet him.

"Hey hey," Michael said in reply. "Hey hey."

"So when are you leaving?" someone asked.

"Right after New Year's," Michael said.

"God, I think that's brave of you," Lee said. "I don't know if I could look at all those children. It's too tragic."

"Well," Michael said.

"Are you staying right in the camps?"

"Yes."

"God, I admire that," Lee said. "We're all so involved in our own little worlds. We think that if we don't have this by twenty-eight, or this by age thirty, we'll be living in deprivation. We don't even *consider* other people's lives, let alone do what you're doing."

Michael was going for four days to Ethiopia. It was the year of the drought, the terrible famine. The relief song, "Do They Know It's Christmas?" had just been released, and the networks had started to cover the situation on the evening news.

They'd shown clips of the desiccated land, once arable, now desert, and of the people, skeletal tribes looking as near to death as the prisoners rescued from Auschwitz. Several celebrities had traveled to the refugee camps to show concern and call attention to the severity of the hunger. Michael would be going with a group of politicians and actors.

The trip, Peter knew, wasn't merely one of the DNC's publicity ploys. In fact, the job working on low-income housing wasn't either. Michael cared. Or seemed to. No, Peter told himself, he does. But then how can he hang out with people like Roberto and Annette? How can any of us do what we're doing? How can Lee flirt on the topic of mass starvation? But *Roberto and Annette*? Their families were fucking dictators! They fled with their fortunes! And if they feel any remorse, it sure isn't oozing out of them.

Oh, lighten up, Peter, he cut himself off.

"I really think it's noble," Lee said.

But she was edged out of the conversation by a woman who seemed to be a data bank on the expansion of the Sahara. The woman knew that since 1972 Lake Chad had shrunk from nine thousand square miles to nine hundred. She knew that each year, in the nations bordering on the Sahara, one thousand square miles of land was deforested. After each statistic Michael responded, sounding distressed.

Soon Lee appeared at the kitchen counter, asking Peter if he'd bought the party favors. She'd wanted water guns for all the guests. The guns would be set beside each plate, to add a touch of whimsy to the dinner, to encourage frolicsome behavior.

"I think we should put them out," she said.

He filled them at the sink while she laid them on the table.

"Okay," she announced, into the living room. She squirted her pistol up at the ceiling. "The artillery's on the table."

No one moved. After a minute, though, the idea caught on.

Almost everyone was armed. The statistician was in the midst of telling Michael about the drought of '73—that three and a half million cattle had died—when they were caught in a crossfire of streaming water. They ducked and grabbed guns of their own.

Meanwhile, Peter had come out of the kitchen and was trying to introduce himself into the fray. His shots generally weren't returned. And the longer he stayed on the periphery of the battle, the more it seemed full of flirtation and innuendo, if not something closer to overt sex. He grew hesitant to take aim; damping a woman's shirtfront—when she wasn't going to fire back—began to seem akin to an old man's stealing a squeeze of a stranger's breast on a crowded street. He was conscious of shooting less and less frequently. Other people ran to the sink to refill their guns. Occasionally a woman yelped or fired briefly at him in reply. Once, he and Annette exchanged a quick volley during which he forgot his hesitance, wetting her neck and breasts. Laughing, she protested that his marksmanship was too good. "It's this special orange gun," he said, but she'd turned toward another adversary.

Michael, of course, was at the center of the action. Both men and women either teamed with him or attacked him in ambushes. They said to him, "Let's get Melora," or to a friend, "Get Michael." Peter heard Lee's slightly low yet girlish voice repeatedly saying these things. He heard her childlike shrieks and raspy laughter. One minute, he saw her up on her toes, whispering some plot into Michael's ear; the next, she was on the receiving end of his attack. Her shirt was already dotted and crisscrossed with dark watermarks, but now she glanced down and said, "Michael, look what you did." The shirt wasn't particularly thin, and she wore a bra underneath; nevertheless, one distended nipple showed. He aimed directly at it. "Michael!" she cried.

Fuck you, Peter thought. And then, more distantly, Do you have to be so obvious? And then, again, Just Fuck You.

Fantasies converged on him. He grabbed Lee's upper arm and yanked her—almost slammed her—against the wall. "What's wrong with you?" he yelled, his coal-hot face inches from hers. "What the fuck is wrong with you?" He punched Michael hard in the stomach, and when Michael, taller and stronger, swung back, he, Peter, broke a beer bottle for a weapon.

He ground the jagged glass into Michael's intangibly handsome face.

Or he walked wordlessly from the apartment. Never spoke again to Lee, Michael, or any of the rest of them. Until a year or two later, when he'd succeeded the way he wanted to succeed. At what mattered. Then Lee or Michael would call to invite him somewhere, to a party or dinner or for a drink, and it would be as if he hardly remembered them.

But in fact, Peter pretended not to notice Lee's playful cries, her nipple, and the direction of Michael's gun. Standing in the living room, he glanced around him as if looking for something, then pretended he was out of water and slipped away to the kitchen. When a few of the guests wandered toward the sink for refills, he went into the bathroom.

Women did this, he thought. Upset in public, they closeted themselves in the bathroom to weep and brood. It was not a manly tack. Yet here he was, perched on the seat cover, nurturing rage and self-loathing. He had no real wish to be macho, but discovering himself this way didn't add to his self-esteem.

Why didn't he forget Lee, forget Michael? That was what he asked himself. Why didn't he go back to his life of two months ago? What had he done worthwhile since meeting them? Had he finished a song? Come up with a melody? "What do you *do* all day?" he muttered out loud, staring between his knees at the white porcelain base. What? You wait for Michael to call. You wonder if you should call him. You will if he hasn't by

3:45. No, by 3:52. 3:45 is too obvious—it'll be too obvious you waited till exactly that time. *Michael Marr, please.* Yes, very nonchalant. And then you say to him, *Hey, mahn,* adding your ridiculous Rastafarian twist, hoping to be casual. Or you think about Lee. You sit there holding your guitar, hunched over it, forgetting your fingers on the strings, thinking about sex with Lee. And *then* you try to write? To come up with *lyrics?* What have you written besides pleas, pleas to the gods to let you bring her dead clitoris to life? "Peter, leave," he said aloud again. Just walk out of here. Just go.

After the main course, as everyone sat digesting their watercress soup, Luxembourg salad, and chicken with orange and leeks, Lee realized that they'd forgotten heavy cream. Michael offered to go.

"No," Peter said, with the slightest tinge of sarcasm. "Relax. You're the guest of honor."

"I'll walk you," Michael said.

Lee lived on Delancey Street in a building owned by a Chinese entrepreneur. On the second floor was his Ko Wong's Beauty Center. Before-and-after photos were scotch-taped to the door. Skin could be blanched, eyes widened, noses lifted.

"Can you believe this?" Peter said. There was something eerie about the cheap Polaroid pictures with the dingy, wrinkled tape across their corners, and about the heavy, steel door. Michael let out a brief groan. "People," he said, "are fucked up."

"Yes, they are." Peter laughed, sensing that Michael meant something about everyone's worst instincts, that his friend was self-aware and insightful, that they had a deep, tacit understanding after all.

They pushed through the front door. The night was damp but, for December, warm. Mist hung in the air, and the streetlamps seemed to have halos. Workers in masks and full jumpsuits were high up on a scaffold, cleaning the facade of a building. With long instruments like blowtorches they blasted either sand or air at the brick, and grime particles, clouds of them, rose off the building, billowing in the light of the workers' lanterns. The blasting made a racket, a violent, high-pitched, incessant roar, and of course the soot would not vanish—it would float and soon resettle as part of the patina of the city; yet the sifting of the dust clouds through the mist was an mesmerizing as an industrial sunset.

They walked. The streets were almost deserted. They spoke off and on. Peter asked about a woman Michael had met last week, a fashion editor at *Elle* who'd been none too attractive or flatteringly dressed, but who'd seduced him with recitations from Henry Miller interrupted by blatant metaphors for what she would do for him in bed. Michael joked that he didn't know if he could see her again, that he didn't know if he could survive—she'd completely lived up to her own billing. He didn't ask Peter about Lee. He almost never had. Nor, since the first two or three times he and Peter had talked, had he asked Peter much of anything about his life—Michael seemed too distracted, deciding about the congressional race, or perhaps he'd had too many life stories poured out to him, perhaps, in moments both private and public, too many people had tried to impress him with their successes or despairs, perhaps he simply couldn't listen anymore. Sometimes Peter thought his friend's disinterest was an unconscious compliment: Michael didn't want to shut him out the way he shut out everyone else.

In any case, Peter didn't mind the lack of queries. Certainly it was easier not to talk about what he was working on; it would barely have been true to say he was working on anything at all. Once, early on, Michael had asked to hear one of his tapes. (Michael had never made any mention of Zadeh, as if he'd never heard Peter's confession that he'd come to Michael's party in hopes of getting Michael's godfather to listen to his songs.) Peter had promised, instead, to play Michael some new songs as soon as he got them finished. That had been the end of it. The songs remained incomplete, their scattered parts seeming less and less promising, their faults less eradicable. But these facts could be forgotten. They would discuss Michael's life, not his own.

More than once Michael had said to Peter, "I haven't told anyone this," or "Just between you and me," and Peter would be filled—in spite of all his skepticism about what his friend would reveal (for he still heard the emphatic strain in Michael's voice) and all his own self-disgust—with elation. He felt something similar now, a warmth spreading over his shoulders, as they returned from the grocery, with a voice calling from a window above and behind them. "Michael Marr!" They didn't glance back. "Michael Marr!"

Peter placed himself in the window and saw them from there: the tops of their heads, their shoulders; Michael, himself.

Lee fished into Michael's pocket for cigarettes. Everyone kept drinking, and at midnight they went to P.S. 5. There they were beckoned through the crowd. To Peter the scene had come to look like some perverse comedy, but thinking this didn't diminish the attraction of being a side-star within it, of stepping through.

Inside, the decor's motif was the end of the Roman Empire. In the first display rooms, along the sides of the wide, dimly lit entry hall, there were actors wearing sandals and loose white smocks, drinking from chalices and laughing inaudibly, eerily, behind the heavy glass. In another room a black-haired woman, also draped in white, sat alone and motionless in her bedchamber, staring unblinkingly at her reflection in a dressing-table mirror. A fourth display was of an executioner, who stood, dressed in black with a black hood, above the prostrate body of a deposed emperor. Still in his royal cloak, the emperor lay on a stone bed which ended at his shoulders; then there was a gap; his forehead rested on a scarlet pillow which cushioned a separate stone slab. The executioner held a thick-bladed sword at his side, and the actors playing both men barely gave away the fact that they were alive.

The main rooms of the club showed the empire in much further decline. Surrounding the dance floor and scattered through other areas were crumbling pillars and archways and the facades of gutted buildings—fabrications of the ruins in their contemporary state. But near the dance floor was a vision of the old civilization.

There was a sunken pool. Another black-haired woman, also still as a mannequin, lay beside it. Her robe seemed to have been torn off her; she was naked to the belly. Three men, dressed like those in the first displays of revelry, knelt around her. Baby squid were strewn over her stomach and sternum and breasts, and the men speared them with small, pearl-handled forks. They were gentle, the men were, their tines never pricking her skin. Still, the scene was painful to watch, especially because there was no glass in front of it, nothing to make it seem at least slightly unreal. Some of Michael's entourage shifted past, grimacing; others stood and winced.

Michael shook his head quickly as if to clear the image.

"This is disgusting," Lee declared. "This is *hideous*."

They moved on toward the anteroom, where there was a party to which they had all been invited.

A hundred or more people were packed inside. Michael was subsumed. Lee started forward into another of her enthused and seemingly ironic hellos. Peter leaned against the bar. After a while, Michael and Lee appeared, together, and in the bathroom the three of them finished Michael's stash of cocaine. In the anteroom again Michael was embraced by new arrivals and Lee's hellos were even more histrionic. Peter spoke with two men he'd known vaguely at college. When he returned to the bathroom, this time for its traditional purpose, he nearly blacked out.

Waiting on line, he glimpsed Lee's black heels under a stall door. Next to them, *between* them—for the heels were spread apart—where Michael's brown bucks. Peter didn't react right away. It was as if every molecule in him were suspended for an instant, held rapt by the stillness of those shoes, but as one spiked heel shifted less than an inch, scraping sideways on the tile floor, he was released, his head reeled, he saw and simultaneously didn't see, he sweat and felt cold, paralyzed, he ducked suddenly from the line into the dark, vibrating air near the dance floor. He had to be wrong. He'd just seen them in the anteroom. Did they have him that confused? No, he *had* been wrong; he'd imagined it; back in the anteroom Michael was there with Annette and Roberto; Lee was chatting with one of their dinner guests. He walked over to her and joined in, joking successfully. Then the three of them talked about the excesses of the club, repudiating the scene by the pool. His image of Michael and Lee disintegrated and dispersed. Only when Peter was back in her apartment did it recoalesce.

Her bed was a low platform. She knelt beside it, beginning to undress Peter, who lay on his back. Next she straddled him, one foot on the floor, the other on the bed, her body bent from the waist, her earrings dangling across her cheeks, her breasts floating against the neckline of her shirt, as she unfastened buttons, exposing his stomach, pulling his shirt-tails free of his pants. When he did a half sit-up, arm out to bring her down for more kisses, she softly warded off his hand, smiling. The backs of her fingers dragged lightly from the hollow above his collarbone to the hollow below his ribs. His throat felt tight as a vine wrapped around itself. Again he sat halfway up, this time to hold her legs, covered in black tights below her black skirt; again, gently, she brushed his hands aside. Her fingers were faultless with his belt buckle, as with the rest of the fastenings. She walked slowly to the end of the bed, took his pants by the cuffs, tugged, almost as if she were a nurse undressing a patient. And he lifted his buttocks, complicitous. There were other roles he would rather have played, but it was as if by evading his kiss and deflecting his touch she had relegated him to this one.

He watched her fold the pants over her arm. She glanced sidelong at him as she draped them across the bureau. He sat up fully, kissed her crotch through her leather skirt. Then, pushing him lightly down again, one foot on the floor and the other on the bed again, she pulled slowly at his shorts until his penis, caught by the waistband, was at a nearly painful perpendicular. She held him with one hand, while with the other she stretched the elastic over.

His penis davened. Meanwhile, images came intermittently to mind: Michael aiming at her nipple; her hand after the cigarettes; the two of them in the bathroom stall, the shifting of her heel, her mouth open and throat tight, as his were now.

She was skilled. Her manipulations, her elicitations, caused slight seizures. Just before his contractions, she stood, removed her clothes, took him inside. Returning to full consciousness, his neck was limp, his hands seemed to consist of water. Haunted again by the images, he reached and placed one watery hand between her legs. She let him stroke her there. All he could read in her eyes was tolerance. After a minute she drew his hand away, kissed the back of it, laid it on his stomach, and said, "Sleep."

Nine

PETER WOULD WIN. HE'D KNOWN THAT. NOT AS SOON AS HE'D HEARD *about the contest, or as soon as he'd sent in his tape, not that early; but when they'd been picked to play at the finals, he'd known. He could barely contain his confidence. He'd told his bass player he could quit his job, his drummer he could quit school. He'd sung to them in a shouting growl, making up the crazy-happy lyrics as he went,*

> *You can throw away your textbooks*
> *Throw away your plumber's wrenches*
> *We're gonna play the Tillman*
> *Goodbye to the roadhouse trenches*

and then burst into the Big Bopper,

> *Hoooo! That's what I like*

And during rehearsals before the finals, just running through the first bars of a song could set him off.

"That," he declared, "was hot."

"You're right," his keyboard player said, "it was."

"We are hot," Peter reiterated.

The keyboard player agreed with an ecstatic run of chords.

"And let me distinguish the nuances of 'hot,'" Peter went on. "I don't mean 'hot,' as in hey hey, we can play the Rusty Nail in Hadley or get three encores in Brunswick, Maine. I mean, hot. I mean, we are fucking hot. I mean—"

"Down boy down boy down," Wyatt, the bass player-plumber, had said, laughing.

Wyatt. What had happened to Wyatt? Thirty-seven years old with two kids, his wife had just said no, no moving to New York, find some other college boy to play with on Friday nights. Huge blue eyes that looked both mischievous and dazzled—lost—above the nose that had been badly broken; ropes of hair he raked back with his fingers from his flat, bony forehead; those white overalls he always wore onstage. Uncle Wyatt, the rest of the band had called him. Out at his tiny new house, one end up on cinder blocks because the foundation or the ground beneath it had just fallen away, out on the wooden stoop he and Peter had sat till six in the morning, Wyatt telling him about his first wife, who'd left after three months (exactly ninety-two days, Wyatt still remembered the number), and later, on no sleep at all, Peter had written the ballad they'd closed with at the finals and then before Jackson Browne.

> *. . . Then I heard what put me across*
> *Old stories of old pain, violent traces*
> *The way he hurt you, it kept me lost*
> *In childhood daydreams of dangerous places*
> *The helpless heroine*
> *The conquering hero*
> *That we needed in a certain sense . . .*

Well, Wyatt had saved his first wife, and his second wife had saved him, but she'd been the more forceful savior; she'd kept him; and no way he was quitting his job, no way they were leaving that four-room house he planned to build a new foundation for.

Smart. Because things hadn't turned out too easy, and after a year one Palmer College boy had decided to go into real estate and another had gone home to work for his father's furniture company. And that had left Peter.

But there had been a moment there.

> *You can throw away your textbooks*
> *Throw away your plumber's wrenches . . .*

There had been a moment.

> *Hoooo!*

When he'd known.

Sometimes Peter let himself relive the past to make sure it had been real, and that's what he was doing when the doorbell rang. He sat on the floor, his back against the base of the couch. He'd been listening to Sam Cooke, hoping to trick himself into coming up with the missing half of a verse, because, much as he liked Sam Cooke, his playful sad-sweetness was a long way from the sensibility of Peter's own song. Sometimes that worked—bombarding himself with what he *didn't* want. So he was listening to "Cupid" and "With You" and "Little Things You Do," and coming up with nothing, and eventually the tape had run out, and Peter had checked the past for traction against the fast-sliding present. And then the doorbell rang. It was Kevin, showing up for his lesson. Peter realized that right away. But for a moment he didn't go to the door. For a moment he stayed frozen. And another. And another. The bell rang again. And again. Get up, he urged himself, figuring he could tell Kevin he'd had his headphones on and hadn't been sure about the bell. But he didn't budge. Instead, he stifled his breathing, as if Kevin might hear it outside the wrought-iron gate. Or as if to suffocate the voice of his own recriminations. Because as soon as Kevin had almost certainly gone, and Peter inhaled fully, the accusations started.

Oh, give yourself a break, he thought finally. You just couldn't deal with that shit today. He'll live. You'll live. "Just give yourself a fucking break," he yelled.

A half hour later, he dialed the boy's number.

"Hey, Kevin. It's Peter."

"Oh. Hi." Kevin sounded surprised and diminished over the phone, with a lot less hard attitude than he had in person.

"Listen, dude. Sorry about this afternoon. I got stuck downtown."

"Oh. That's okay."

"Well, no. Not really. No, it's not. Next time I'll remember the subway takes fifty minutes to go sixty blocks."

"I had a shitload of homework to do, anyway." Now Kevin sounded more like himself.

"All right. Well, practice those runs and I'll see you next week."

"All right."

"Have a good week, Kevin."

"All right."

"Take care."

Peter hung up. There was a minute of utter nausea, and in the next minute he'd never felt better, cleaner, more full of determination. As if, by betraying the boy, he'd put all his money on a single bet. It was all in. As if, by hiding from his student like some kind of insect, he'd bought himself a kind of freedom. Or an absolute need. He felt solidified. Reduced. Whole.

Now you're going to get something done, he told himself. Now you're going to finish this song. Now . . .

The phone rang. It was Michael.

That night, in a bar called the Alibi, Michael told Peter he'd decided to run for Congress. The Alibi was a restored downtown tavern, with a twenty-foot pressed-tin ceiling and narrow booths with high wooden backs. It was the kind of place where throngs of young Wall Streeters try to behave with the disheveled charm of old immigrant men. Twenty-five-year-old stockbrokers in flashy suspenders dealt hands of hearts and, every so often, bellowed out the chorus of "Just One of Those Things" or "Pennies from Heaven." Michael said he'd been going there since before it had become so "obnoxiously yuppie." "I'd rather fight than switch," he said, though the patrons would have blended in perfectly at one of his parties.

Anyway, that was where he told Peter his decision. He'd just returned from Ethiopia. "God." He shook his head. "The first morning we were in these safari tents they had us stay in, and all of a sudden we wake up hearing these hoofbeats. It sounded like a zillion animals were racing across the desert. So we look outside and what it is is that the Red Cross shack has just opened, and everyone in the camp is racing to get their handful of grain. And there are no voices! It's total chaos, but there's no yelling. Not even babies. And the feeblest-looking kids, with legs like this, are just silent, getting shoved aside. Getting trampled on! It's dead silent except for their feet that sounded exactly like hoofbeats. Scott Legros named it 'The Stampede of Hunger.' Which was perfect. He's going to do a documentary and call it that."

Michael stopped, held Peter's gaze. As often as Peter had noticed it before, the question behind Michael's eyes surprised him. There were the layers of Michael's own eyes Michael seemed to be begging his friend to peel away. There was the truth of Michael's own experience Michael seemed to hope his friend would uncover. Peter didn't doubt that Michael had witnessed such starvation, but Michael himself seemed to.

"I don't know," Michael went on. "After four days of that I just thought: Maybe I'm being incredibly selfish. Maybe it's *not* going into politics that's self-indulgent. Because what does it matter why people vote for me? What does it matter if people vote for me because of who my father was? People *want* me to run. And the only reason I won't is because I'm worried about why I'll be elected! I'm telling you, the more I thought about it, the more I felt like a serious heel!"

Again—the utter uncertainty couched within Michael's steady eyes, the lurking need for confirmation that he had in fact thought and felt these things.

"Well," Peter said, "maybe that's right." And he wanted to believe it—that Michael had truly had this revelation, and that he belonged in office. But willing as he was, he felt like a dumping ground for his friend's superficial soul-searching, Michael talking and talking about needing to escape adoration, avoid what was mapped out for him, and going right on plucking the preordained fruit. Why don't you try a little harder, Michael? Peter had sometimes wanted to say. Why don't you face up to yourself, Michael? You're full of shit, Michael. Why don't you think a wee bit more deeply about the way you live your life?

But Peter hadn't said these things, pointed out the rationalizations and fluid failures of will, and he didn't say them now. Why? Because beneath his anger, he told himself Michael was the most deeply troubled person he knew. So why be that hurtful? Peter himself had his music—even if things weren't going well—at his center; Michael had nothing. Nothing of his own. Why be that cruel? Michael was too fragile, too dependent on his flimsy delusions. He would disintegrate, and Peter couldn't bear the possibility of causing that. Of seeing that.

Anyway, he thought, didn't shrinks stay silent, make no judgments, let their patients talk themselves toward their own realizations? Couldn't he help Michael that way?

"And I mean, I thought a lot about my father," Michael said. "And I kept thinking, *that's* why he did it. That's why he ran for Congress, that's why he ran for Governor, that's why he ran for President. Because of what he could do for other people. And I thought, that is exactly what *public servant* means. Serving the people. That's why people loved him."

"Right."

"I don't know. It just made me realize I should run. It just made me see that selfishness was the only thing keeping me from doing it."

There was a pause. Michael waited for Peter to respond.

"I think you should," Peter said. "Though you're running for Congress—" he smiled—"not sainthood."

He held the smile, feeling its sting, as if he were inflicting harm not only on Michael but on himself.

"All right," Michael snapped, looking genuinely wounded. "I'm not saying I'm a saint."

"That's good."

"Was I saying that?" The hurt in his friend's gaze confirmed Peter's sentiments. Michael was too vulnerable. Too frail.

"No, Michael. Calm down. I was joking; I was joking. I think you should run. I think you should run."

Ten

"FIRST OF ALL," LEE SAID, "HIS REAL NAME ISN'T STEVENS. THAT'S HIS middle name, plus an *s*. His real name's Minkowitz."

"*Minkowitz?*" Peter said.

"Minkowitz."

They laughed as they walked along Fifty-ninth Street, held hands. They'd just been to a dinner thrown by this Bobby Stevens.

"And he's changed everything about that apartment," Lee continued. "Everything. I mean obviously it was all ruined in the fire, but there isn't a single reminder in there of what it used to look like. And he's always complaining that his grandmother's trying to give him things his parents gave her. You should hear him. 'She's haunting me, Lee, she's haunting me. That's the third time she's called about that couch. The upholstery on that thing is gold, Lee, *gold*. It's the Jewish vision of royal grandeur. With tassels dangling off the arms. It's tackier than a pimp's rearview mirror.'"

She was a perfect mimic. Peter smiled, squeezed her fingers. They'd reached Central Park South and strolled beside the stone wall, the darkness of the lagoon to one side of them and the glow of the hotels across the street. This was one of the times he liked best to be with her—after parties or nights in clubs. She'd spent most of the evening squealing hellos and whispering secrets and feigning seriousness while she listened to fools, and he had lingered at the edges, both self-conscious and scornful, but now, in private, she was in solidarity with him, mocking the people she'd carried on with earlier, wrapping herself and Peter together in a cocoon of criticism.

He had asked her how she could carry on with these people so happily. "What do you want me to do," she'd said, "sit around the sidelines like some kind of chaperone?" Which was exactly the way he sometimes felt: like one of those old Spanish grandmothers on the verge of death. And later he'd stared down at his hands as if they were already brittle, no longer connected to him by the flow of blood.

Not that he didn't defend himself to himself. What do I care what these people think? How they see me? Still, there was no avoiding the way he saw himself, or what he felt when he did shift in from the edges, or found himself drawn in (for he was recognized as Michael's close friend and never completely ignored): alive. Alive! Offering some pustule of gossip, or taking part in the deconstruction of someone not present, he felt exhilarated—uneasily, but ecstatically nonetheless. It elated him to be in the thick of this crowd.

Even now, alone with Lee, what added to his happiness was that he could contribute this and that to the gossip about their host—he'd been involved enough to come away with information.

"He told me," Peter said cynically, "that he redecorated the way he did because the memory of his parents is too painful."

"Oh, please," Lee sneered. "More like the memory of his

parents makes him cringe. You should have seen him when we were in college. On vacations? When I came to New York? If some of us would go to his apartment, he'd usher us straight from the front door to his room, and as we passed the paintings and tables with things on them in the hallway he'd mumble, 'Not responsible. Not responsible. The chotchkas in this hallway do not represent the aesthetics of Bobby Stevens.' And they weren't just chotchkas. I mean, they weren't high art, but they were these little animal statues his grandmother had had returned to her after the war. But Bobby thought they were the tackiest things on earth, and he finally terrorized his mother into taking them off the table and keeping them out of sight. And now the whole apartment looks like his remodeled bedroom did then—ten-thousand-dollar-pieces of black plastic for furniture and Keith Harings on the walls."

"What about right afterward?" Peter asked.

"You mean was he upset? Have I ever told you exactly how it happened? He was out cruising the town with his boyfriend—and don't think this has anything to do with him being gay; coming out has never been an issue for Bobby; according to Katrina he came out in fifth grade; and his parents have never been bad about it, so don't think for a minute his attitude has anything to do with that—anyway, he was with his Peruvian boyfriend, this snaky guy named Umberto, and the two of them were living with Bobby's parents, so it was thanks to Badlands or the Boy Bar or wherever they were that they weren't in the apartment. They might be dead, too. Or they might have been awake when it started and been able to save his parents. That's what would haunt me. I'd never be able to forget I might have saved them. I'd never be able to really forgive myself. But Bobby? Two nights after the fire I saw him at P.S. 5."

Peter laughed, shaking his head a little.

"It's true. He was accepting everyone's sympathy, looking

very grim, but you could tell he wasn't exactly shattered. And by the end of the night he was dancing away in his little loafers. His parents were like a blemish on his conception of himself—with them gone there were no more traces of Bobby Steven Minkowitz. There was only Bobby Stevens. It's sick. It's truly sick."

Peter didn't say anything.

"He's a truly sick human being," Lee reiterated. "A truly sick boy."

But now Peter was thinking less of Bobby than of Lee, that on the surface she might be frivolous, but that that was truly deceptive—underneath she had her head on straight, her heart in the right place.

And thinking this, he was overcome by a desire to kiss her. Nothing could have been more necessary. The desire registered in his stomach, his chest. It felt like a weight pressing from inside his forehead. As they walked, he put his hands on her shoulders to stop her.

"Hey, you want a ride uptown?"

They looked toward the street.

"Free o' charge!"

It was the driver of a horse-drawn carriage, the kind that tours children and vacationing couples around the southern third of Central Park. At this late hour this one seemed to have escaped its usual tedious track. Blithely it occupied a lane of Central Park West near Seventieth Street, and from the driver's attitude as he leaned across his bench and called again, "Come on! Hop in! Free o' charge for a beautiful-looking lady and her handsome escort!" it seemed he hadn't been responsible for the horse's direction, that the horse had said to him, "To hell with the park; I want to trot uptown," or at least that having steered the horse this far amidst speeding Saturday night taxi traffic (and probably risking a fine, Peter guessed) he had renounced responsibility—the situation was out of his hands; he was just along for the ride. To Peter, he didn't look like a man who could afford such recklessness. Tufts of white hair protruded below his top hat, and the flesh on his chin was loose and bumpy. His eyes seemed vague, layered with good memories and recent sadness.

"You sure about this?" Peter asked, standing below the old man, as a car honked and swerved past.

"Sure I'm sure." The driver sounded gruff, insulted by Peter's question. "Now be a gentleman and help your lady up to her seat!"

So Peter put out his hand, and Lee made a show of balancing herself on it as she climbed into the carriage. He slid in next to her on the velvet bench with its elegantly curved and scalloped back.

"Where can I take you, sir?" the driver asked.

"Anywhere," Peter said. "As far uptown as you're headed."

"Does he always talk in riddles?" The driver looked over his shoulder at Lee.

"Ninety-seventh between West End and Riverside," she said.

"Yes, ma'am."

The driver faced forward, sitting straight and sending a quick ripple along the reins to the horse's bit. The night air was crisp but still, and the horse's steady trot caused only a slight breeze; the buggy's big wooden wheels turned the roughness of the pavement into a series of coaxing sways. Taxis kept racing past, yet it was as if the carriage proclaimed an older world, one more purely glorious. From their high perch, Peter and Lee gazed at the entrances of the grand apartment buildings, at the marble pillars and gold light streaming out under the canopies, and at the uniformed doormen with white-gloved hands. To the other side they stared into the park; paths coursed through the trees lit by old-fashioned lanterns on wrought-iron poles. And letting their necks fall back they looked at the buildings again, at the high balconies with their girdings of intricate stonework, and at the towers and turrets, and above them at the sky, where, in spite of the city's luster, a few stars were visible. Then, as their eyes dropped, they glimpsed someone—a silhouette small as a pencil—leaning out over a balcony of what they realized was Michael's building.

They counted floors, up from the lobby, but lost track. There were too many rows of windows and ledges. They tried counting down from the top, but it was impossible at so steep an angle. Still, they had a sense that it was him. Separately, privately, they felt as if they saw him—the pale gray eyes—and, though they knew it was impossible, they had the dim, half-conscious sense that he was aware of them as well, and not the way they imagined him, etching in his features. They sensed he could see them in clear detail.

"This is how things used to be," the driver announced, his dark-coated shoulders rigid despite the motions of the carriage. He didn't turn around. "In the old days."

At Ninety-sixth he turned west, then went north for a block on Broadway, and trotting past the budget clothing shop, the video store, the pizza place, Peter and Lee felt illicit, like joyriders.

"Well, what can we pay you?" Peter asked, in front of his building.

"Can't pay me anything," the driver said. "Was my pleasure."

"Come on," Peter said. "Let us give you something. Hay money. Whatever."

The driver chuckled and took Peter's ten-dollar bill.

"Help the lady down," the old man instructed, and Peter did, and in his living room, after waving goodbye, he and Lee were like kids, their disbelief was so genuine.

And maybe it was this elation that was responsible. Or maybe it had to do with Peter's appearance in *People* the week before ("Michael Marr and friend Peter Bram party in the Greenroom at P.S. 5")—no doubt Lee was deeply affected by that, warmed and thrilled by it, much as she denied it to herself. Or it could have been sheer luck, positions evolving fortuitously, touches and rhythms in perfect sequence. The grazing of a thigh, the grating of abdomens, the addition of this or that pressure. In any case, Lee came. It wasn't the most eventful climax Peter had ever witnessed. Still. She'd made a small choking sound, then giggled sharply and flinched away from his finger, and yanked his hand away from her crotch.

They were on the living-room floor, on cushions they'd taken from the couch. He lay curled behind her, his knees to her knees, chest to her back. Occasionally, she kissed the fingers of his hand that was under her cheek.

"Are you sleeping?" he asked.

"No," she mumbled.

"No," he said. "Wake up. I'm wide-awake."

"Shhh."

He kissed her shoulder, which smelled faintly of the wine they'd had at dinner—alcohol evaporating with a sweet dead-flower scent through her pores.

"Maybe I should play for you," he said.

"What?"

"Maybe I should play for you."

"You finished something?"

"No. Not really. But maybe I should just play for you. Anything. Something old. I could do that."

"Okay."

"Okay?"

"Sure."

"I mean, if you want."

"I do. Let me get in bed. You can play for me in bed."

He'd never played for her before, in bed or anywhere. But just now, curled on the cushions behind her, he'd realized

something. Or no, not realized it—*understood* it, *knew* it, for
the first time in months. His old songs were good. 'Great
Jones Street,' 'Limited Love,' those songs were good. He
heard them in his head and they *sang* back to him. And so was
the one he'd been working on. Yes, it needed a sharper break,
a new line on the chorus—but the lines he had, sung slightly
flatter than the reaching chords—hearing them in his head he
felt his pores open, his *pores* were listening.

All he had to do was trust himself. Get doubt out of the
way. Tomorrow he'd finish the song. Let the changes come.
All he had to do was relax, not chase his talent away.

And his last tape. How many places had he sent it last fall?
Three? Four? Christ! What had happened to him? When had
he lost faith? When had he forgotten what Rudy Wells had
told him, that making music your life was like playing some
kind of roulette: talent qualified you, got you your own
number, then you just had to keep betting till your number
came up, and "hope that happens before you bet your strength
broke." Well, he wasn't broke. He had the number, and he'd be
there when the wheel hit home.

His guitar was in the front closet, and, in his shorts, he
carried it in its case into the bedroom. Lee was on her back,
her head propped on two pillows, the blankets tucked under
her feet and bunched under her chin. Rarely had he seen her
like this—innocent, content—and when he had it had never
fully included him. Now it did. Her eyes flicked upward from
his thighs to his face, inviting him to slide the covers off her
and replace them quickly with his body, or to cinch the
blankets protectively and kiss her lightly.

"All right," he said. He sat on the side of the bed, tuning.
The olive skin of his back caught the overhead light. His
shoulders were broad, sturdy even when distorted by his
posture with the instrument. "All right," he said again, and
played a song most people knew from the movie *Midnight*

Cowboy. On the sound track it was smooth, the voice fluid and effortless, the instrumental work gentle. But Peter's voice didn't have Nilsson's nasal, laid-back quality, and he didn't try to emulate it. His was raspy, deep, apparently incapable of reaching the song's one vaulting note, and he exaggerated the seeming lack of range, undercut the song's sentiment with a stoic edge. His pick work—the notes at the start a little too forceful, then the not-quite-consistent, almost staccato strumming, and the silencing of the strings against the heel of his hand—had the same restrained effect. And he sped things up, played and sang a fraction too quickly. A verse was almost gone before emotion, without warning, without announcement, coalesced in the room.

> *Everybody's talking at me*
> *I can't hear a word they're saying*
> *Only the echoes of my mind*
>
> *People stopping, staring*
> *I can't see their faces*
> *Only the shadows of their eyes*
>
> *Going where the sun keeps shining*
> *Through the pouring rain*
> *Going where the weather suits my clothes*
> *Banking off of the northeast wind*
> *Sailing on a summer's breeze*
> *Skipping over the ocean like a stone . . .*

And what are these lines on paper other than bad poetry—clichés of loneliness followed by the most predictable kind of hope? But sung the way Peter sang them, with the music he played behind them, they were personal and precise. They told a story so suddenly and completely that its sadness and deluded dreams nearly ruled out the beating of your heart.

Peter sensed this. He was aware of Lee, her stillness. She was transfixed, maybe disbelieving. He really is good, she thought. I was starting to have my doubts. But he really is. And she lay there, head propped on the pillows, watching, listening, motionless.

For a moment, her appreciation swept everything else away, and he was hardly conscious of his fingers or voice. Then he heard himself and was back inside the song, coming to its vaulting of octaves, up to "breeze." The trick was not to slip into falsetto. And he didn't. The trick was to keep his voice flush against a barrier, all its pressure against its own ceiling.

He continued, after pausing, into a song of his own. He'd written it last October, after sending out his last tape. He'd adored it, then doubted it, then detested it, as he'd grown to detest practically everything he did. But on the cushions in the living room, he'd gotten things back in perspective. Now he made his voice stretch and trail on the verse lines, come to sharp stops on the refrain, communicate what finally can't be explained.

But Lee groaned. Motionless with memories, not entranced by his singing, as he began a third song, which he intended to be his last, she heard her father in the auditorium at Humes. It was the Wednesday before Thanksgiving, a special assembly. Every year he took the stage with his guitar and pick and *capo*, and strummed and sang one or two folk songs, usually sing-alongs. As a child, years before enrolling at Humes, she'd gone to these assemblies with almost unbearable joy; when her father strode out from the wings you could have snapped her small body in two—she sat beside her mother, rigid with pride and anticipation. And when he sang, and all the students accompanied him, she felt as if they wanted to be part of her family, to have what she had. Her mother said, "I think your father is the most popular teacher at school" and "He has a marvelous voice."

Disillusionment was gradual. In fifth or sixth grade, possibly earlier, she caught glimpses behind her own adoration. A year or two later, it was clear she'd been deceived. And somehow her realization—one every child must have—became an urgent, permanent disgust. By sophomore year—the year she sought out Dr. Stocklin—she sat in the back of the auditorium, rigid with dread. It was that assembly she remembered as Peter played: her father strolling out from the wings; her father strumming through his standard repertoire; her father, after the final chorus (for which far less than the commanded "Everybody!" joined in), announcing that he had one more "number." *Number.* She recalled his saying that, and heard the first chords of a current hit, and was aware of the whispered sarcasm surrounding her, and stifled what leaped out now, this groan, which shocked her as much as it did Peter. Right away, she was sorry. She started to apologize, to explain that she'd been distracted, thinking of her father, not listening to Peter at all, but her lips wouldn't move to produce the words, and in the silence her sentiments began to shift from sympathy to a sense of duty. Maybe she'd done the right thing. Even if it hadn't been on purpose. Maybe the only thing to be was honest.

She glanced at the skin of his back.

How else could she help him?

How else could she keep him from becoming a failure and a fool?

Eleven

A MINUTE, A MONTH, A YEAR. THAT WAS HOW LONG GIVING UP took. In a way it happened in the instant of Lee's groan, or in the moments after that were filled by her abortive apology, his anger, their silence, and the beginnings of her coaxing, her advice. She told him about her father. Not everything. Far from everything. Nothing to alter the image of her idyllic childhood, to blemish the record of her father as beloved teacher, and nothing, certainly, to betray the extent of his effect on her. But just enough to let Peter know there were similarities, and that the comparison wasn't flattering. It didn't take much. A bit about her father's early ambition to be a writer, a bit about the fact that teachers weren't respected as much as they "really should be," all of it adding up to a brief history of her father's disappointment. "And I just worry about you," she said to Peter. "I just don't want *you* to be disappointed. Twenty years from now, I don't want you to have to be playing in bar mitzvah bands, playing 'Hava-nagilah,' or giving guitar lessons."

No, she assured him, she wasn't saying he wouldn't make it. How could she know? she said. And yes, she'd liked his song—she'd groaned only because she'd remembered her father ("making a *slight* fool of himself," she joked the truth of her feelings away). She did not tell Peter she'd hardly heard his song (she couldn't have repeated a single line, or hummed the melody even), and so the tepid tone of her praise stood as condemnation.

What she said unequivocally was, "I just think you should have something to fall back on."

In his agreement there was both hatred and relief.

The next month was devoted to the discussion of alternatives. And the possibility that came up constantly was law school. It was the obvious choice. They could list almost endlessly the number of their friends who'd gone or were going or were about to go. A few went out of interest, the rest by default. There was an old Clash song the defaulters sang as a joke, "I fought the law/ And the law won." For Peter, it was the predictability that made the prospect dimly tolerable. The comedy of it was so clear! Of turning himself into a walking cliché! It was too blatant a cop-out to buy into, too ludicrous to be taken seriously.

He took the LSATs and did alarmingly well. More comedy. And Lee laughed along. But she also took him to dinner to celebrate. They gazed out over the East River from the River Café. He, too, was pleased by his performance, but thinking about the near-perfection of his scores was like looking at some bright, dazzling television graphic that stayed and stayed on the screen, some beautiful and sickening diagram of facts.

Was this what he was cut out for after all? Were the scores some kind of sign?

He wasn't ready for Lee's next idea. Why not apply late to Columbia for the following September? Instead of waiting a year. His scores were strong enough. She had a friend who'd done it.

He balked. He glanced up from his menu and delivered a firm no. He said he wanted to spend another year full-time on music. Give himself that chance.

She didn't argue. She only suggested he might want to get it over with. If things weren't going that well for him, then maybe now was the right time. "And you know," she said, "maybe you should give the right side of your brain a little rest for a while. Maybe that's exactly what it needs. Maybe you should think of law school as a kind of vacation."

He laughed—partly at her reasoning, partly because he sensed himself about to accept it. Well, why not? he thought. Why not play the joke for all it was worth? Think of it as a swimming pool. He could jump in, creating a splash of hilarity, or walk in, stirring a mere ripple. And why *not* think of it as a vacation? (Here he began to take her rationale more seriously.) He'd already considered it that way himself. Three years of just marching along. Hup-two-three. Three years of Torts, Civ-Pro, Corporations. A kind of rest. And he thought of the way he sometimes wrote, bombarding himself with what he *didn't* want. Maybe this was like that. Maybe law school was the blitzkrieg he needed.

He was accepted in June. The day he got his letter of admission, he ran into Glickstein on the street.

"Yo, homie, what's happening?" Glickstein greeted him loudly. They were on lower Broadway, and Glickstein, in his green poplin suit, carried a bagful of foodstuffs from Dean & DeLuca's.

"Well," Peter said. Though he'd seen Glickstein at a number

of parties over the past months, he hadn't managed to mention the new, temporary turn in his life.

"*Word*," Glickstein replied.

"Other than that I'm about to enroll in the vocational training school of the upper middle class . . ."

"Say what?"

"Law school, Derek. Law school."

There was a pause before Glickstein exclaimed, his voice somewhat weak, "Peter, that is funky!"

It was impossible to tell what this meant, "funky" having many definitions, let alone Derek's possible misuses. At least, doubt lingered for a moment. Then Glickstein asked, "Why?" slanglessly and sadly, and looking disoriented.

So Peter assured him it was a short-term thing, training toward a lucrative sideline, not a career. "It's like learning to be a high-priced carpenter," he said. "It's a trade." And Derek's surprised sadness helped Peter believe this. Heading home, he felt happier than he had in weeks. Once again, he realized, Glickstein had given him back a little faith.

Meantime, there had been a shift in Peter and Lee's sex life. That night after Bobby Stevens's party, in the moments after Lee's orgasm, a hint of boredom had crept in behind Peter's joy. A battle had been won. There was a slight twinge of letdown. "Well," a small voice inside him had asked, "now what?" The voice had faded quickly in his happiness. Boredom had said a quiet hello and a swift, furtive goodbye. And Lee's reaction to his musical performance had banished it. Their discussion of future "options" had banished it. As had the general drift of his life.

Too much was at stake now, when they were in bed, for boredom to become a factor. Now that he was going to law school, Lee—as well as Michael—often seemed to be all he had. Pleasing her, letdown was a long way from what he felt.

Nevertheless, there *had* been a shift. It was that she *could* be pleased. Frequently she still tended to him, and would hardly let herself be touched; but then there were the nights when she dangled at the short-breathing edge, and the nights she dropped over. Her orgasms calmed him in a way his own certainly did not.

Other things, too, reassured him and seemed to draw them closer. First, over the summer, Lee was fired from her job with the brilliant Phil Orestes, creator of the Endymion campaign and, more recently, of the "Make Your Night" ads for Harbinger beer. He called her into his office, said her work had fallen off, wrote her a check for two weeks' pay, and told her she was free to go. "My *work?*" she railed to Peter, later that night. "Waiting at his apartment for his new couch to be delivered? Picking up his silk jackets at the special place he *has* to have them dry-cleaned? Creative assistant? I'm his *personal* assistant! We're his personal slaves!"

But then Peter pointed out that she was in the wrong tense, that it was over, past, finished, that starting tomorrow or starting next week after she took a vacation she was going out to look for a new job. She broke quickly into wails as loud as a wounded child's. "Lee, Lee, Lee, why are you crying, why do you care?" he comforted her, held her, felt the tight rattling of her sobs against his chest. "The guy's an asshole. The guy's a jerk. This is *better* for you. I know it's hard. I know it's hard. But he didn't fire you because you weren't good. It's just another one of his power plays. This has nothing to do with how good you are."

"I know," she mumbled through her subsiding tears. She sighed tremulously. "I don't know. I don't know."

She said she felt used and scared. "Sometimes you get used," he said. "Sometimes it happens. Sometimes you *let* it happen.

And maybe that's the best way. Because if you let it happen, that means you can *un*let it."

And he assured her she would find another job, one that was far better.

But two months of interviews brought no offers. Finally he convinced her to change tactics. "It's time to turn the tables. Time to use *him* a little bit." Instead of playing her firing as one of the ad world's typical sudden changes, she should relate a few untypical facts. "Don't sound vindictive. Don't sound overheated," he insisted. "But tell them, very calmly, that your pay was extremely low, and that you and the other assistants were promised a share of the agency's profits, and that you feel you were fired because Mr. Orestes wanted to avoid giving you your percentage. There must be plenty of people in the business who think he's a shmuck, and they'll be only too glad to hear your story."

The plan worked like magic. And she was all gratitude. Three weeks later, at Josephine's (the small, intimate club that had supplanted P.S. 5), she told everyone how happy she was with her new job, how smart her boss was, and how interesting her accounts were, and, as Peter stood beside her, she beamed and said he'd coached her through.

And then, during the autumn of Peter's first year at law school, there was another crisis. The problem was both slight and startling. They were at the opening of a Tribeca bar called the Garage. Waitresses with extremely white skin and severely sculpted hair passed trays of Jamaican finger food—bits of spicy hacked chicken and curried goat and fried plantains. Late in the evening, Lee yanked Peter away from a conversation.

"We have to go," she said.

"What?"

"We have to go."

She pushed quickly through the crowd toward the door. He followed, turning hurriedly from the circle he'd been talking with. He thought she was sick; he thought she'd been notified of some tragedy; he thought one of her parents had died; he didn't know what to think. On the street, he ran several steps to catch up with her.

"Lee, what happened? What's wrong?"

"Nothing," she snapped. She kept walking, fast. "Absolutely nothing."

"Lee!"

"I've just had enough of your friends."

"What?" *His* friends?

"Nothing. Forget it. Let's just skip going to the Puck Building tomorrow, okay?"

"Okay."

"Let's just skip going to all these things."

"Okay."

His arm was around her shoulders. They slowed.

"Now will you tell me what happened?"

"Nothing."

"Lee."

"Look, Peter, he's *your* friend."

The two sides of his rib cage felt as though they were gripping each other like fingers, tightly locked. Had he made some play for her? Suggested some arrangement? Kissed her, felt her up, fucked her in some corner of the party?

"Who?" he asked.

"Michael."

"Lee—" he could fire a gun directly into Michael's face, he thought, he really could—"do you want to explain yourself?"

"No."

"Lee!"

"Nothing. No. I just asked him—" She was crying. Her words were lost.

"Lee, what are you saying?"

"I just asked him to buy me a drink and—" More lost words.

"And what?"

"He looked me dead in the eye and said, 'No,' and just—" her voice cleared for a vehement burst—"*walked* off."

There was a pause. He almost laughed. He tugged her closer.

"Oh, honey," he said, "he probably didn't even see you. You know how he sometimes gets at the end of the night. When a zillion people have been crowding around him. He barely recognizes anyone."

"No, Peter. He hates me."

"Honey."

"It's no earth-shattering news."

"Honey, that's crazy. He likes you. I would know."

Another pause.

"Honey honey honey honey honey," he coaxed. "It's true . . . it's true."

So the next evening he put on his tuxedo, and she her low-cut black gown that made her breasts look like a great white shelf, and they went to the Puck Building. In the ballroom, she made her irrepressible rounds. "How *are* you," she said to people she saw less frequently, and "How are *you?*" she said squeakily to people she saw all the time; and she exchanged dozens of cheek kisses, many accompanied by quiet *mmmm*s; and she talked about her job and criticized another agency's campaign and said she was worried about Jenny Clemens because Lex had just broken up with her and wasn't he just a typical Italian scoundrel and they should really take her out and cheer her up, and, when someone asked and Peter was gone, she said, "Well, he doesn't exactly *love* it, but it was time to face the music," and she laughed.

Off and on throughout the evening, Peter mingled along with her; at other times he stood with Michael or chatted with people he'd come to know during nights like this. He got off a few good jokes. He rated himself a reasonable success. For a while, though, he took a break. He leaned against a wall and watched. He watched Lee. He thought of last night, how he'd comforted her; and now she maneuvered easily, from cluster to cluster, and clusters formed around her. She laughed and gestured. She swept her blond hair dramatically back. Earlier, she'd even flirted, as ever, with Michael. She'd drawn a finger across his short, angling forelocks. She'd touched a fingertip to a button on his shirt, as if pressing for an elevator. And yes, Peter had felt enraged at that moment. But for the present he was calm and vaguely, pleasurably sad, and he had the impression that the two halves of her, public and private, were utterly separate, or at least that for her, and maybe for everyone, the private self hardly mattered when it came to what was done out in the world.

Glickstein was at the party, and Peter watched him as well, and listened as he spoke with a friend nearby. Glickstein talked about the prices of lofts below Canal Street, and about skiing in Europe. There was no sign of his errant, overzealous slang, no hint that he'd once dreamed himself a person very different from this. Yet he seemed oblivious and content, comparing accommodations in Austria to those at Stratton and Vail.

And Michael, standing there with Roberto and Annette. They actually engaged him. He didn't wander away from them or look distracted as they spoke. He smiled, trading barbs and sarcasm, or, like Glickstein, discussing vacations. The children of deposed oligarchs, the son of America's mourned liberal—maybe the similarities mattered more than anything. *Here.*

"It's not only what they represent," Peter had railed at Michael, not long ago. "It's not only where their money comes from. It's what they *believe*. They'll tell you, straight out, their families were good for their countries. Everyone has their place. You heard her when we were talking about South Africa. 'The blacks aren't *equipped* for government.' *Equipped*. Or Roberto saying they're moving out of their neighborhood because the ethnics haven't moved out as quickly as they were promised. Ethnics? It makes you realize the depth of their self-deception. But really, it's *too* deep not to be hateful. They're hateful people, Michael. I don't know. Maybe you can ignore that."

Michael had looked stunned, as if he'd never considered Roberto and Annette's politics before. "No, you're right, Peter," he'd said quietly, shamefully, his eyes full of anxious, doelike fear of his friend's condemnation. "I guess they're pretty awful."

"Well," Peter had said.

"I know." Michael had shaken his head. "It's fucked up." The conversation had taken place in a bar, and during it Michael had toyed miserably with a bowl of pretzels; he'd tipped the bowl and stared under it, as if hoping for a place to hide. He seemed so sensitive to Peter's criticisms, and in the moments of decomposing Peter couldn't stand to have such power over him.

"Well," Peter had said, telling himself he'd made his point. "It's not that bad."

Yet here Michael was, at the party, flanked happily. And hypocrisy was too easy a word for it. Hypocrisy was the wrong word. Could you blame Lee for her whirling, frivolous ease when only last night she'd been fragile and insecure? Or Glickstein for his bland, anonymous coping? Or Michael?

Look at yourself, Peter thought. Lee introduces you to some friend from work or college, or some nightworld celebrity—the D.J. from the Palladium or the manager of Josephine's—and you're overjoyed to impress them, to get off on a strain of snide wit and hear their dry, crackling laughter.

With the D.J. from the Palladium, a half hour earlier, it had turned out they'd lived in adjacent Westchester towns, and that as kids they'd played in the same baseball league. And Peter had entertained him, and the rest of their cluster, by recalling the league's umpires—the man with the pitted face and peg leg, and the one who always brought along his mongol son.

"It was like a side-show at a fair," Peter said. "Come see the umpire with six heads! I used to have nightmares about those guys."

Well, you were pleased with yourself, Peter thought. And he remembered Michael's words, "I know. It's fucked up."

Maybe that was all you could say.

On his first day of law school, several weeks before that party at the Puck Building, Peter had listened as the dean welcomed him and his three hundred classmates. Two lecture halls had been opened into one; a vast semicircle of new students sat before the dean and the faculty. Peter stood with a few others at the back. Yet the dean's words drew him in, made him feel he had no business leaning against the wall, that he belonged in the middle of things, sitting in some center row, that this was something he wanted a part of. Service to society, intellectual rigor, the difficult and often painful decisions of justice—as the dean spoke, the law wasn't a career, it was a calling. "In 1922," the speech wound toward its close, "the future Supreme Court Justice, William O. Douglas, hopped freight cars from the stockyards of Minneapolis to the doors of this law school. And today you, too, have come through those doors." Peter knew better than to buy such exalted oratory 100 percent. But for something to fall back on, he thought, this will be pretty damned great.

Then the students were released into the hall and made their way upstairs to wait on line for locker assignments. This was a very different gathering. They compared colleges and majors and mutual friends, and downstairs again, after claiming their lockers, they organized into fresh clans of nervous acquaintances to have lunch before their classes in Legal Method. It wasn't that Peter couldn't imagine the young William O. Douglas scurrying to make first-day friends, saying anxiously, "Let's see what J.P. is up to," or, "How long are you guys gonna be at Anna Lee's?" It was just that by the time Peter left the building to get lunch, the law school's doors had lost some of their hallowed quality.

He went back and forth. Through September, for four—or at least three—hours a day, he forced himself to sit in the library with one of his texts or casebooks open in front of him, and though he spent much of that time on recriminations (What was he doing here? And then, Why, since he *was* here, wasn't he concentrating?), he did manage to absorb a fair amount of the material. In Civil Procedure, he was called on and gave a case recitation that the professor, booming from his podium, declared "one of the best I've ever heard." Peter blushed with pride.

But the startling thing was that people complimented him and clapped him on the shoulder and glanced at him with envy after this classroom triumph. The startling thing was how much they cared. They weren't what he'd expected to find— the defaulters, here for every reason besides desire, singing the old Clash song as a sad and self-mocking joke. Or if they had been when they'd applied, they'd been transformed. For now desire was what they had in abundance, a pure, powerful form of it, a vibrating need to do well. They'd arrived on the first day in full sprint, and a month later Peter was still sitting on the infield, laughing, watching them run round and round, he doing a minimum of work, yet more or less keeping up, which was all he figured he had to do, since the intensity of their wanting made him want this less and less. His classmates were already talking about the firms they'd like to work for, and the names: Paul, Weiss; Davis, Polk; Fried, Frank; Milbank, Tweed—and the corresponding information about types of

practices and associates' hours—sounded interchangeable, and he thought of the firms as obscure constellations, arbitrary formations in the sky that could not possibly add meaning to his life. Even the scattered discussions about public interest, coveted positions with this or that defense fund, blended with the general chatter of desire, from which Peter felt so remote.

And as his classmates ran, the infield on which he sat turned gradually to quicksand. The legal concepts he was supposed to know he didn't even study, and the ones that came up constantly in class he heard like an incessant birdcall—"Promissory estoppel, promissory estoppel, promissory estoppel." His Civil Procedure professor barked out his name and a question one morning in November, and Peter said, "Can I take a rain check?" He waited for laughter and heard a horrified hush.

"Don't you *ever* come into this class unprepared without giving me a note!" the professor yelled, and Peter realized his own lips were twisting, that he was snarling like a sullen teenager, as if he were about to lead a student mutiny, but no rebellion was brewing, the class wasn't about to rally to his side, and, he thought, why should they? He's the most respected scholar of federal jurisdiction in the country. They want to be here. You want to be somewhere else.

Peter had shifted from a daily to a weekly quota of studying, which was far easier to blur and circumvent; soon he'd abandoned quotas altogether. As exams neared he tried to race through cases, then switched strategies and tried to learn just a few cases well, all the time thinking about how little he knew, and how achingly little he cared, how he was too far down to dig himself out, and about how much he couldn't *help* caring. Just no P's, he urged, before pleading, as if to the grading scale itself, which went Pass, Good, Very Good, Excellent. And then, Why not? Why not a P? Or a No Credit? This wasn't his life!

For weeks, *Why not a P?* became his personal slogan, and repeating it to himself, in the library or eating at Mother's or walking home past Rat Park, he could barely keep himself from cackling.

The grades were posted on computer printouts in the school's lobby, course by course, as the professors turned them in. His first was a G. The remaining three went up a week later, on the same afternoon: a VG, an E, a second VG.

He was stunned. He was ecstatic. He felt ill.

He pushed out through the thick glass doors and sat on a bench above Morningside Park.

Well, why not an E? he thought. Why not Stone Scholar? Or Kent, if he worked a little harder? Why not *Law Review?*

He called Lee and reported his success, and the following Sunday she took him to another celebratory dinner at the River Café. That morning, they had gone to Lee's church on Fifth Avenue. Every Sunday, unless she and Peter were away for the weekend, she went to hear the Reverend Timberlake's sermon. It didn't matter how late they'd been out on Saturday night; the next morning at nine she was up and getting ready, putting on her long skirt with the print of purple leaves on the black background, or her matching top and long skirt with the delicate pawlike patterns in white on the dark blue background, or her sweater dress with the red-on-black snowflake design, or, at Christmastime, her scalloped red skirt and red, brass-buttoned vest. It always startled Peter to see her in these clothes. From bed, he watched her pull them on, and with every article she added his desire increased. It was a different kind of need than what he felt at night. The innocence of these clothes dazzled him; seeing her in them it was as if she'd been touched by a wand, remade, and he thought, I don't even know her, and the notion of her complexity made him want to kiss her, his hands on the purple leaves or red snowflakes.

But it wasn't only the clothes that drew him; it was the

churchgoing itself. She adored Timberlake and his down-to-earth wisdom, and often, if Peter met her afterward and they spent the afternoon together, she paraphrased that morning's anecdotes and aphorisms. The church was Unitarian, and Timberlake didn't talk much about God or Jesus, or quote frequently from the Bible. Instead, he discussed nuclear war in terms of the effect it would have on the deer who came to drink from the pond at his country house in Cornwall; or white-collar crime in terms of his stealing apples, as a child in Washington State, from his neighbor's orchard; or charity in terms of a fossil he'd found while hiking in the Catskills—the thoughts it had evoked about the humbling age of those mountains. Sometimes these moral lessons struck Peter as terribly easy and optimistic and simple—they trusted no higher authority was needed, asked only that everyone *mean* well—but, on the other hand, they were *something*, weren't they? and, he asked himself, Just how wonderfully moral a person are you?

A few times he'd gone to church with her. He'd have gone more often, but he was Jewish, and though he hadn't been raised religiously—he hadn't even been bar mitzvahed—he thought that if he were going to worship in his adult life it ought to be in a synagogue. Otherwise he'd have heard more of Timberlake's sermons, which calmed him despite their pre-chewed quality. The minister was only in his thirties, the youngest leader of any of Manhattan's large churches, and he combined the questioning of the 1960s with the wholesomeness of his upbringing in the Pacific Northwest. He communicated with the young and the young middle-aged, and he appealed to the elderly because his lessons—experimental without being threatening—made them feel youthful. As he spoke, everyone was comfortably engaged. Everyone was uplifted by a sense of cogent, controlled enlightenment. Including Peter.

On the Sunday of Peter and Lee's dinner, Timberlake's sermon was entitled "You Can't Always Get What You Want." Peter rolled his eyes and cringed at this cooption of the Stones' lyrics, but he was affected by the minister's message: "Take stock of what you have."

It was partly this saying, and the flickering pleasure of his grades, and the mere symmetry of the dinner's setting (almost a year ago, they'd been at this same restaurant, celebrating his LSAT scores), that inspired Peter to propose. He hadn't planned it; he didn't even have a ring; but it wasn't as if he hadn't been thinking about marriage, or as if they hadn't talked about it, and suddenly, in the restaurant, the idea of asking came into his head, and the place seemed perfect for it, and Lee's sharp features were superimposed on the view of black water lit in shifting slivers and vanishing shapes; and their engagement began.

They planned to be married the following November.

Why not an E? Why not Stone Scholar? How long did such optimism and resolve last? It left him in ebbs, interrupted by surges, every five, fifteen, thirty days, of certainty and determination. These periods of intent (which could be extremely brief) might be sparked by his reading. A case in one of his books—Hamer v. Sideway or Fire v. Balm—might interest him, or the story behind it might move or amuse him, and he would argue himself into believing that his involvement was general. Or his resolve might have nothing to do with his reading; he might be in bed or in the shower, warm and removed, and decide—simply decide—that he liked the law. But no matter what the process of persuasion, and no matter how long its effects (whether two minutes or two days), inertia invaded him more and more thoroughly, and for his second semester exams he relied largely on the help of his classmates. For some it was his musical past, for others his association with Michael; for some it was the fact that he did almost no work (there was a course in which he never saw the professor's face until exam day, and one in which he never bought the casebooks), for others it was in spite of it; at any rate, a good number of students were drawn to him. They were generous with their forty-page outlines, detailing the material. They tried to coach him.

His grades were sluggish, middling, unattractive things. Seeing them posted, he was repelled first by the grades themselves and next by his own disappointment. Had he studied during the term? Had he even made a real last-ditch effort? You asked for it, he told himself accusingly, and then, flippantly, You asked for it.

Flippantly. At clubs, at parties, and afterward with himself, flippancy became his standard tone. That summer, he took a job in the corporate department of Walker, Gottlieb, and spoke as if it were no more relevant to his future than the work he'd done as a kid, caddying and mowing lawns and sweeping the bleachers at Yankee Stadium. In the same way he'd made his friends laugh about his supervisor at the Stadium, who'd followed him from 12 until 6 A.M. every night, making sure he used the proper sweeping technique ("There's a right way and a wrong way to use a broom, boy"), he entertained people with accounts of the associates at the firm. They were frenetic flunkies, straining to distinguish themselves, scheming to demoralize and derail each other. Or he told a story about the new partner who'd called him into his office to show off the furniture and bookshelves and track lighting he'd just had installed. Everything was sleek Danish modern and leather and chrome, but the *"pièce de résistance,"* as the new partner had said, was the desk that could be adjusted to tilt upward like a drafting table. "In our line of work, Peter," the new partner had advised, "you have to be creative. And I believe it helps sometimes to just tip the contracts up, to look at them in a creative way." "How creative can you be about filling in the blanks on a boilerplate form?" Peter asked at the party, and went on to describe the man down on his knees under his nifty desk, wrestling with its malfunctioning crank.

Of course, he didn't share these portraits with many of his lawyer acquaintances. For them, he would have taken things quite a bit too far. He steered clear of them at parties. But the nonlawyers were certainly glad to listen and laugh.

And in the mornings he went to work. Since he was only going into his second year of law school, his position was vague—something more than a paralegal, something less than a summer associate. He was not yet a recruit, to be coaxed with dinners and "dream nights" and *pro bono* assignments. The partners gave him real work, like reading through the blue sky statutes.

Such reading was anything but sunny. The last thing that had interested Peter was one of the first he'd found out, that the laws' name derived from a supreme Court decision concerned with "speculative schemes which have no more basis than so many feet of blue sky." This had made Peter laugh. He'd imagined people buying shares of empty atmosphere, people giddy with expectations, and he'd become giddy himself. From then on, there hadn't been much levity. Each state had different requirements for issuing new stock, and each code had to be studied to be sure the client company conformed with regulations. He was progressing alphabetically. He'd been at it two days. He was on Delaware.

That night, he confided in Lee as he never quite had. No stories about his colleagues or flippancy about himself. "No, leave the light on," he said. They were in bed. He wanted to see her face as he spoke.

"Earth to Peter, earth to Peter," she broke in, and she continued, ending each sentence with a singsongy inflection.

"It's a jo—ob. Jobs aren't always won—der—ful." And later: "You have to *make* yourself interested. Put something into it. Just try. Just for now."

One of the myths still existing between them—no matter if either of them believed it—was that in two years, after he graduated, he could always go back to music exclusively, or write songs while working as an attorney, or that he might practice law in a better way than at Walker, Gottlieb. Not that Lee wanted him to veer off onto many of the paths she delineated. Marriage to a defender of the disadvantaged was not what she had her heart set on. And certainly she hoped that they would soon treat the old Peter, the singer/song-writer, as a comic figure, a bygone character in their marital folklore. Yet the mind adjusts, desiring one thing in order to obtain another, opposite wish. On conscious levels she just wanted him to be happy.

And increasingly, at parties and clubs, he was. He com-manded plenty of attention. Clusters formed around him. He felt exhilarated, even triumphant. At the end of a night, stepping out onto the street, he loved the city's blanched darkness. It seemed to quicken and lift everything. And the forces of friction and gravity seemed to doze.

Meanwhile, the press was speculating about Michael's run for Congress. He'd made no announcement; he'd refused to answer reporter's questions. This was all part of the DNC's plan. Let rumor and hope build around his silence. Then, in late November, he would officially declare his candidacy.

One afternoon, as Peter read through the blue sky statute of Tennessee, he received a phone call.

"Peter?"

"Yeah."

"Doug Schraeder again. From *Newsday*."

"Hey."

"Listen. I figured it's been two weeks. It's time to let me give you another try."

"Doug," Peter said, "at this very moment I'm working on the most beautifully named and *the most boring* legal problem known to man. Believe me, I'd like nothing more than to meet you for lunch. But I can't, Doug. I have nothing to say."

"Well, how about this? How about we keep it soft? Stay off politics. Character. Ambitions. Private moments. Bullshit. Whatever."

"Doug."

"Source unnamed, Peter."

"Doug, I know nothing."

Not that Peter couldn't have given out harmless observations—to Schraeder or any of the other reporters who called. Plenty of Michael's coterie did. Profiles were meaninglessly fleshed out with such quotations. But Peter was the only friend who knew for certain about Michael's plans, and the only one who knew how his candidacy was being engineered. (He hadn't even shared his knowledge with Lee.) And of course, about personal things, Michael confided in him in a way he didn't with anyone else. So Peter did his part to maintain the distinction. His role spread over him like a soothing camphor. He said absolutely nothing to the press. Unresponsive, he felt himself the protector of his friend's privacy, the guardian of a territory within which Michael could freely exist.

After dealing with Schraeder, he called Michael, who was already at home. They were supposed to go bike riding that night. Michael said the doorman had rung up, that four photographers were posted outside the lobby.

"I hate this shit," Michael said.

"Well, maybe we should smuggle you out."

On his way home, Peter bought a bike messenger's satchel,

and, riding over to Michael's, he wore blue shorts, of which Michael had an identical pair, a red windbreaker with a hood (luckily it was beginning to drizzle), and the helmet his father had bought him two years ago (this was its first use). Sticking out of the satchel was a poster tube.

He locked his bike across the street from the Helmsford and walked past the photographers into the lobby. The doorman, who'd been clued in to the plan, nodded Peter through. Upstairs in the vestibule, Michael donned the jacket, the hood, and slung the empty satchel.

"Do I make a convincing bike messenger?" he asked.

Peter stepped back. "The mug is a little too visible," he said. "Here." He tugged the hood strings and tied them across Michael's chin. The hood was cinched down across Michael's forehead. He was as hidden as an Eskimo or an astronaut.

Michael went out into the marble hall and was gone into the elevator. They would meet at the statue by Columbus Circle in twenty minutes. Peter found himself with ten minutes alone. He wandered into his friend's bedroom. This wasn't the first time he'd snooped in the apartment, aimlessly opening drawers and closets, or simply standing, at once idle and furtive, in the middle of a room, or searching, without any precise purpose, the compartments of Michael's rolltop desk. He'd read letters from Michael's aunt and statements from his accountant, letters from lovers and supplications from strangers. And in brief, panicky flashes, he'd expected to see something from Lee. If he did, he knew that would be it. The marriage. Michael. Everything. If he found out they'd slept together, it would be over. He'd be gone. But not before he dealt with Michael. Without pulling back. Without pity. And it wouldn't only be what he, Peter, would say. He might not say anything at all. It would be what he'd *do*. The lesson he'd inflict. When he considered it, he worked himself quickly into such a rage he couldn't picture the scene coherently. He saw it in tight glimpses of wild violence. The leaving, the getting out, that much was definite. The goodbye gesture was undecided. Except that it would be dreadful.

But in Michael's apartment he hadn't found anything.

Tonight, though, stepping into the bedroom, he noticed on the floor a stack of *Life* magazines, and he felt, long before he understood it, a wave of sympathy. The one on top was open to a full-page picture of Michael at his high school graduation. Several of the issues had him on the cover (at age twelve, sailing with his cousin; three years ago, receiving his Palmer diploma); all of them contained stories about him. Peter had seen most of the photographs before. It wasn't the images themselves that kept him sitting on the bed, flipping through; it was the surprise that Michael owned these particular issues, and that, minutes or hours earlier, he'd had them out. Peter imagined him studying them. There was something especially futile in it—Michael's trying to track himself down in the photographs of magazines.

It was time to go. Peter arranged the pile the way he'd discovered it, took Michael's bicycle and the windbreaker Michael had left him, and headed downstairs and out into the drizzly summer evening. When he reached the statue, Michael put up a hand for a high-five to their evasion.

"It worked?"

"Yes, indeed," Michael said, grinning.

It had stopped raining. They decided to bike over the Brooklyn Bridge. They sped downtown on Second Avenue, racing the traffic on the hill above Forty-second Street, their tires *shushing* on the wet pavement. They rode slowly, circuitously, through the deserted park at City Hall.

On the upper level of the bridge, which they had all to themselves, Peter recalled a story from when he'd lived in the Heights, before his family had moved out of the city. A kid he'd known had climbed the cable to the top of one of the bridge's towers. He told this to Michael as they pedaled over the walkway's uneven slats.

"Shit," Michael said, craning his neck and gazing up at the ascending cable.

"I know. There are handrails, though. I mean, workmen must have to go up there sometimes."

"But with harnesses."

"True."

"You game?"

"Right."

"I'm serious."

"Michael, forgetting the fact that heights do *not* attract me, forgetting the fact that when I was a kid I used to get scared looking down at the water from *here*, seeing the little specks of it between the slats of this nice safe walkway, there is another problem. MICHAEL THE MOUNTAINEER: Marr Arrested in Bridge-Scaling Stunt. The DNC would not be pleased. No, they definitely would not be psyched."

"Fuck the DNC."

"Michael."

"I'm serious. Let's do it."

"I'm serious, too. Let's not."

But they locked their bikes. They pissed nervously onto the wooden slats. Peter decided not to go second. He negotiated the barbed wire—meant, he thought, to discourage suicides—and stepped onto the girding above the car lanes.

Their tires humming on the road's steel grate, cars whipped past a long distance down.

"We can't do this, Michael," Peter said. "It's been raining. It's wet. This is fucking stupid."

"It's dry, Peter. Don't get hysterical. If you don't want to do it, just wait here."

Peter stepped onto the cable. He kept glancing to his left. There was the walkway, only six, eight, twelve feet below. This wasn't bad. The cable was no tightrope. It was about a foot in diameter. And even if he slipped, how could he fall if he kept hold of the handrails?

The answer was on his other side. He fixed his eyes on the cable and refused to let them focus on the car lanes or, farther out, the water. He would not would not would not glance down. He kept his strides cautious, steady. Just one foot in front of the other. Nothing can happen. Just make sure of your handholds. Don't let go before you grab on with the other. Tight? Okay, let go. Grab, let go. Grab, let go. Don't look down. You're fine. No, no, no, no.

He did. He looked. The incessant wavering hum of the tires seemed to force him, and there were the car hoods flashing past on the brightly lit roadway and—he hadn't yanked his eyes away in time—the water, glinting between the girders and shifting indifferently, intimately in the distance. He felt as if the tendons in his wrists had been stretched, as if he could no longer clasp tight to the rails. The cable. Just focus on the cable.

A truck backfired. He started. He knew what it was, but imagined it was someone in a car, shooting up at them as a prank. Or a cop, trying to get their attention. The images made him weaker. Every *thought* made him weaker. Any thought was closer to *the* thought—that he could misstep, sneaker sliding off the cable's curve, or trip, toe catching one of the cable's joints, and at the same time he could lose hold of the rails or—and this was the thought sneaking in behind every other—he could cause these things to happen. Just one lapse. Just one impulse.

Okay. He tried to calm himself. Okay. Just empty your mind. One foot in front of the other.

He stopped. He gazed around him—not down, *out*. Enjoy the view. Ferry glowing in the harbor. Enjoy the view. Lights of Verrazano Bridge. Enjoy dark roofs of Brooklyn, people beneath them eating watching TV. The thought again. Letting go.

"Peter."

He didn't turn, didn't answer.

"Peter!"

Cautious of any movement that might jar him, checking his grip on the rails and the dependability of his knees, he glanced over his shoulder. Michael was farther back than he'd thought. "What?" Peter said quietly.

"I guess this wasn't such a great idea."

"What?"

"I guess this wasn't such a great idea."

"No." He could barely make himself yell. His own voice threatened his balance. "You can turn around if you want."

A delicate iron ladder led from the end of the cable to the top of the tower. The top itself was flat, a rectangle of pavement. There was nothing at the perimeter, no railing, no rope. Peter stayed low, wary of his balance, his sanity. From here the cars were smaller than his hand, but the moaning of the tires vibrated through his chest. He lay on his stomach at the outside edge. The river, directly below, coaxed. If he pushed himself forward, if he placed his palms on the stone of the tower's side and pushed himself forward until his neck, shoulders, chest were over the edge, if he persisted until his belly was suspended over water and air, at that point nothing else, no retraction, would be possible. He ground his chin on the cement. He crouch-walked back to the ladder. The sight of Michael on the cable, approaching slowly, step by meticulous, terrified step, left Peter helpless with sudden laughter. He tried to squelch it when his friend reached the base of the ladder, but Michael's eyes were too startling, too empty, too desperate, a hundred times more eerie than Peter had ever seen them, a thousand times more hollow; rigid, depthless, petrified, Michael's eyes gazed up at him, and Peter struggled and let out a last chortle of near-hysteria before getting control of himself and saying, "Michael, Michael, just keep your eyes up here. Just keep your eyes on me. Just keep your eyes on me."

There was a difference in their fears. They talked about it later. Peter explained his, the voice of curiosity or desire, or something between them whispering about how easily he could cause his own falling. But Michael said it hadn't been like that. For him there hadn't been any tempting voices.

"It was like nothing," he struggled.

"What do you mean?"

"It was like I was *already* dead. And I just happened to be on the cable. . . . It was like with the next little puff of wind . . . it was like I would fly off . . . it was like I would just be air."

Twelve

PETER AND LEE SPENT LABOR DAY WEEKEND AT THE MARR CAMP ON an island on Seaver Lake. Peter and Michael, and, as it turned out, Roberto and Annette, drove up on Wednesday evening. Lee had to wait and fly up on Friday—she had a bridal-gown fitting scheduled at Bergdorf's, where her maternal aunt, who had always disdained Lee's father and pitied Lee, had bought her gown.

On Wednesday afternoon, Peter and Michael met for lunch downtown, and afterward Michael had the idea that he should buy a mountain bike for the trails around the camp. The bulky, low-geared, fat-tired bikes were just becoming popular; there was one hanging in the window of a small shop, and Michael said, "I should get one of those for the dacks" (the "dacks" being the Adirondacks, where the Marr camp was), and they wandered in.

The shop was narrow and cramped and dim, an anomaly on the Soho side street of bright, plate glass–fronted businesses—a bakery, an art gallery, a store that sold only hats and lingerie. The window in which the bike hung was dark, and gazing through it, one might have seen the store as an old and long-uncleaned fish tank, its air tinted a greenish brown and its colorful bicycles looming in the murk. The front door had no window at all—it was simply a plank of red-painted wood. When Michael opened it, a bell tinkled loudly.

As Peter followed his friend in, it took a moment for his eyes to adjust. There were standing lamps, but their light seemed absorbed by the floorboards, which were painted green, and by the walls, which were the same color except where they were decorated with bicycle posters. Opening a counter door, a young woman emerged from a back room, slipping past a customer, a boy in a Hawaiian shirt.

"Can I help you?" she asked Michael.

Peter noticed that in spite of the darkness the shop seemed to be doing well. It was crammed with new bikes; there was hardly an aisle; wheels encroached at knee- and head-level. When the boy in the Hawaiian shirt left, Peter had to squeeze between sets of handlebars to make room, and a man trying to wheel in his bike to be repaired caused a minor crash and a complicated tangle of spokes and pedals, brake levers and derailleur cables, which Peter helped unsort. Behind the counter in back was a black man, a Rastafarian, in a red, green, and black leather cap. He came out to wait on a new customer, a man in a business suit who looked to be in his forties.

"No, Josh," he said to the customer, in a voice that was startlingly high and thin, either faintly effeminate or simply gentle. "That bike is for chumps. Save yourself seventy dollars and buy the Centurion. It's the same bike."

"Okay. But that's no way to get rich."

"Oh, don't worry, Josh. I'll find myself a chump."

Meantime, Michael was questioning the young woman. She was short and thin, with straight, dark hair that fell almost to the waist of her black Spandex shorts. She had on some sort of quirky, toylike earrings—big, stick-figure cats, Peter thought they were. She'd asked Michael about his plans for the bike and suggested two models. She'd hoisted them down for him to try, and he'd tested them, riding along the block. He'd wanted Peter to try them as well. Peter had liked the first and been doubtful about the second, but now, inside again, Michael was gazing at other bikes.

"What's the difference between the Ultimate and the Ross?" he asked. And then, "What about the Baja Team?"

"Well, the top tube is a thicker gauge, so it's a little bit stiffer. And there's more stiffness in the seatstay. And it has an upgraded Com-Tam crankset. It's a racing bike. Definitely a racing bike."

Watching, Peter couldn't tell if Michael were really considering the eighteen-hundred-dollar Baja Team to tool around on, or whether he was only extending his conversation with the woman. He seemed to be flattening his eyes in his mode of ennui and enticement, and she seemed almost fluttery, tense with self-restraint as she recited the high-grade components. And she *was* cute. Huge brown eyes. Small-breasted and sexy in her midriff shirt. And then there were the funny earrings, which were definitely cats, with a tiny fish suspended in each of the round bellies.

He helped her haul down the Baja Team. He tested it and had Peter test it.

"I don't know, Michael," Peter said, catching the woman's eye. "Doesn't seem like the competition's going to be that tough, pedaling by yourself around that island."

She laughed.

"But couldn't you tell the difference?"

"Barely. I guess I'm not worthy of such a fine machine."

Within ten minutes, Michael had chosen the Baja Team and brought out a credit card. And now the woman was definitely nervous, as if, in the midst of their transactions over charge slips and brochures and warranties, she were debating whether to slip Michael her number.

"Well," she said, smiling, when they were through, "I guess I'm due for a raise."

Michael's lips curled minimally, and he dealt her a stare containing the full force of his seductive indifference. "Okay," he said, starting to guide the bike out. "Take it easy."

"Enjoy it," the Rastafarian called, from the repair room in back.

"You don't remember me?"

It was the woman, and, turning, Peter glanced from her to Michael, waiting for his reaction.

"You're Peter Bram," she said.

She smiled easily, her nervousness diminished, like an old and self-assured lover confronting Peter with some knowledge of himself.

"Sorry," he said. "I—"

"Oh. No. I don't know why I asked that. There's no real reason you should. I mean, I used to go hear you all the time. When you were at Palmer."

"Oh."

"I even followed you home one night. In one of my more mature modes."

"Well, you should have just gone ahead and knocked," he ventured.

"Let's not get carried away."

"Sorry," he joked, feeling strangely calm, and nearly oblivious of Michael behind him, pushing out the door with his new mountain bike.

"Where are you playing now?"

"I'm not."

"Oh."

"I've taken a slight hiatus."

She smiled, then seemed to become distracted, thoughtful. She twisted her full, kind of comical lips.

"So what would happen if I followed you home today?" she asked. "And knocked?"

"Mmm. That probably wouldn't be a good idea."

"Why?"

"Because I'm engaged."

"I see. Then that *would* be pretty undiplomatic."

"Right."

"Well," she said. "Good luck with your hiatus."

"Thanks. What's your name?"

"Karina."

"Okay. Well, I'm glad we finally met."

Michael and Peter picked up Roberto and Annette, and they drove out of the city. This was not a ride Peter looked forward to. Frequently he felt Roberto and Annette truly deserved to be put in front of a firing squad. All too often, though, he found himself laughing along with or trying to impress this couple he wanted to have shot.

Annette, in her semi-British accent, said, "Oh, Michael, did Roberto tell you who we ran into when we were out at the Packers'?"

"No."

"Doug Friedman," Roberto said.

"Dougie." Michael shook his head and laughed.

"But not at the Packers'," Roberto said. "At Indoline."

"At about six in the morning, or some god-awful hour," Annette added.

"Yes, well, it was our last day, and we were leaving that morning. It's a beautiful course. Michael, or Peter, if you ever take up golf, have Jillian take you out there.

"At any rate," Annette continued, "we were on one of the

162

greens, and all of a sudden we hear this 'Hi, guys,' and there's this man standing beside a lake below us—with a scuba mask on his head, and wearing a swimsuit and flippers. Dougie. He's standing beside some sort of contraption. And he tugs off his flippers and comes jogging barefoot across the rough and up onto the green. So he says, 'Hi, guys,' again, in that eager-beaver way of his, and insists on standing there and having a little chat. Apparently he free-lances for a company that does secondhand golf balls. He dredges them off the bottom of lakes, and the ones the machine can't find he dives for. 'Twenty cents a ball,' he says. 'Mmm, good money,' we say."

Everyone laughed.

"But of course that's not what he's really doing," Roberto said.

"Still painting?" Michael asked.

"Yes." Annette let out a tremendous sigh.

"Apparently he's living in some shack in Montauk," Roberto put in.

"Do you remember those paintings, Michael?" Annette asked. "Those shiny gorillas, or whatever they were?"

"Oh, my God, I know," Michael said. "You know what I always thought he should do? I saw a 'Sixty Minutes' once about this. Velvet painting. These illegal aliens just churn these things out—jungle scenes, naked women, all this shit—on black velvet, and the paint glows. I guess they sell like hotcakes in Nebraska. I always thought Dougie would have a talent at that."

"Well," Roberto said, chuckling. "He looked sort of like an illegal alien when we saw him. He looked like he'd just swum across the Rio Grande."

When they'd drained Dougie of conversational value, Michael mentioned that he'd seen Beth Wichterman at Josephine's. "She is *not* a happy camper," Michael reported. "I guess every business school she applied to turned her down. Even Fordham gave her the boot."

More laughter.

Then Peter played his trump.

"Well," he said, "do you all remember Cliff Lighthauser?"

"Yes!" Annette managed to combine excitement with jaded weariness.

Michael didn't remember him.

"Oh, I think he dropped out right before you came," Annette explained. "Suffice it to say he was the best-looking boy at Palmer."

"Well, Annette, I'm sure he'd be happy to have a nice, long talk with you," Peter said.

"Where did you see him?"

"In Union Square. Carrying a sign that said, 'Did You Want to Talk About Jesus?'"

"Peter, clarify yourself. *Please.*"

"He's born-again, I guess. He was milling around with a little platoon of these people, all carrying these signs. *Did* you want to talk about Jesus? They hadn't gotten the tense quite right. Anyway, this woman had a microphone and a little amp, and she was trying to sing hymns over the boom boxes. And there was Cliff."

Everyone was thoroughly amused.

"Did you talk to him?" Annette asked.

"No, he was busy chatting with someone who *had* wanted to talk about Jesus."

In fact, as soon as Peter had spotted Cliff, he'd considered saying hello. This impulse was not like the one he'd had two summers ago, when the city had seemed to fill with religious recruiters, and when Peter had yearned vaguely to speak with them, to be convinced by them, to immerse himself in whatever rigors they were devoted to. No, Peter had considered approaching Cliff in order to improve his story for

Roberto and Annette. All the better if he could repeat some born-again inanities Cliff would utter.

The Marrs owned an island (about two miles around) at the south end of Seaver Lake, and theirs was one of the oldest Adirondack camps in the area. Michael's grandfather had bought it in the 1930s from the original owners, who had built its expansive yet rustic main house, and its satellite cabins, fifty years earlier. During the thirties and forties, the Marrs had gradually razed most of the cabins and made extensive additions (a hexagonal, fully-windowed kitchen and dining room connected to the house by a covered walkway; a library and a solarium connected by another walkway; a larger boathouse; a second-story billiards room on top of the boathouse; a wide deck, on stilts over the water, to be used at cocktail hour at sunset); but everything had been done with impeccable discretion, no building deviated blatantly from the log-cabin motif, and with all the obvious luxury there remained a sense of the frontier. On the boathouse was a shingle bearing the name of the camp, "Keenahog." As Michael and his party arrived from the mainland, in the dark, in the Marrs' Boston Whaler, they drifted under the sign and were greeted by the family's old black caretaker.

The caretaker's nickname, Chaz, had always struck Peter as incongruous with his silence, his spindliness, his tattered chamois shirts, and his virtual invisibility during the times Peter had visited the island. Chaz lived alone in the woods, in one of the few old cabins left standing. He helped people with their bags when they came and when they left; in between he nearly vanished. Occasionally Peter had run into him working on the grounds around the house, and had tried to start conversation. Chaz had seemed to warm to him, but had resisted going past the pleasantries. When Peter had asked how many years he'd been living on the island, Chaz had said, "Oh, a long time," and that had been that. And when Peter had asked Michael about Chaz's history, Michael had looked as if he'd never given it much thought, saying only that Chaz had worked there as long as he could remember.

On Thursday morning the huge lake was still, unruffled by wind, and unripped by boats. By Saturday entire clans would fill the seven other camps at that end of the lake, and family and more friends would be at Keenahog, and there would be perpetual action—windsurfing, sailing, fishing, canoeing, sculling, and, for the other families, though not for the more purist Marrs (who did their best to avoid motorized recreations), water-skiing and para-sailing. But on Thursday Michael and his guests had breakfast on the deck, and things were so empty and quiet and unresort-like that Annette and Roberto's accented voices, formidable in any social place, sounded surprisingly frail. They seemed to sense this as they remarked on how gorgeous the house and water and surrounding mountains were. After a minute or two of speechlessness, Annette said hurriedly, "I'll clear," and Peter had a moment of sympathy for them both.

They recovered a bit of their poise as Michael took his guests for a cruise on the family's old wooden fishing boat. Almost wide-eyed and curious, they asked scattered questions about the formation of the lake and the history of the camps and what the few people did who lived there year-round, and they murmured and exclaimed as Michael talked about glaciers and ice fishing. When he docked the boat again, they said they would rest.

But in the late afternoon Roberto had a burst of vigor. He was ready to fish and canoe, and Annette, guiltily inert with a copy of *European Travel and Life,* said she would cut flowers and start cooking dinner. She went down to the garden. While Michael went in to change, Roberto and Peter (who was going to try sailing in spite of the fickle breeze) followed her.

In her swimsuit and matching chiffon cover-up, she knelt in the hillside flower bed. From above, her frazzle of black hair looked almost shrublike in the shadows. She cut several zinnias, stripped the stems of their leaves, and shifted to another part of the garden. Her shins were dusted with dark soil. She'd left the leaves scattered in the dirt, and one of them clung to her knee. She seemed unaware of it and knelt again, snipping, stripping, stripping. When she was through, she held a bouquet of zinnias and dahlias and snapdragons, and the lower halves of her legs were caked with earth.

As she started back to the house, she said, "Darling, would you gather those leaves and throw them in the trash by the shed?"

"Oh," Roberto said, as Michael came down the hill, "Chaz will take care of them."

Not three feet away, Michael continued right past on the path to the boathouse.

"True," Annette said, walking languorously off.

Roberto moved to follow Michael down.

"You can't be serious," Peter said.

Roberto turned briefly, and Peter considered, for an instant, breaking his exotic, bladelike nose.

"Why not?"

"Here," Peter said, though Roberto wasn't waiting for his answer. "I will pick up the leaves—" he annunciated with mocking emphasis—"and put them in the garbage."

There was no wind. While Michael and Roberto had canoed out of sight into an inlet, Peter had managed to tack the small sailboat around an uninhabited island, but on the far side the breeze waned and the sails luffed. He could always motor home; for the moment, though, he let go of the tiller, leaned back, and drank one of the beers he'd brought from the boathouse bar. He kept thinking about Roberto's nose and what a pleasure it would be to bust it with a single, square-on punch. He knew he had to calm down, that there were three days left to get through. And he knew he couldn't goad Roberto into a fight, that he would only look like a fool trying to do it—Roberto was slender and sly, and Peter outsized him by three inches and thirty pounds. Still, the fantasy satisfied and gnawed, and he kept imagining various lines he would deliver before and after the blow. The punch itself, which always followed some hapless swing of Roberto's, was solitary and decisive, its justice unmitigated by scuffling. *Boom* and it was done. The nose nicely crumpled. A spurt of Roberto's aristocratic blood.

He continued thinking along these lines through a second beer. Then he had to pee. This was no problem. It was windless and he was far out on the lake; he simply stood with the boom against his arm and pissed over the back of the boat. It was a heady, free feeling to pee outdoors in this way, and his headiness gave way to an idea. In his state of slight drunkenness, he followed it. He turned, and peed on the white Fiberglas wall of the cabin. He peed into the cabin. He aimed his piss up onto the cabin's roof and managed to pee on the mast.

It was dusk. He sloshed a few buckets of lake water to wash the white Fiberglas (realizing that if he didn't, and if his piss did dry visibly yellow, and Michael noticed the strange stains in the morning, it could easily be Chaz who would end up cleaning them). Still, Peter smiled openly on the desolate lake as he motored home.

Thirteen

Dear Karina,
Maybe if I followed you home.
                                        Peter

THIS AND HIS PHONE NUMBER WERE ALL HE PRINTED ON THE NOTE he mailed to the bike shop. And addressing the envelope, he could use only her first name, since he didn't know her last.

All of which made him feel as if he were merely playing a game. It was the Tuesday after Labor Day. His wedding was hardly two months away. Dropping the note into a mailbox on his way to school, he rebuked himself, but happily, thinking, Stupid, Stupid, Stupid. And as he neared the law school's squat, faceless building, he felt immune to the depression that usually hit him frontally like a soft and heavy wall. Nor did the depression sneak up behind him and pat him on the shoulder as soon as he'd passed through the thick glass doors.

Beyond attraction and lightheaded curiosity and the blend of calm and elation he'd been overtaken by during their two-minute talk amidst the encroaching bicycles, there was another reason he'd written the note. He thought of his infidelity (if that was what ended up happening) as a kind of insurance. If Lee was ever unfaithful, or if she had been already, especially with Michael, and if Peter found out, he would need a betrayal of his own to remember and protect himself with.

But this last, frightened reason was separate from his central, happy impulse. He'd left the bike shop in a momentary bliss of ease and affection, and he'd sensed right away he would try to get in touch with Karina.

On Thursday she called, and suggested they meet on more neutral ground. She lived in Brooklyn, in Williamsburg, but she had the next day off and would be on the Lower East Side. It was supposed to be a nice day, with an early thread of fall thinning the city's air, and they decided on Tompkins Square Park.

He spotted her amidst the park's outdated punkers and eternal, elderly chess players and basketball players who looked either prematurely haggard or truly too old for such pickup games. She sat motionless on a bench, alone, looking comfortable and unconcerned about attracting or avoiding attention. She wore a white T-shirt and white suspenders. There was a black lunch pail beside her narrow, blue-jeaned hip. When she saw him she didn't wave or stand or say anything as he neared. She just kept still.

"Hey," he said quietly.

She shifted the lunch pail to the other side of her, like a kid making room for a friend whose place she's saved. The sleeves of her T-shirt were rolled up into cuffs. Her arms were thin, pale. Her hair—long, straight, unstyled—was perfectly, radiantly black.

He sat down, and neither of them spoke. He leaned back on the bench. Shutting his eyes, he tipped back his head as if tilting his face to the sun (which was behind clouds), and as if he and Karina had met merely to keep each other company while they got tan.

"So," he said, straightening.

"So." Her voice was sly at the edges, the way it had been in the bike shop. The faint hint of a private joke between them seemed to surround this echoed word, *so*. Then she sighed, briefly, nervously. But when her lips came together, something about them, the way the upper one had that deep dip, made her look inwardly humorous, restful.

"So is that really yours?" He glanced across at the lunch pail.

"Yunh–huh." She twisted this utterance playfully, giving it a sort of hillbilly drawl.

"Well, then you probably get enough clever little lunch-box jokes. So I'll just ask. What's in it?"

One bench over, a game of speed chess was being waged. The old men snapped down pieces and slapped at their timer every two, three, five seconds. It didn't matter that everyone in the park seemed utterly detached from time—the out-of-vogue punkers whose boots and chains would eventually become timeless, neither in nor out of style; the basketball players who had nowhere to be in the middle of the afternoon; even the chess players themselves who seemed unaware that at this rate they would finish innumerable games—countless matches and meaningless championships—before nightfall. They jabbed furiously at their clock.

"Earrings," Karina said.

"Earrings?"

"That's why I was over here today. Hawking my wares."

"Successfully?" He felt almost drugged—at ease in spite of his uneasiness.

"Four cats and four anteaters," she said. "These are the anteaters."

She tucked her hair behind her ear, though the earring was large enough to be noticeable anyway. It was a wooden outline of an anteater painted bright yellow, and suspended by tiny hooks inside its belly was a wooden square painted to be an ant farm. The square was yellow with black mazelike lines, and tiny black ants crawled obliviously, happily, along the paths.

Peter laughed. "You made these?"

"Yunh–huh. And these are the cats."

She opened the lunch pail. These were the earrings she'd been wearing in the bike shop. They were done in the same way as the anteaters, except that the cats, each with a fish lodged in its stomach, had fully articulated faces that were mischievous and pleased. And the fish weren't so happily oblivious as the ants. They were mounted at an angle that made you think they were leaping, trying to get out. But by the cat's self-satisfied expressions, it was clear the fish weren't making much progress. The scene was like a cartoon, but somehow, for being frozen, it was both more gleeful and more evil.

Also inside the lunch pail were mice mounted within boa constrictors, obese women painted minutely inside of svelte, curvaceous ones, and earrings of Jonah in the belly of the whale.

"These are great," Peter said.

"Thanks."

"We should celebrate. We should celebrate your sale."

"Well, I didn't exactly sell them. A store *took* them. I get a percentage *if* they sell. I'm not exactly the Paloma Picasso of casual jewelry."

"Still."

172

She said there was a bar she usually went to, a few blocks away. She led him down the three cracked steps to the entrance. The place was completely empty.

"Hi, Karina," the middle-aged Polish barmaid said, her smile girlishly pleased, her voice abrasively nasal, heavily accented. Her face was small and squarish. Her hair was in a squat, moderate beehive.

"Hi, Wanda."

"Hey, Wanda," Peter said.

"Hi! Hi, I remember *you*. You move? Gone! *Poof!*"

"No. Just no more band. You remember my friend? Blond curly hair?"

"Yes," she said emphatically. "Sure." She cocked her head, bending to the bar so her ear nearly rested on the wood. She made a bridge with her thumb and forefinger and mimed taking a shot at pool.

"Right," he said. That was the way Sifkin had always shot, ear practically touching the felt and nose close enough to sniff the cue ball, as if aiming required extra senses, hearing and smell as well as sight.

"Drummer," she said.

"Right." He'd started with Peter after Peter's first band had disintegrated. He'd played the way he shot pool, leaning forward and turning and tipping his ears eccentrically close to his drumheads and cymbals, as if he couldn't hear his own beat. He'd just about clock himself on the head with his sticks. He'd been a very good drummer. "He's the one who used to live in the neighborhood. Over on Avenue B. He's in L.A. now. Trying his luck out there."

"You?"

"What?"

"Still music?"

"No," he said. "Not now. I'm taking a little break."

Behind him, he heard the rumble of pool balls dropping

into the gutters of the table. "Watch out," Wanda said to him, pointing at Karina and smiling.

He brought two beers and set them on one of the laminated luncheonette-type tables in the booths that lined the room. The benches were red vinyl, and the walls, which had probably once been papered gold, had faded to shades approaching a cigar-leaf brown. In one corner was an old-fashioned phone booth with a wooden seat and a wooden floor, the lone quaint, if decrepit, detail; otherwise the place was simply dim and narrow and in disrepair, the floor mop-smeared and the mirror behind the bar about as clear as a shower door's frosted glass. This was the 5&7 Club, one of the few spots on the Lower East Side where slumming or struggling youth coexisted companionably with the neighborhood's elderly Ukrainian drunks. All around it the dives were thronged with would-be poets and performance artists. But the 5&7 was for some reason largely ignored, and it maintained its desolate balance.

"So," Karina said, racking the balls. "A regular in your previous life."

And that was the way it seemed, familiar but jarring, as if standing here were an experience of *déjà vu* rather than something he'd done two or three nights a week a few years ago. His band had rehearsed at Sifkin's apartment for his second tour of New England college bars. The first had been the autumn before the Tillman gig, when Peter was on his brief way up; the second, at least in Peter's view, had been a confirmation: that the Tillman, the near record contract, the scattering of good New York gigs, meant nothing. On the road, the band had slept five to a motel room, or in the frat house of one of the band members' younger brothers, or in the dormitory of the campus radio station's manager, or in their van. And shaving in some of those collegiate bathrooms, Peter had felt as conspicuous as a dinosaur. At twenty-four, he'd sensed himself closer to the sixties fallout and other aging ne'er-do-wells who subsisted around the edges of the campuses. Not that the nights didn't provide slight celebrity. Not that a college girl or two didn't take him home. But leaving a girl's dorm in the daylight he felt like an aging loser who'd masqueraded as a star, now sneaking away after a quick screw.

Anyway, he and Sifkin had shot pool here before that tour, and after it again, when they'd had the Tuesday night gig at Tramps. Erratically, unpredictably, those performances had been euphoric or dismal, tight or clownishly careless (Peter losing track of his own lyrics; half the band coming in with some other song), not really because of drinking or drugs, though there was some of that, but mostly because Peter had thrown up his hands. He was playing to fourteen people and being paid forty dollars and he just hadn't expected things to work out this way. So he quit expecting anything of himself. He handed his performances over to fate, and what recklessness returned him was sometimes beautiful, other times droning. And all the time deadly.

Incredibly, though, the club's manager hardly noticed. Or maybe it was just easier to have a house band on Tuesday nights. In any case, Peter had finally quit. He'd talked it over with Sifkin, and the idea was that they needed a break, that Peter would work on new material. Then they'd put together another band, line up better gigs. And Peter would send out a new demo. But somehow the new band was never formed. As for the demo, it made minimal rounds. For the second time, Leonard Cohen's publisher had called to encourage him. But so what? There was nothing except praise to cling to, nothing except an affirmation of his talent, his promise. After that, he hadn't hustled the demo at all, except by going to that party at Michael's, where he'd hoped to meet Zadeh.

Still, here in the 5&7 what came back to him was relief rather than bitterness. Here he'd felt removed. After the

175

rehearsals or the gigs at Tramps, he'd stowed his guitar with Wanda behind the bar and had spent hours shooting pool.

"You breaking?" Karina asked.

"Go ahead."

"You sure?"

Her arm, in the loose, rolled-up T-shirt sleeve, was like a pale, frail piston. One sudden snap and the rack splintered, balls caroming and clattering and spinning, finding their way toward pockets and falling with quick, dull thuds.

Peter and Wanda exchanged glances. "I told you," she said.

"How often does she come in here?"

"Two in the side, Peter," Karina said.

"Every night."

The two went down.

"Back at ya," Karina said, and banked the five. Then she drew the cue ball off the three, splitting the balls at the table's center. The four was a long rail, the seven had to be coaxed between stripes. She made them both. "Okay," she said, not entirely successful at restraining a grin, and, kicking the cue ball gently off the rail, she tapped the eight into the corner.

Peter applauded. Her half-suppressed smile cracked into a quick laugh. Good as she clearly knew she was, she seemed surprised by what she'd just done, as if this were a recent talent. "I just ran the table," she declared, half to herself, and spun on one foot three-quarters of the way around (she was a much better pool player than she was a ballerina), and at that moment Peter, who had no idea what he was doing with this childlike woman in this seedy sanctuary of a bar, knew as certainly as he could know anything that he wanted to kiss her.

"I guess you better let me break," he said.

They were not unevenly matched. She didn't quite get back the precision of her first run, and he, though it had been a while, saw the balls the way he always had. For him, that was what it was—a way of seeing. A buffer seemed to form around him as he aimed. There was a level of concentration he felt himself lowered into.

He won the second game, and she said they should quit while they were tied. They sat and sipped their beers. They talked about the neighborhood, the bar, the shop where Karina worked, the ludicrously expensive bike Michael had bought to ramble around on. They talked about her family— her father, who was a Palmer security guard, and her mother, who'd worked at the Omni hotel downtown. "That's my pedigree," she said. And they talked about how her mother had left when she was nine, vanishing to Natchez, Mississippi, with the vice-president of a paper company (whom she'd met at the hotel during a paper-products convention), and about a game—"It was called 'The Unfairness Game,'"—Karina's father had played with her and her two brothers and any of the neighborhood kids who came over.

"What it was," she said, "was that my father would sit in the middle of the living room, on one of these kitchen stools we had that swiveled, and we'd do whatever we wanted around him. Do a flip off the couch, or pretend to be shot, pretend to faint. Or imitate some cartoon character on TV, or rattle off the names of every state. And he'd sit there in the middle, swiveling, and scoring what we were doing. And the only rule was, you couldn't yell 'That's not fair.' He'd yell, 'Ten points for Jeffery Lyons!' or 'Twenty point penalty for Karina Lyons!' or 'Two *hundred* points for Karina Lyons!' And there was no system to it. One minute you could do a back flip off the couch and get ten points, and the next minute you could do the exact same thing and get penalized a thousand. And we loved it. My friend Tracy Orkin would call every afternoon and ask, 'Are you guys gonna play The Unfairness Game tonight?' And we'd beg my father, 'Please please can we play The Unfairness Game?' And we'd promise him anything—wash his car, help fix the basement. Just so we could play this game."

177

Listening, Peter imagined her then, romping across the wall-to-wall carpeting. And he thought of her now, making her quirky wooden earrings and learning to play pool in this drearily peaceful bar. He set the tips of his forefinger and thumb five or so inches apart on the edge of the laminated table. He shifted them steadily across, five-inch section by five-inch section.

"What are you doing?" she asked.

"Measuring the width of this table," he said flatly.

"Why?" she asked.

"So I can lean across it."

Which he then did.

Fourteen

THE WALK FROM THE BEDFORD AVENUE SUBWAY STOP IN WILLIAMS-burg to Karina's apartment made Peter feel as if the flow of blood through his body was fuller, slower, easier. There was a physical slackening, a loosening of muscles and a slight but sweet reduction of the heart rate as he stepped from the top of the station stairs onto the street, just as there is for city vacationers when they duck out of their cars into a night of crickets and stars. But there was a serious difference. This tranquility, the one that washed over him in Williamsburg, was the product of decay, of dingy, unflourishing industry, and of poverty, pure and thoroughly entrenched.

A half block in front of him now, as he headed to Karina's apartment for the second time, were two gas stations. One was new enough at least to have square-style pumps and a logo-bearing signpost, though it looked as depressing as only unmaintained urban gas stations can. But the other, the other was truly in keeping with the neighborhood. Its pumps, a plain and very faded red, had the old rounded tops, and they could have dispensed any gas imaginable—the station had no sign at all. Alongside the garage were dry, in-curling viney growths that might have sprouted from cracks in the pavement or been akin to tumbleweeds. And the pavement in front of the garage was so battered and broken that the big, dull-colored cars parked there for repairs (for the station *was* in business) nosed and tipped like boats on a choppy lake. Behind the station was a narrow fenced-in lot, fringed with weedy grass. A gutted Greyhound bus was locked preciously inside.

Farther on was a small, blackish, unlabeled warehouse, with busted windows on its second floor, from which, nevertheless, the clanging and grinding of manufacture could be heard. And Peter walked by another fenced-in lot, coils of razor wire and three "Beware of Dog" signs lending extra protection to the seven totaled cars inside. There was no dog to be seen. Nor was there any hint of a proprietor, any indication that the cars hadn't sat there for years as they did today, torpid in the late-summer sun, intermittently remembered by their owner, who had once or still planned to turn them into profit.

These, along with the scattered bodegas and bars, and the drug dealers lingering at the corners, were the functioning or semi-functioning businesses of the neighborhood. As for the homes—tenements next to decrepit shells of buildings, or tiny row houses (divided into three or four apartments) with hard plastic awnings, like visors, over their front doors—they had the same muted spirit. And indeed it was mutedness—silence—that pervaded the blocks Peter walked on. Yes, there were loud radios, and laughter from two men, one in his twenties in a tight, sleeveless shirt and the other jowly, unshaven, some elderly relative, standing outside a Puerto Rican social club. And yes, tires clattered over loose steam grates, and, for no clear reason, a mother yanked her little girl brutally to her side, as if the violence of the yanking were meant to equal the danger of everything in the world the girl might be warned against. But it was silence that Peter was aware of. A suffused hush.

It was the quiet of a place where ambition is hardly an issue. Here, for better or worse, people were simply existing. Even the drug dealers were like that. They sure didn't look like they were amassing mini-fortunes. There were no beepers on their belts or gold chains around their necks. They were sixteen-, eighteen-, twenty-two-year-old men, and a few women, loitering on the corners, waiting for buyers with the despondency of used-up prostitutes. They were barely distinguishable from their customers. On what they sold they subsisted and probably got themselves high.

When Peter reached Karina's building, she called down from the roof. She lived on the top floor of one of the small, hunched row houses. Peter glanced up. She leaned over the roof's low wall, smiling, but seeming to know something extremely private, hidden, about him, as if she'd been watching him from a long way off. He glimpsed as well the beige head of Karina's dog, Tyler. His paws on the low wall, he tried to peer over the edge in imitation. Karina threw Peter the keys.

He climbed the building's stairs. Narrow and bowed and linoleum-tiled, they smelled powerfully of disinfectant. Peter's tongue recoiled as if to block his throat, the backs of his nostrils clenched. A moment later, when he began to adjust, he forced himself to breath deeply. He inhaled the ammonia, the landlady's attempt to keep her house distinct from the decay outside.

He let himself into the apartment, ducked out the window, and climbed the rungs of the fire escape. He thought about whether he'd kiss Karina hello. No. They'd spent the one afternoon together on the Lower East Side, and another here, mostly in Karina's bed. That was the whole history of their affair, and now he was shocked to realize how relaxed he felt. Still—did she want to kiss him? Sleep together again? He was pretty sure she wanted both. He figured he'd leave the question unanswered, leave the tension in the air awhile.

As soon as he stepped onto the roof, Tyler, a two-year-old lab with a beige, almost white coat, scrambled across the glistening, pebbly tar, paws scuffling, and hopped and panted at Peter's hip.

"Tyler," Karina ordered. "Sit."

And she kissed Peter—long and full, her tongue sliding between his surprised lips.

The phone rang downstairs. She went to get it. Peter was left with the dog, gazing over the neighborhood and off at Manhattan. He could have been seeing the skyline from Nebraska, he felt that removed. Below him a dealer, a heavy-thighed woman in striped stretch pants, leaned idly against a railing, and Peter smelled again in his memory the ammonia on the stairs, imagining the landlady whose ambition came down to acrid cleanliness. And he glanced at Tyler who two months ago, Karina had said, had let himself be led over to the bathroom and shut inside by the burglars who'd broken in through the skylight. Oh, there was an excess of crime here, and real danger. And the view from the roof could be one of hollowing sadness. Yet how calm Peter felt staring from this desolation to the skyscrapers across the river! How ludicrous and desperate Manhattan's architecture seemed! All those eclectic facades, sleek or Lego-like, cylindrical or slanting or nothing but tall, each one created from the crazy need of some architect to declare himself.

But here? What? A last-minute, meaningless detour before his marriage? The chance of something else? He considered what exactly he was doing here—momentarily, vaguely—then *refused* to consider it. He lifted the lid an inch on everything beneath these questions, then dropped the lid back into place. He would think later about what was under it. Not now. Why ruin this feeling?

* * *

In Karina's apartment, about an hour later, they stood, still fully clothed, her slight body stretched, her small breasts seeming to create pockets for themselves near the base of his rib cage, the warm insides of her elbows against the sides of his neck, their kisses untactical except when he tongue-traced the perimeter of her lips, one of Lee's techniques, or slid his tongue along the topography of her ear, or rode his hands up the sides of her chest and crushed gently upward and inward against her armpits and the tops of her breasts, untactical, that is, on her part, her mouth open and unwithholding, her hands on his back now pulling tight as if to fold him around her, her eyes soft in their focus, unrestrained. He was the technician. His tongue decorated her collarbone. Through the ridgy spandex of her biking shirt, it circled her nipples, his hands pressing deftly beside her breasts as if nurturing them. He shifted her to the bed (a mattress on the floor) and ran his tongue in scythelike patterns over her lower ribs.

By the time he unbuttoned her jeans, kissed the tops of her thighs, slipped his tongue beneath a ridge of elastic, she was wet, so much so that it surprised him, though he'd slept with her once before and been surprised then also—her hips were so narrow he could practically have spanned them between forefinger and thumb; her pubic hair was sparse; such wetness, such openness, at the center of such a slender, undergrown place, shocked him, made something turn over inside him, made him groan the way she had already begun to.

With his tongue he retraced his path—thighs, ribs, clit again, collarbone, mouth. Standing, they undressed each other, then she pulled him back down to the bed and he slid inside her, just slid in, no guiding by her hand or prodding at the periphery, no second or three of fumbling to find the right spot, no pause while she responded and widened, he just found himself in, thoroughly, a kind of miracle, all that heat so suddenly and eagerly given, and her mouth fully on his, her tongue deep, as if she were straining to make the contact more complete.

It was strange, though. By the time he came, he was somewhat detached, undepleted. And coming at all had been, in the end, a bit of a struggle. He'd ridden above her orgasms, overjoyed by them, soothed by them, stroking and grinding and rimming her into them, two, three, four of them, but at a certain point he'd felt compelled to show that he was just as entranced as she was, and unfortunately he wasn't. Guilt? Was it guilt that was keeping his cock's sensations dim? Thoughts of Lee? Maybe. But if it was, the guilt was working in a secretive way—Lee crossed his mind fleetingly, without eliciting a great deal of remorse. Or was it simple mechanics? Was Karina's cunt just too big, too frictionless? No, it fit snugly enough, and what it lacked in tension it made up for in pure heat, and anyway she was skilled with it, clenching its lips around his prick and tipping her pelvis to brush his hood along her walls, and now, in an effort—openly acknowledged by her smile—to make him come, she was lightly fingering his balls and when that didn't work turning up the tempo and gripping his ass, but even with the aid of a fantasy or two it took a solid five minutes for his orgasm to close creepingly in (meanwhile she had another), and when the ejaculation did at last arrive it was like local anesthesia. It affected only the necessary part of him. His cock quivered. The rest of him stayed disconnected.

Still, when he held and kissed her afterward—lovingly, gratefully—there was no deceit.

"Hey," she said. "I almost forgot. I have something for you."

"What?"

She stood, not answering.

184

"What are you doing?"

"I was looking all over for this."

She put a tape into the stereo and slipped back into the clothes that lay crumpled by the bed.

"What is this?" he asked. "One of those success tapes?" All he heard were faint waves of static. "Are they programming us subliminally?"

"My production skills were a little weak."

"Wait a second. What is this?" And then, annoyed: "Where did you get this?"

"Made it. Now, here, I finally got the levels right."

The volume leaped. Music lurched from the speakers.

"Okay," he said.

"Why?" To him, her voice sounded full of false innocence. He pushed himself off the bed and punched "Stop."

"Well," she said, "I was going to walk Tyler and leave you here in reverie."

"I'll just sleep."

He lay down only until she'd put a leash on Tyler and followed the lab out the door. Then he went to the window and watched her vanish around the corner, after which he did what he'd dimly known he would, even beneath his annoyance. He returned to the stereo. He turned the volume knob to the left, almost to zero. Adjusting the volume gradually upward from there, he listened.

It was a tape of the Tillman gig. There was the rough, scratchy bass line Wyatt had opened with. There was his own guitar driving in over it. And then his voice, grainy, gruff, its sadness forced somehow to bitterness by the speed of the song, a tempo that didn't have time for sadness but that seemed to let it back in behind his singing, beneath it, boosting it, the song gathering momentum and lifting above both despair and the bitterness as Wyatt came in on harmony and together they hit a plateau of pain that stretched just far enough to turn into pure beauty before they snapped it off, cut their voices, and ended the song suddenly, isolating the plateau against a stark drop-off of silence.

They'd rehearsed that abrupt ending dozens of times, but now, listening to the tape, it caught Peter off guard; he'd forgotten that was how they'd done it; always, before that concert, they'd finished the song another way, repeating its refrain; so hearing the final line done once only, stretched and stopped sharply, he felt as stunned and utterly vulnerable as the audience had, carried and then suddenly dropped.

A moment later, here in Karina's apartment, he let out a quick burst of laughter, and applauded. He clapped in the empty room. He stopped the tape. He tugged on his pants, figuring that if Karina were going to catch him listening he should at least have the dignity of clothes. He got himself a beer from the fridge, took a pillow from the bed, and sat against the wall near the stereo. He turned the volume higher, higher, his body slouched but tight, his beer forgotten, his arms folded across his stomach as if he were cold or ill, though certainly he was neither of these.

When Karina returned he merely smiled, shrugged. "Well," he admitted, "I was curious." He took a long sip of beer.

"You know," she said, "I just want you to know. I could probably get you a gig at the Central."

"How?"

"I know Bob Garavelli."

There was a pause. He seemed to consider it.

"No." He shook his head, speaking slowly, almost wryly. "No. Definitely not."

And he snapped off the tape.

Karina rode the subway back to Manhattan with Peter, the LL across Fourteenth Street. She was going to sell T-shirts. This was another of her pursuits. She made jewelry, sold bicycles three days a week, and had designed a black and white T-shirt, a series of them, with sketches of Tyler printed on their chests. There was the "Doggie Gym" shirt, with Tyler's head popping up over a set of barbells, the "Diner" shirt, on which Tyler's face loomed above an empty counter appointed with ketchup bottles and metal napkin dispensers, and the "Taxi" shirt, on which the dog rode alone through a nighttime Manhattan. Like the earrings, the sketches made Peter laugh, for no particular reason. There was nothing aggressively funny about them. But Tyler's face was cryptically endearing. In each portrait, he wore a pair of dark sunglasses. He seemed a cool, very urban dog. On the other hand, the speckling of his jowls and the slight tilt of his head gave him a thoughtful, possibly forlorn, expression. He seemed to combine a rakish attitude with a lonely, lovesick spirit. It depended on how you looked at him.

On the subway, Peter and Karina rode with her folding red table leaning against their legs, and she sat with the box of T-shirts on her lap, the cardboard coming up to her chin. There were sixteen shirts in the box, she said. This was the last of the series, and she wanted to finish them off today. Then, for a while, she planned to concentrate completely on her jewelry, though a friend of hers was fixing an old loom, and they might weave scarves and sell them during the winter.

"I'm in the fast lane of arts 'n' crafts," she said.

The joke won him back. Listening to her scattered plans, he'd been repelled by her indirection, by the fact that no one thing seemed crucial. And he'd shrunk, too, from the sense that she was laying some claim on him, tricking him into something, even as he reminded himself that *he* was the one about to be married, that he was the one in control.

She asked if he wanted to help with the T-shirts.

He checked the time and said he guessed he could, that Lee wouldn't be home until seven anyway.

"Lee," she said. She had a special way of pronouncing Lee's name, and a habit of repeating it once, as if dangling it in front of him, whenever it came up in conversation. The first few times the pronunciation had been musing, faintly teasing. Now it sounded close to outright mocking, as if she knew something he didn't. It grated.

"That's her name," he said.

"Ooo," she said. "Sorry."

They stepped off the subway. He smiled to cover his sudden flare of anger.

"I thought this was a careless little frolic," he said. This was the definition they'd agreed on when, on the phone two days ago, she'd asked what precisely they were doing.

"Correct," she said.

They walked downtown on Sixth Avenue and set up her table a block from Washington Square Park. Around her were a vendor of cheap, silver-plated jewelry, a man who did quick charcoal portraits, a Muslim selling incense and tiny vials of perfume, and a couple who may have been marketing or merely exhibiting a number of hand-woven Indian-style blankets. (The couple, behind the other vendors on the wide sidewalk, sat on one of their blankets. They had the others spread directly on the pavement around them, with no apparent sense that people might not want to buy anything that was strewn over a city street.) Karina said they should open her table next to a man selling discount cassettes. "He's the only one who gets steady business," she said. And she told Peter to act like a customer, to mill around in front of her table, hold up the shirts, pretend he was ready to buy.

Soon she had a constant stream of customers. A basketball player, strolling up from the West Fourth Street courts, bought a T-shirt for his girlfriend. A woman lamented she was too heavy to wear T-shirts, but Karina suggested she get one for incentive. A policeman, who ordered all the vendors to shift back farther on the sidewalk, ended up with two "Doggie Gym"s, one for his wife, he explained, and one for himself, since they'd just bought a Muscle Master for their basement. He paid Karina and said he'd return in half an hour for the shirts, at the end of his beat.

During a lull, not long before Karina sold out, a tall, husky black woman turned from browsing at the cassette table. Her Afro was an unkempt thatch. She wore a tank top that revealed heavy, strong arms, the top tucked neatly over her thick midsection into the waist of her jeans. She stared a full minute at Karina's shirts.

"You made these?" she asked Peter. Peter was now behind the table, no longer needing to generate business.

"She did."

"You drew this dog?" the woman asked Karina, then glanced toward the benches a half block away. "Hey, C.J.!" she called. "Hey, C.J.!"

"What?" her friend snapped.

"Come here, baby."

"Shit." C.J. stood. She was short, wiry, light-skinned. Her face was all sharp angles. It looked harshly worn, though she might have been only thirty. She walked a pit bull terrier on a tight leash. "What?"

The tall woman waited until her friend came over. "I just want you to look at this dog." She pointed at Tyler's portrait. "Just look at this dog. This is a *dog*," the woman said, as if continuing an earlier argument. "And you want to know why?"

"Shit," C.J. protested.

"'Cause this dog's got inner life. Even behind those sunglasses you can tell. That's what I've been trying to tell you about your dog. That's the problem. No inner life."

"Joanne," C.J. said, starting slowly away, her pit bull heeling with martial precision, "what the fuck are you talking about?"

Fifteen

PETER TALKED TO MICHAEL ABOUT KARINA, AND TO KARINA ABOUT Michael.

He said, at first, "It's just a little last-minute poontang." And Michael, as usual when the topic was Peter's life and not his own, said next to nothing. Or rather, he switched the subject to his own concerns. His voice covered by the bar's jukebox, he said, "Peter, I'm getting some serious cold feet. I mean, in two months my life is going to take a serious turn for the worse. Because as soon as I make that announcement, Jesus, that's it. I mean, in all honesty, Peter, you're the only person I can have a real conversation with. How can I talk to anyone, when all they're thinking is, Michael Marr is talking to me? Believe me, I want to have a serious relationship. I've gotten laid enough times. But the minute any chick gets around me it's like she turns into a geisha girl. How can I please you, Mastah Mahh? I mean, you should have heard that chick Jessica Baker the other morning. She cooks me breakfast, brings it in, wakes me up, and then she's right in my face while I'm eating, going, 'I think you need a Jessica in your life, I think you need a Jessica in your life.' She's like a bird chirping away in there, 'I think you need a Jessica in your life, I think you need a Jessica in your life.'"

Well, Peter had heard it before, knew it already, but to be pronounced Michael's only confidant was again to be elevated, in a sense, into a state of grace. It was to feel one's head reel a bit. It was to lose one's vision momentarily. It was to glide to the bar for more beers; it was to feel accounted for, taken care of.

Yet at the same time, he was about to clue Michael in to a few long-unstated facts. Namely, one, that he *let* the Jessicas surround him and that there were other options, i.e., people who couldn't give a *shit* who he was; and two, re politics, that he shouldn't feel so obliged to run, that there were plenty of potential candidates praying he wouldn't, and that anyway running did *not* mean he had to let himself be packaged as the perfect replica of his father, everyone's long-awaited fantasy. Michael, Peter was about to tell him, you know, you can have a fucking say in your own life.

He was about to assault his friend with all these truths, or at least hint at them, but their discussion was interrupted. A woman stepped over from the bar and introduced herself as the daughter of Michael's aunt's college roommate.

"Can I join you?" she asked.

"Sure," Michael said tonelessly.

To Karina, when she asked whether he knew Michael from Palmer, Peter said, "No. I met him a couple years ago. At a party. By a kind of fluke."

To which she replied, "Michael Marr." She used the same

musing, lightly teasing tone she had, early on, when pronouncing Lee's name.

Peter let the subject drop.

And said to Michael, about a week later, "I'm actually kind of into her. I mean, she's a serious flake. But."

"Maybe you just didn't do enough sampling before settling down with Lee."

"No, Michael. I really don't think that's the issue. And I should correct myself. I misused the word 'flake.'"

"Peter," Michael asked, as if cutting to the heart of the matter, "how is she in the sack?"

And Karina said, "Michael Marr," starting to dangle the name in front of Peter now when Michael came up in conversation, dangling it the way she dangled Lee's name, mockingly.

So Peter snapped, "Could you curtail the sarcasm?"

"Sorry," she said.

"Because in spite of everything, he *is* a friend."

"Sorry," she said.

"Because hard as this may be for you to believe, he is not some corrupt species."

She laughed.

"He's self-aware, he knows the whole scene around him is a fucking sickness, if anything he's kind of miserable. And the irony of it is, everyone thinks he has everything, and that if you're with him what you have is him. But with Michael and me, that just isn't the case. And I think if you pressed him, he'd say the same thing. He'd tell you, that isn't the way our friendship works. Because the truth is, it's the opposite. And he's said this exactly. What *he* has is *me*. I'm the only person he can be himself with. The only friend who sees him the way he is. And yes, it feels good to be in that position. And yes, it matters a little who he is. I'm not going to deny that. How could it *not* matter? But the *need*, Karina, the need is the other way around. What he has is me, Karina, what he has is me."

"Sorry," she said. "My apologies."

While Michael, suddenly more responsive as Peter kept talking about her, said, "Peter, calm down, the woman is not the Good Witch Glinda."

"You know, Michael, maybe I have to make myself clear. She—"

"Makes jewelry, sells T-shirts on the street, she needs to do a little time-traveling, this is not the Summer of Love."

"Michael."

"Look, I'm sorry. I just don't see what you're so worked up about. I've seen the girl. I just didn't think she was that attractive. Believe me, if I had I'm sure I could have gone for it. I mean, the chick was practically batting her eyelashes at me when we were outside testing bikes."

"Pity," Peter said to Karina. "Sometimes I think that's what our entire friendship comes down to. From my side. I've just ended up feeling incredibly sorry for him."

"Mmm."

"Look. Can you just listen? For once. Listen. I spent three years of my life avoiding him. The semester we were at Palmer together? Nothing. No contact. While friends came running up to me asking, 'Guess who I just got high with?' 'Guess who I just rode home with?' 'Guess who? guess who? guess who?' And when I was in New York I'd still get calls from these people, and they'd drop in their little exploits with Michael, as if they actually didn't realize what I thought. But the fact is, he's not to blame for that. He's not *above* it. I'm not saying he hasn't played into it. But that doesn't rule out pity, Karina."

"Mmm."

"Mmm. Mmm. Such subtle insinuation. Karina, let me ask you, since you're so far above everything, why were you flirting your little head off in the bike store?"

"What?"

"Should I repeat the question? Why were you flirting with Michael in—"

"I wasn't flirting with Michael."

"Then why did you look like you'd never written out a sales slip before? Why so nervous dealing with him?"

"I wasn't nervous because of him." She laughed. "I was nervous because I wanted to meet you."

"Besides which," he said, on the phone one afternoon, "I think I'm going to let her get me this gig at the Central."

"So that's what this is all about."

"No. But nevertheless."

"Peter, are you sure you know what you're doing?"

"Yes."

"I mean, you're getting married in six weeks."

"Yes, I remember."

"So what are you planning to do?"

"Flee the state. Go into hiding."

"Peter, this is serious."

"And in the meantime do this gig if I can get it."

"What are you planning to tell Lee?"

"That I got a gig at the Central."

"And nothing about Karina?"

"I hadn't planned on it."

"And the wedding?"

"I don't know."

"And who's going to this gig? Both of them? Karina hiding in the background?"

"If I'm lucky Lee won't be here. She has to go to Wyoming to work on that Elaro ad."

"You know, you are a guiltless son of a bitch."

"Maybe."

Michael waited.

"I don't know," he said. "I don't know. I just think this has a lot more to do with your music than you realize."

"Well, maybe. Maybe that's right. But maybe that's what relationships are partly about. About what they let you do. I go out to her apartment in Williamsburg and I think, Fuck, why did you quit? Because all your Palmer friends were off doing something else? Succeeding at something else? Marching along their preprofessional paths? Hup, two, three, four? She doesn't care about that shit. She barely *knows* about that shit. And it's a relief, Michael. It's a relief."

Michael waited again.

"I just hope you're not setting yourself up to get hurt."

"And why would I be?"

"Listen, I don't want to tell you what to do. Believe me. All I'm saying is, you've been through this before. That's why you went to law school, remember? Because things didn't work out the way you thought they would, remember? You had your one concert at the Tillman, and then you spent three years spinning your wheels. Remember?"

"Yes, I do."

"Believe me, Peter. I'm not trying to tell you what to do."

"And maybe three years just wasn't long enough."

"Maybe not."

"Because everyone has this image. Musicians are either the ultimate successes or the ultimate losers. And the losers are laughable. But people spend ten years playing hole-in-the-wall bars before they even start to make it."

"I'm sure that's true.

"But," Michael added quietly, "say you spend two or three or four more years, whatever you decide, and things still don't work out. You'll be thirty."

"That's right," Peter said. "I'll be thirty."

"And what if Karina isn't bargaining for that? All I'm saying is, right now she sees you as the person you were four years ago, five years ago. You're the guy who opened for Jackson Browne. The guy she followed home. But take it from me, Peter, that is the shallowest kind of love you'll come across. And what happens if there are three more years like the years you already went through? She might be the queen of craftsland, but that doesn't mean she doesn't think like everyone else."

"Thank you, Michael."

"I'm sorry. I just think someone better play devil's advocate here. I just think you better think things through. You've been with Lee for how long? You can't just throw that away for someone you've known three weeks."

"Okay, Michael. All right. Maybe that's right. And don't think I haven't had those same thoughts. What if I try again and nothing happens? What if I got seriously into something with Karina and it turned out she saw me as something I'm just not talented enough to be? See, I have to give you credit. Because that's exactly what I've been thinking. But maybe that's the point. Maybe you just have to take that risk. Thirty years old, thirty-five years old, forty years old and nothin' doing, nothing happening, *nothing*. Nothing. Maybe that's just the bet you have to make."

"But that's what I'm saying. You don't. You can do exactly what you're doing now. Or a month ago. Because really, this other girl is just a side issue."

"No. Wrong."

"Why? Tell me why that's wrong."

"Because. Because if I marry Lee, and stay in law school, the idea that I can do that, and still write music, that's bullshit. I don't know why. But it is. Maybe for someone else it would work. And maybe Karina *is* just a side issue. But it's all tied in together. If I stay in law school that is going to be my life. *That.* And sometimes I feel like if I do that I might as well cut a line down the middle of my chest, from the bottom of my neck to the bottom of my stomach, and empty everything out, and sew myself up around nothing but air."

"Oh, Peter," Michael said. "I just don't think that has to be true."

And Karina—after another of their sessions of lovemaking; she enthralled, he melted by her pleasure—asked, "So what was the fluke?"

"The what?"

"You said once you met Michael by a fluke. So what was the fluke?"

"Oh, well, actually I ended up going to a party at his apartment because Stephen Zadeh was supposed to be there."

"Who's Stephen Zadeh?"

"He runs Continental Records. Michael's godfather."

"Oh."

"Anyway, going to this cocktail party was about the last thing I wanted to do. But I figured I better. And that's where I met him."

"Michael."

"Right."

"But not Zadeh."

"No. He wasn't there."

There was a silence. The late afternoon sun cast a rhombus of light across the bed where they lay.

"So has Zadeh ever heard your stuff?"

"Nope."

"You've never asked Michael—"

"No, I haven't."

"Has he ever offered?"

"No." Peter stared at the ceiling, waiting for her to respond, some quiet insinuation.

"And given that people are always hoping to use him in some way—" he started to explain.

But, like an elusive and subtle enemy—almost a submissive one—Karina had drifted into sleep.

Sixteen

FOR A FEW YEARS NOW, THE CENTRAL HAS BEEN REESTABLISHED AS the best and most diverse of the live popular-music clubs in New York. Tracy Chapman brought her husky, sad, angry, hopeful voice there for a weekend not long ago, and Lyle Lovett and John Hiatt have packed the seventy-five-table house with their special brands of country. And throughout the Central's past there have been visits, some announced and some surprises, from serious stars. Bruce Springsteen, who performed there early on in his career, has stopped in for several unadvertised sets. Paul Simon played there twice during the period between "Kodachrome" and "Graceland," when his popularity was on the wane and he wanted to try out new things. There have been performances by the Talking Heads and an endless list of impromptu collaborations in which the very famous—Jagger, Dylan, Ronstadt, Turner, King, Collins, Costello—have come up from the tables to join old, not-so-famous friends on the low and very intimate stage.

And a steady stream of second-tier yet long successful musicians have made the Central a regular stop on their tours—Bonnie Raitt, Joe Cocker, Randy Newman, Joan Armatrading.

But when Peter, with Karina's help, got his gig there, the club was just starting to reemerge from three or four years of rough times. It had still been getting its occasional guest appearances by big names, but the second-tier players had no longer been able to fill the house. Suddenly it seemed there weren't a thousand Joan Armatrading fans in New York to be divided over a weekend's four sets. And the third tier drew audiences that were thin at best.

It would be impossible to say what exactly had caused the downslide. Partly it was MTV and the spread (beyond saturation) of the city's nightclubs, because if there were two common denominators among nearly all the Central's acts it was that their songs were not ready-made for videos, and that they would never make the play lists of P.S. 5's D.J.'s.

In any case, it was at the beginning of the Central's revival—when twelve-inch fast-play dance discs were no longer the hottest thing in every record store, when Madonna had become an ignorable fixture rather than an overwhelming new presence, and when there seemed to be a glimmer of a trend toward more musical depth—that Bob Garavelli, the Central's part owner and Karina's friend, booked Peter Bram for one set on a Wednesday night in October.

It wasn't that big a deal. At least, Peter could try to tell himself that. He'd had New York gigs that were almost as good, and this was for a Wednesday night. His name in the ads wasn't going to cause any Klondike stampede at the Central's box office. The place would be nine-tenths empty.

On the other hand, it *was* the Central. Things could happen if he could get himself booked there again. People would see him. Industry people. Or Garavelli might help him out.

He had ten days to put together a band.

Ten days. If everything went wrong, if the whole thing was a disaster, one thing was lucky. Neither Lee nor Michael would be there. Lee would be on an Indian reservation in Wyoming, helping to coordinate a campaign for Elaro, a new perfume. Things had been going well for her lately. In addition to her upcoming wedding, she'd recently been promoted; she was partly responsible for giving the perfume's TV and print ads the desired look, the right combination of decrepitude and sensuality. In one sequence, a tourist, played by the model Melora Reardon, was to be followed along an unpaved street by an increasing throng of young Indian boys in tattered clothes, and Lee would be in charge of choosing these child antagonists/seducers, of finding eyes that were incipiently sinister and mouths that were appropriately lush.

Michael would be meeting with Roy Kramer, two speech-writers, and various members of the DNC, to go over the announcement speech that had been written for him.

For which Peter was thankful. Lee and Michael were the last people he wanted in that audience.

Karina found him a drummer, an ex-boyfriend of hers named Torch, who seemed to be doing pretty well for himself, getting regular studio work, touring with a couple of acts. Truth be told, he made Peter a tad wary and jealous, because Karina had appraised him as "a major asshole but a decent drummer." Peter never trusted people's intentions when they called someone an asshole. A woman calling a guy an asshole was like announcing he was the man of her dreams. In this case, Torch certainly didn't look like a dreamboat. A sparse beard did nothing to obscure his pockmarked cheeks. His nose both hooked and bulbed. Still, he'd been unfaithful to Karina, who'd told him "right away" that she was "gone if he kept pulling that shit." Another doubtful declaration. She *had* left, clearly, but Peter had to wonder about just how quickly and willingly. And Torch's presence made him wonder, too, just how enamored Karina would be if the twenty-two-year-old who'd gone over at the Tillman turned out to be a twenty-seven-year-old going nowhere.

Obviously, she had a thing about musicians. And he recalled Michael's line: "You're the guy who opened for Jackson Browne. The guy she followed home. But take it from me, Peter, that is the shallowest kind of love you'll come across." Obviously, she'd be gone at the first sign of failure.

But Torch, who had a sullen edge and a streak of outright belligerence, was all compliments about Peter's songs, and Peter converted his own uneasiness into an offhanded, easy camaraderie.

And then there was Wyatt, Uncle Wyatt, Peter's old bass player, who'd come down to New York for the gig. Even with his disarranged face and disheveled hair, his way of looking like some quietly and maybe dangerously demented redneck, there was no chance of mistaking him for an asshole. Not during the years Peter had known him, anyway. At forty-one, he was the kind of man of whom women say, "He's such a sweetheart." Or whom they call teddy bears. And with Peter and Torch he played a bit of the eager lapdog, a bit of the abused clown. He'd written two songs he hoped Peter would sing. They ran through them. Peter might not have had the heart to reject them both, but Torch had gazed at Wyatt and said simply, "Bro'," and Wyatt had clutched his chest and stumbled back in an imitation of gunshot death that struck Peter as far more sad, and delicate, than funny. But they'd all laughed.

Peter had called a keyboard player he'd worked with on one of his demos. Together, the band ended up with four days to rehearse. They set up in Karina's apartment. The drug dealers on the corner didn't appreciate Peter's style. They turned up their boom boxes—their salsa, their rap. Peter couldn't blame them. His voice was flat, and Torch's drums seemed to hack relentlessly, as if punishing the others for lost beats, botched chords, muddled harmonies. No matter how far they got into a song, it seemed inevitable there would be a blurring of rhythms, a missed note giving way unrescuably to droning, the band crumbling to a halt or clamoring dismally on. Peter shut the front windows. "That's for the dealers' sake," he said.

Even Karina sounded doubtful. "Even if it *is* a national disaster," she said, "you're good, Peter. Trust me, you'll get other chances."

And when Lee called from Wyoming, and decried the poverty of the tribespeople, and didn't ask a thing about the band, her disinterest seemed merciful.

On Tuesday Peter heard what he took to be a sign. In a bodega a block from Karina's apartment, the cashier's radio was playing a song Peter planned to cover. It had been a hit the summer before last. It had played constantly at P.S. 5. It was all studio gimmickry, all sound effects. Artillery. Radar. The singing was attributed to a one-shot performer named Terry Gee, though the original human voice hardly mattered—it had been transformed by machine into a machine itself, the simple melody and twelve words' worth of senseless lyrics repeated and repeated with immaculate precision. A week ago, Peter had hit on distilling the song to a single acoustic guitar and his own rough voice. He sensed he was coaxing sentiment hidden mysteriously, unwittingly, within the music, or that he was creating sentiment around it. Now, ordering sandwiches for the band as the radio played the dance-track version, he felt as if he must be right, as if this was a sign that he wasn't fooling himself.

He'd planned to open with the cover at the Central, and now he was sure. Or sur*er*. So what if the radio was playing a year-old hit? How unlikely was that? And even if the chances were one in ten million, no one was up there speaking to him through some radio D.J.

But he was willing to think, Maybe. To be encouraged.

And anyway, he decided, he would definitely open with the song. It was the one thing only he could fuck up. No piano, no bass, no drums, no harmonies. Just him. Voice, guitar.

Turning the corner onto Karina's block, with his bagful of sandwiches and second, threatening-to-tear sack of sodas, beers, he was stopped by one of the dealers. "Hey, that's you singing up there?"

The man had a thin mustache and a wispy goatee. He was short, reedy. He wore a T-shirt that said "Tennis Pro." He looked physically defenseless, which made him seem all the more dangerous. The danger was hidden. He'd crossed the street, from the railing where he leaned with two of his colleagues, to confront Peter.

"Yeah. I have to admit it."

"Well, I don't want to bother you, man," the dealer said. "I just want to tell you you're starting to sound pretty good."

"Thanks."

"You practicing for something?"

"Yeah."

"For what? You giving a concert?"

"Yeah."

"Where?"

"A place called the Central."

"The Central? Hey. Listen to me. You want me to tell these dudes to shut up so you can rehearse?"

"That's all right," Peter said.

"No, man. Listen to me. You can't hear yourself. Hey!" He turned to the dealers across the street. *"Cállense, coños! El tipo está tratando de practicar!"*

His colleagues leaned, dumbfounded, a glitter of congas,

plucky guitars, and snappy, high-pitched horns blasting from the radio at their feet. "No, no," Peter said. He held up his free hand, as if to tell the others he hadn't put their partner up to this. But the one with the goatee stepped angrily across the street and snapped off the radio. Maybe it was his. The others didn't protest.

"See?" he called back to Peter. "You should listen to what I'm telling you. That's what you need. Peace and quiet. I know. Listen to me. I'm soundproofing this whole street for you."

Before Peter could dissuade him, the dealer started to march down the block. Peter felt obliged to wait for his return to thank him. He edged toward Karina's stoop. He didn't feel too comfortable across from the others, now without their music, but when he glanced over, ready to shrug or roll his eyes, they were in the midst of doing business, one of them bending, reaching between the bars of the railing for their stash. Peter slid his eyes past. He watched his new guardian, who didn't seem as powerful halfway down the block. The dealer strutted back. "They'll shut up quick," he said, "if they know what's healthy."

"No, no," Peter said. "Thanks. This is great. Believe me."

"Listen to me," the dealer said.

"Okay," Peter said. "Thanks. Thanks a lot."

"What's your name?" the dealer asked.

"Peter."

"Raymond."

They shook hands. The dealer toughened his eyes like a TV criminal sealing a pact, which gave Peter the sense, however fleeting, that he wasn't a criminal at all, that he was only pretending. Peter had a quick thought, dismissed it, then brought it back. He said, "So should I get you a couple tickets to our concert?"

"What are you talking about?" the dealer asked.

"That's if you want to come. I could put them at the box office for you. Free."

"Listen to me," the dealer said, not quietly, but confidentially. "I said you sounded good for what you play, I didn't say what you play is what I like."

Peter smiled, laughed. The dealer did, too. The dealer put up his hand, and when Peter reciprocated with his own the dealer slapped him a high-five.

"Rehearse good," the dealer called sharply, from the middle of the street, and Peter said, "Okay," and gave a small wave and went inside.

Luck for once, whatever luck is, was truly on his side. On Wednesday night, when the band returned to the Central after their sound check, half the tables were taken and there was a line at the box office. With Karina, he pushed through to the bar, baffled. Most of the ads hadn't even carried his name, only "To Be Announced," and the opening band, hammering through a dogged version of "Little Sister," sure didn't sound like a major attraction. They spotted Garavelli at the far end of the bar. Famously obese, he wore a blazer, a madras shirt, and rounded, tortoise shell glasses.

"I didn't know I was this big a draw." Peter smiled, leaning forward, shouting over the music, as the owner put out his bulbous, small-fingered hand to shake.

"You're not." Garavelli rubbed the bridge of his nose, pushing back his glasses. He looked unexcitable. He'd booked acts as different as the Clash and the Malian National Choir. He'd dropped out of Wharton fifteen years ago to start this place, and he seemed utterly subdued within it, resigned or confident or just hidden within his obesity.

"So who's headlining?"

"You are."

dddd

Peter took another look around. The crowd hadn't gotten any smaller. "Is it bat night?"

Garavelli laughed. In fact, he practically cracked up, which made his shoulders bob. No, he said. No, but there had been rumors. Van Morrison was supposed to play. Or Tom Waits.

Instead, an hour later, Peter walked out onstage.

He came out with the house and stage lights off. As planned, there was no announcement. In the dark, he took his acoustic guitar from its stand and fixed its strap over his shoulder. He held the guitar lightly across its neck, to damp any errant sound. He wanted to go abruptly from silence into the song, the cover of the dance track. No tuning, no tampering, no preamble of nervous notes or little chitchat routine at the microphone. He wanted his opening to be perfectly stark, his first chord to be sudden and almost angry, his strumming to be insistent and somewhat thrashing, his singing, chantlike, to leap immediately to longing, to leap there before anyone in the audience was ready for such intensity, to make them catch him, to come at them before they could be amused or appalled that he was doing this song that, the summer before last, had blared from every boom box in New York, before they could think, Oh, how clever, before they could take his version for earnest commentary or slapstick gag, because he had no intention of mocking the original, no, what he wanted was to pare the song down to nearly nothing, to the desperation he'd found at its center or at its circumference.

He turned to the microphone. Two of the stage lights came up. And he got what he wanted. He took all those studio effects and reduced them to a strum that always threatened to be erratic, and from those twelve words' worth of lyrics he created something cryptic and mournful, aggressively persistent, an assault that became an admission that wrapped over the room.

He quelled the strings and quit singing as suddenly as he'd started. The band came on. The rest of the stage lights came up. He counted the others into a song he'd written three weeks ago, the first he'd finished in almost two years. And when that song was done, he said into the microphone, no expression on his face, "That was for Karina. And now a word to the wise. My name is Peter Bram, and unless you know something I don't there will be no special guests tonight. It's just you and me, folks."

Then he continued, his hoarse voice rising from behind the piano's descending chords, then Torch striking a slow, quiet beat on his cymbals, then guitar and bass kicking in. The song swelled, swelled, as did the entire set, and when they were through, after two encores, people were up by the low stage, shaking Peter's hand.

He sidled toward Karina's table. He felt watched, his shoulders, neck, the sides of his skull teased by the pressure of glances. He was tempted to burst out laughing, felt on the verge of turning to everyone and saying, What are you looking at? That wasn't me!

But of course, it had been. As he sat with Karina, Garavelli made his way over to chat, to congratulate him. Clapping him on the shoulder with one of his small, obscenely fat hands, he said, "Call me next month so we can get you back here."

Garavelli left the table. He sent over more drinks. All Peter wanted was to get out of the emptying club, finish his beer and get out before he did something, anything, he didn't know what, to ruin what had happened.

Torch was ready to stay. Why not drink as long as the liquor was flowing?

"Torch," Peter hissed, "if you'll leave now, I'll buy all your drinks for the rest of the night, and for the rest of your *life*, anytime I'm with you, no matter how much you drink, I'll buy."

Torch thought this over.

"Anytime?" he asked.

"Anytime."

"No matter how much?"

"Torch, I'll buy you a case of Cuervo if we can all walk coolly out of here within the next five minutes."

They left.

Outside, around the corner, they stood waiting to load the plumbing van Wyatt had driven down in. "Well," Peter said, as Wyatt unlocked the rear doors. And, handing Karina the equipment he was carrying, Peter ran, vaulting a series of parking meters, flying through the pale glow of the street-lamps, and doing some sort of ecstatic, James Brown convulsion halfway down the deserted block.

Seventeen

T HE FOLLOWING NIGHT, PETER WAITED FOR MICHAEL AT AN UPPER West Side restaurant called Timmy's. It was a large, plate glass–fronted place with a sleek and vast interior. There were silver rails and rose-tinted carpeting, and the room was divided into an endless array of levels, platforms that were one step up or two steps down. There was no perfectly horizontal way to cross the restaurant, so that, if your table was in the rear, getting to it was something like backpacking—you had to climb and descend, descend and climb, before you reached your camp. But a sense of the wilderness was probably not what Timmy or his designers had intended to evoke. More likely they'd meant to maximize the suspense and attention surrounding entrances and exits, and at this, to be fair, they'd succeeded. Partly there was suspense as to whether anyone would trip negotiating the numerous stairs. And the young patrons (among them many bankers and lawyers in their twenties and early thirties), like fraternity brothers and their dates at a formal dinner dance, would occasionally whoop and applaud at such stumblings. "Hey," a blue-suited young man might yell. "Where'd you learn to walk?" But again, to be fair, suspense and attention were also created by the illusion of importance, of celebrity. That is, the newly grown-up professionals felt momentarily like stars as they traversed the uneven terrain. They felt so fully watched, so fully exhibited as they paraded across the various plateaus.

It was not a restaurant one would have expected Michael to choose. One would have expected a darker, less open place, more covert in design and a tad more sophisticated in its clientele. Yet Timmy's was one of his regular spots. And it had something in common with the Alibi, the old downtown bar Michael went to. The patrons here were not too different from the guests at the parties Michael threw or the people who tended to surround him at clubs. Oh, there were the exceptions like Annette and Roberto, and others with exotic lineage or daunting looks or intriguing jobs, but the rest of them, who clung helplessly like a thicket of tiny nails to a child's magnet, and whom Michael complained about constantly, were the types who filled the Alibi and Timmy's. They—the ones who made it onto Michael's guest lists—might have had a bit more polish. They'd learned how not to look too blatantly overawed in Michael's presence. And one way or another, they'd got themselves on the invite list of the new club, Josephine's. Basically, though, they were the same. The men had the same fresh, puffy faces, and the women dressed like vamps but never quite succeeded in being other than pink-skinned and post-collegiate. And it wouldn't have been beyond a few of them to yell, "Hey, where'd you learn to walk?"

So why did Michael eat regularly at Timmy's? First, he said, it was convenient. Second, he knew the maître d' from St. Paul's, and his friend always seated him at a back corner table, one of the few tables with a degree of privacy. Third, he liked the pasta primavera and the Cajun crabcakes. But when Peter had teased him, implying that these were hardly the reasons—that he enjoyed the trek across the platforms—Michael had looked like a desperate child, became defensive, and Peter, fragile in the face of Michael's fragility, had retreated quickly, gently.

Tonight, Peter sipped his beer at a back corner table, waiting. He could see the patrons enter and leave, or cross to the bathrooms, happily tense with their high visibility. As Michael came in through the glass doors and stood talking for a minute with the maître d', Peter could sense the room's transformation. The voyeurism of the diners, always partly the delusion of the person making his entrance or exit, was now thoroughly real. As Michael approached, ascending and stepping down, stepping down and ascending, everyone was aware, almost everyone watched. People with their backs to his path twisted in their chairs. At a table of birthday celebrants whispers replaced bellowing. And Peter, waiting at the end of Michael's journey, was to be the recipient of all this importance. The open attention Michael got rarely surprised him anymore. The shock of witnessing it at close range had worn off. But the pleasure never had.

"Hey," he said, half-mumbling.

"Hey," Michael said, and thanked his friend, the maître d', who had shown him to the table.

They couldn't talk about the announcement speech Michael had gone over the night before, since there was no loud music to cover their voices, and anyway Michael seemed anxious to talk about Peter's gig. On the phone, Peter had recounted how well it had gone. He'd said he didn't know what was going to happen with anything, except that he was going up to Dean Milligan's office next week to withdraw from the law school.

And now Michael said, "Peter, really. I'm glad this thing went well for you. But I just don't know if you should make such a drastic move."

"What would be so drastic about it? I haven't set foot in a class since the second week of the semester."

"That hardly means anything." Michael laughed. "I mean, given the bullshit you got away with last year."

"True. But bullshit is a kind word for it."

"Peter."

"It's just not what I'm cut out to do."

"But how can you know that?"

"Time for a legal pep talk?"

"Peter, look. This is the last time I'll say it. After this, you're on your own."

"Thank you."

"What happens if this guy doesn't give you another gig?"

"He will."

"But what *if*, Peter? Or what if he does, and things *still* don't happen?"

"Then I'll deal with it."

"You'll just keep playing in these two-bit bars?"

"And sending out demos. And doing whatever I have to."

"And doing what to support yourself?"

"I've done it before, Michael."

"Teach guitar? Do bar mitzvahs?" Michael laughed. "Peter."

"Right."

"Hava nagilah, hava nagilah, hava n–" Michael sang quietly.

"Let's try to keep the latent anti-Semitism to a minimum," Peter tried to joke.

"I'm not being anti-Semitic. I just don't think Karina fancies herself a groupie at the Beth Israel community center."

"That's a good line, Michael. Except I don't think she fancies herself a groupie anywhere."

"You know what I'm saying."

"I might. But I don't think it's true."

"It's always true, Peter. You're the one who told me about that guy Torch. She goes after musicians. That's her m.o. And as soon as one comes along who's more successful, she'll be singing 'Goodnight, Peter.'" He let out another burst of dry laughter.

Peter shook his head, smiling faintly, straining to dismiss Michael's words. But he was struggling, dazed by this assault.

"Anyway," Michael began again softly, as if the argument were over and he wanted to point out that he had Peter's happiness in mind, "do you really want to spend your life singing 'Billie Jean' to a bunch of Jersey thirteen-year-olds?"

"No. And that's exactly the point. Because I don't think I'll have to."

"But what are you basing that confidence *on?*"

"On the fact that I'm good!" Peter almost screamed. "On the fact that I just did the best fucking concert of my life and that Bob Garavelli told me to call. Small things, Michael. Tiny fucking small things. But those are the things you have to go on."

"Okay, Peter. Okay. I guess I'm wrong."

"Okay."

"I guess I've just never thought you had the temperament to be a musician."

"And what temperament is that?"

"I don't know. Maybe you're just too normal. Too sane."

"What!"

"I don't know. I mean, musicians drive their cars into swimming pools and drown. You're a nice normal kid from Larchmont and Brooklyn Heights."

"The goddamned *Beastie Boys* come from Brooklyn Heights!"

"That's not my point."

"Well, then, what is?"

"I don't know. Maybe you're just not self-destructive enough to be a musician."

"Let me get this straight. You don't think I'm self-*destructive* enough to be a musician?"

"Sometimes I think that. Yes."

"Unbelievable. You—" But then he stopped. He didn't know what he was going to say. *You son of a bitch* or *Why are you trying to undercut me?* or *I don't need to drive my car into a swimming pool because I have you* or *Fuck off* or, weakly, *I really don't want to have anything to do with you.* It was this last, lame reply that pushed in front of the others, and so, trembling, his muscles clenching, his eyes almost watering, he made no reply at all. "You don't think I'm self-destructive enough?" he said finally, grinning painfully, still trying to make a joke of this.

"Peter, calm down."

"You want to know how self-destructive I am?"

"Peter."

"Let's go." He signaled the waitress.

"Peter, I'm sorry. Don't get all bent out of shape."

Peter put the cash under his beer glass. His eyes had watered now. It wasn't the beer glass that was blurring them. "Okay," he said. "Let's go."

"Peter, believe me."

"Let's go."

Outside, he hailed a cab. Michael protesting, they got in. And Peter told the driver to go to Chambers Street, to the end of the Brooklyn Bridge.

"Oh, Jesus, Peter."

"What's wrong? All I'm going to do is climb to the top of that tower again."

"Don't be an asshole."

"I'm not trying to be."

"Look, I'm not going to beg you not to."

"That's good. 'Cause I'm certainly not hoping you will."

"More power to you, buddy."

"Good."

"Though I really don't think this has to do with anything."

"That's right," Peter said. "It doesn't. But that's what self-destruction is all about."

The cab took the West Side Highway to Chambers Street and cut across. It was a long ride. Peter stared out the window, then leaned his head back against the seat, slouched down, and shut his eyes as if he were actually going to sleep. The night they'd climbed it the first time, he'd had a dream. It hadn't been about the bridge, but it had been the first dream he'd ever actually died in. He'd seen his body lying on some sort of dirt embankment. A tractor with a huge hoe had been coming noisily down the dirt cliff to scoop him up.

He'd woken, shaken, but not scared. He'd realized what the dream was about, and assured himself repeatedly he would never get back on that cable.

The cab stopped. They walked. The bridge was deserted. Not the car lanes, no, the tires over the steel grate gave their deep, quavery groan, but the walkway was empty. A gust lifted a littered cup and sent it clattering across the wooden slats. Another excuse. Too windy to go up there. But no, he was going.

"Having a few second thoughts?" Michael said.

They headed to where the cable intersected the walkway. As they neared it, Peter stepped quickly in front. He didn't say anything. He tried to keep his mind clear of everything except his anger, figured rage would get him up that cable fast and straight as a machine if he didn't think about anything else. Only thinking could make him fall. Only thinking could cause that dizziness. As long as he didn't think, it was just like stepping one foot in front of the other down any city street. As long as he didn't think of that dream.

Just do it, he told himself, but already he was picturing the view from up there and already his knees were trembling and it felt as if some sort of current were running along his skull, and his head seemed to be pitching repeatedly forward, into the beginnings of slow swoons. Without glancing back, he hoisted himself onto the girding between the walkway and the cable.

Okay, you're fine, you've got it, he thought, and then, thinking of Michael, he laughed. The laughter rose in powerful contractions through his chest, and as he tried to squelch it snot shot out his nose. He stifled the laughter, wiped his nostrils. He leaned forward, stepping onto the cable. He was forgetting everything, forgetting not to look down. He'd been looking down and hadn't realized it, and now he was aware; his head was tilted and his eyes were focused on the car lanes below him, the steel grate glaring a bit in the bridge's lights, the road flat and shimmering and bare for a moment before a car sped past, and so swiftly, so easily, so irretrievably, by doing almost nothing at all he could be falling, and he'd already started thinking, and forgetting, too, to ignore the groaning of the tires, and there, between the car lanes and the interior beams of the bridge, was a glimpse of water, a patch of choppy, glittery blackness that seemed to suck out his stomach and to exert some pull or pressure, making it treacherous to raise his neck and lift his eyes.

He checked the placement of his feet, the steadiness of his impossibly tight knees, the grip of his hands on the rails, and pulled his head upright. He looked up. He looked up the curving, ascending cable to the top of the tower. It was a long way.

"Fuck," he said, not moving.

"Shiiit," he said, louder, grinning over his shoulder at Michael, hoping to play this as if it hardly mattered. He *knew* it didn't.

He stepped off the cable and onto the girding. He jumped

back onto the walkway, his eyes low. His head was still light and reeling, and as it cleared he felt that if he didn't meet Michael's gaze immediately, if he didn't make himself speak right away, he was going to cry. He felt one instant from breaking down. He glanced up.

"That wouldn't have been self-destructive," he joked. "That would have been suicide."

Michael didn't laugh. He didn't crack a smile. "See, Peter," he said. "You're just a nice, normal guy after all."

Eighteen

LEE WOULD BE FLYING HOME FROM WYOMING THE FOLLOWING night, and now Peter rode the subway to Williamsburg to see Karina. Stepping up from the subway stairs to the street of defunct industry and decrepit gas stations, the shock of the poverty and calm of the place hardly registered. He thought of it fleetingly, but felt it only dimly, and when it did start to hit it wasn't as restfulness mixed with a complex sadness for the people trapped here, it was as pure depression. Walking past the fenced-in lot with the gutted Greyhound locked inside, the windows smashed, the wheels gone, and walking past the crumbling shells of warehouses and the fake brick facade of the Puerto Rican social club, he felt it was a good thing he wouldn't be coming here for a while. He felt it was a relief. This was a neighborhood of death. Not crime death or drug death, though certainly there was that too, but the death of distance. The people here were just so far removed. These hideous, becalmed streets were their entire world, and within it life seemed barely possible. The lives Peter sensed around him seemed to clot his head and to make something willed, something burdensome and aching, out of breathing the air.

He and Karina were going to talk. Just talk. Over the phone they had agreed about that. And on his own Peter had decided that this would be the last time he'd see her. Not forever. But for a while. He had to think things through. Maybe in a week he'd be back. Maybe in a week he'd decide to break off the wedding, forget Lee, forget all the arrangements that had been made and money that had been spent, forget everything, and stuff a few clothes into a sack and tie it to a stick and walk down Broadway to the subway like one of those old sketches of vagabond or runaway kids, and show up at Karina's door, and that would be that. But probably not. Ninety-nine percent he was going to get married in November. He was going to have to give that a chance. If the timing had been different, he thought, the whole situation might be different. If he'd met Karina a year ago, or six months ago, or even at the beginning of the summer, then, obviously, it would be another story. He'd have had a chance to really know her, see what they had together, and maybe he'd have had to be up front with Lee and say, Look, I think we need to spend some time apart, I'm just not sure about this. And maybe . . . who knew what would have happened then? But now he was committed. He really was. And he couldn't just give up everything he had with Lee without trying to make it work. He couldn't just throw that away. Just sidearm it out the window. Because that's what he'd be doing if he broke things off now. No way he could ever regain Lee's trust.

But if the marriage was a disaster, and if Karina hadn't found someone else . . . He almost hoped that was how it would happen. A year, six months, in less time than that they could be together. And even if things with Lee were fine, maybe he and Karina could carry on an affair, secret trysts that would go on for years. People did. Peopled lived such double lives.

For now, though, this had to be the last time he saw her. They would talk and he would say all this and he would leave. No sex. Definitely no sex. He probably shouldn't even kiss her. Just explain how he felt and go. And she had to have decided the same thing. That their relationship was futile now. She had to know that as well as he did. That it was the timing.

But he couldn't help worrying about Garavelli. What if Karina were vindictive? Even if she wasn't, as soon as she quit pushing for him, Garavelli might forget him. And he needed that second gig. But he couldn't think that way. He couldn't go on with Karina just until he got his booking. Even considering it—and he certainly did consider it—made him feel as if that was what everything boiled down to. And it wasn't. Karina had changed his life. Altered it. Given it back to him in a major way. Because even if Garavelli turned him down . . . As soon as Lee came back from Wyoming they were going to talk. He would tell her what he'd realized. And next week he would pay a visit to Dean Milligan at the law school, withdraw.

And maybe *that* was what his relationship with Karina boiled down to. What she'd shown him about himself. Somehow, between her full, restful lips and her weird, whimsical earrings, somehow she'd reminded him he could have a say in his own life. And if that sounded like a selfish reason to be half in love with someone, well, it was a good reason. And anyway that wasn't all of it. It didn't account for what he'd felt when she'd said, "I just ran the table," and did that three-quarters pirouette in the 5&7, or when, the week before last, he'd taken Tyler to the vet because Karina had to be at the bike shop. She'd given Peter her keys, and opening the police lock on her apartment door he'd felt illicit, frightened of himself. Why should she have given him her keys? How did she know

221

what he would do? She hadn't known him long enough for this. Once inside, though, his uneasiness had vanished. Tyler had skidded across the linoleum floor to greet him. "Tyler Tyler Tyler," he'd said, and stood amidst the unmade mattress on the floor, and the work table covered with taped-down newspapers and the clutter of brushes in coffee cans and crumpled paper towels and wood scraps and cups of paint and her small jigsaw, and the stripes of sunlight stretching beneath the windows, and he'd imagined this, with no small amount of longing, as home. Then he'd clipped a leash on Tyler's collar and walked him to the vet for his checkup.

So why was he putting an end to it? Turning onto Karina's block, he hardly knew.

She came downstairs to let him in, and in the dusty, dim light of the vestibule he was relieved to notice that her face looked almost jowly. She smiled, but that did nothing to distract from the fleshiness. It only creased it, giving him a glimpse of a repellent, distorted face that had been, until then, hidden from him. Returning her smile, something inside him shrank at this revelation of ugliness. He told himself to be thankful. It would make it easier to leave.

"So," she said, leading him up the stairs.

And he said, "So."

They both seemed determined to keep this scene light, to insist on the definition they'd come up with at the beginning. Careless little frolic.

She got him a beer from the fridge. She sat in one of the director's chairs whose canvas she'd once dyed and had since let become stained and flecked with paint (she never seemed to guard her work as precious, as irreplaceable or worthy of real concern); he took the other. The apartment was in its usual state of dishevelment. Her clothes were mostly draped and piled over, rather that hanging from, the portable clothes rack, and on the floor beneath it lay several crumpled colorful garments. A throw rug was visibly glazed with Tyler's pale, shed hairs. But the bed was fastidiously made. In all the times Peter had come over, it almost never had been. Its blue-and-green woven spread was now tucked neatly around the edges of the mattress, and its pillows were plumped and arranged against the wall. Peter's throat clenched. The made bed was like a closing off. He wanted the top sheet and blankets twisted and ridgy, the pillows in dented, slothful disarray. That was the sight that had usually greeted him when he'd walked into the apartment.

"So," she said, "what are we gathered here to discuss?"

"Discuss? Is discuss absolutely necessary?"

"Yes. I think it was supposed to be the theme of today's visit."

Could we just get in that bed with our clothes on and talk there? he thought about asking. He was barely above begging. There, he felt, with the covers loose around them, he would be able to speak.

It took him a while to get started. And as he did begin to say that this had to be the last time, and as she, stoically, agreed, and as he explained why, her face metamorphosed. If, in the vestibule, it had truly been heavy, jowly, it wasn't now. It was graceful around her inwardly comical, cushiony lips.

He didn't think she would let him. But he stood, lifted his chair next to hers, sat again, and kissed her. She responded only slightly, not resisting though. He slid his hand along the side of her neck, beneath her black hair.

"One last screw?" she said.

He held her by the shoulders and nearly shook her. "God, Karina, please don't say it that way."

They wound up on the bed. He would have rather stayed longer on the chairs, kissing, or remained standing an indefinite, almost endless amount of time, the two of them undressing each other slowly, but she pulled him to the bed. And once there she had no desire for holding, licking, stroking. It was as if she wanted this brutal. She rolled him off her and stood, pulling off panties and jeans together, then her shirt.

"Hey," he said, standing beside her. "Slow down."

"Why?" Her voice was perfectly flat. She lay back on the bed. "Take off your clothes."

He felt on the verge of pleading, Why are you doing this? Why are you being so cold? She lay there naked, motionless, her legs slightly apart. Stunned, saddened, bewildered, he did what she said, took off his clothes. Then he stretched out next to her, ran a finger between her breasts.

"Just fuck me."

He searched her eyes. She stared blankly, then shut them. She waited. Her legs apart and eyes shut, she waited, and he did a semi-push-up over her and shifted himself in. He slid in. Easily as ever. And then something gave way. The sense of her directing him diminished, vanished altogether. He moved slowly, and for a moment, glancing down at her chin tilted back, and hearing her murmurings and the tight, high-voiced, plaintive muttering of his name, there was a metallic blankness in his head and he sensed that he would come or was already coming, but the moment passed and he found himself above her, as if he were glimpsing her upturned jaw from an elevation greater than the actual inches, as if he were *over*hearing her quiet, clutching sounds. There was an interval of near-giddiness. There was the sense of pulling off some practical joke. He tried to lose himself as she was lost. He kissed her hard, hoped to black his mind, feel it reeling as if into a cavern behind her mouth. He tried to concentrate on his feelings for her. He pictured the moments he'd recalled earlier—her pirouette in the 5&7, his taking Tyler to the vet, her saying, "I'm in the fast lane of arts 'n' crafts"—and briefly the memories brought on a glimmer of orgasmic sensations. Mostly, though, they made him feel a great swelling of tenderness. To come, finally, he had to imagine himself with a succession of women, including a bat girl he'd recently seen on the NBC Game of the Week.

Afterward, Karina drew her finger across his chest in quick, sweeping lines.

"What exactly are you doing?" he asked.

"Sketching Tyler's face on your chest," she said. "Giving you an invisible T-shirt." And, a minute later, "Maybe you should just stay here."

"Until when?"

"What would your betrothed think when she found that you had vanished?"

"Don't know."

"Lee Abigail Holt. She wouldn't know where to find you."

"No, she wouldn't."

"And Michael."

"You know—"

"Michael Marr."

Silence.

"They wouldn't know where to look for their little Peter," she said.

"You know, why don't you stop before I tell you to fuck off?"

"Mmm."

They were quiet.

"It was a good idea, though," he offered.

"Let's start again," she said. "I'll redo my sketch." She dragged her forearm across his chest, erasing.

She began to sketch, as if this were any idle afternoon. When the phone rang, she paused, then stood to get it.

"It's for you," she said.

"Hello?"

"Hey."

"What's up?"

"Well, I hate to do this to you."

Michael had a favor he needed done, and Peter had said he could call him at Karina's, if Michael couldn't find anyone else to do it.

"I really don't know about this."

"Peter, you said I could call if it came down to it."

"You couldn't get Becker?"

"He has to work."

"Well, then, tell him to leave."

"Peter, the guy can barely hold a job as it is."

"Then tell him to go tonight."

"He can't. She's leaving at four."

"And you couldn't get anyone else?"

"Peter, at this point I can't get just anyone. I can't *trust* just anyone."

"What about Roberto?"

"Peter, believe me. I wouldn't be calling you if I could help it. I know this is a bad time. If you can't do it, I understand."

"Shit."

"You could go and come back. Her place is right on Twelfth Street. You could take the LL across and be back in Williamsburg in an hour."

"Not exactly."

"Why? I don't see why you can't do that."

"Well, then, think it through."

"Okay, Peter. Okay. You're right. I'm sorry. You're right."

Peter said nothing.

"Seriously. I know. I'm out of line."

"No."

"Okay. I'll let you go. I'll see you tomorrow. Okay?"

"No. Just give me the address."

"No, Peter, seriously—"

"Just give me the address."

"Peter, I don't want—"

"Okay. Okay. Calm down. Just tell me where she lives if you want me to get there before four."

226

All during this conversation Karina had been lying on her back on the bed, where Peter could see her. As with the shape of her face, which had seemed to transform itself earlier, it would be impossible to say what exactly her expression was as she lay there. It may have been perfectly neutral. But what he saw was a paroxysm of rolled eyes and disparaging exhales through slightly parted lips. What he saw was an insinuating child who refused to understand the truth about his friendship with Michael. Now, as he hung up, she was half dressed (in jeans and a bra) and pretending to search through the drawers of her work table. Pretending. She was like an insidious kid who taunts and taunts and then hides behind a wall of innocence.

"So Michael knew where to find his little serf after all," she said.

And the incredible thing about what happened next was that he thought about it first. Amidst all the rage that swarmed in on him, he had a conscious thought, a clear image, a full moment's awareness of his impulse, and no voice came in to dissuade him. Then he hit her. Backhanded, loose-fisted, he struck her eye.

He was screaming, pleading, horrified almost before he'd done it, a series of tight, twisted words.

"I'm fine." Her voice was rigid.

He put out his hands in a half-paralyzed gesture to hold her face, but she took a step back.

"You should go," she said.

"No no no no please. I'm sorry. I'm so sorry. Just let me touch you. Just let me touch you. I can't go like this. Please."

"You can do whatever you want."

"No!"

But that was what their goodbye was like, he placing stiff, cautious arms around a body that felt inanimate.

Nineteen

THE FAVOR MICHAEL HAD ASKED WAS, IN ITSELF, NOT MOMENTOUS. He was throwing a small party the next night, and he wanted, for himself and his guests, a supply of ecstasy, the drug that had recently replaced cocaine. Cocaine had become too dangerous and too democratic—people were dying from it and altogether too many people were doing it. The notion of snorting lines had become crass. It had lost its cachet.

Of course, Michael and his crowd were hardly the first to swallow pills of ecstasy. And soon the use of it would seem too widespread. Anyone talking about the night they'd just spent on "E" would elicit a twinge of revulsion. But for a certain period of time, for Michael and his friends, to take the drug was to feel they were among a knowledgeable and illicit few.

Strangely, the reputed effects of the drug (a combination of amphetamine and mild hallucinogen) didn't have much to do with exclusivity. That is, ecstasy was supposed to make you feel open, generous, friendly, free. As Lee had said once, to one of the poor uninitiated, "It makes you want everyone in the room to put their arms around each other and just talk the night away. It's like the sixties in a pill."

In any case, this is what Michael had asked Peter to pick up. For his dealer's sake as well as his own, Michael couldn't go himself. Too much attention surrounded his comings and goings. And especially now that he was on the verge of running for office, there was no way he would risk getting caught. In fact, he planned to forswear drugs completely after this one night.

So, as the party began to thicken, inevitably, beyond the small gathering Michael had intended, Peter arrived with Lee. Just an hour earlier, she'd returned from her shoot in Wyoming. Peter had the pills, and got to dispense them to the privileged among Michael's guests. Semi-secretively, he handed them to Roberto and Annette, and to about a dozen others, and he called Glickstein into the hall and gave him one. He felt fairly virtuous about this last gesture, since Glickstein hadn't been counted in and was trying to look unconcerned about what a select third of the party was doing.

And the drug started to travel through bloodstreams and brains. It did evoke talkativeness and a degree of generosity. For instance, Roberto and Annette sat happily with Glickstein, on whom they generally practiced their postures of exotic scorn. Peter joined them.

Annette said, "Oh, my God, Peter, it was dreadful. He's still extremely good-looking, but he had this 'Stepin Fetchit' smile on his face. It was dreadful. He said, 'Don't worry, I'll find a safe place for this pup.' And when we came out of the restaurant he went jogging off for the car in his valet suit and came driving back with the 'Stepin Fetchit' smile on his face, and we didn't know what he wanted us to tip him, a hundred dollars or nothing. It was dreadful."

"So is he still trying to act?" Peter asked.

"I guess so."

"Hoo boy," Peter said.

And a while later, Peter told them about running into Barry Lieberman on the street.

"Poor you," Annette offered.

The commiseration made him hesitate a swift instant. He didn't want to catch himself sharing too many of her opinions. But he wanted to tell the story. He said, "Protesting for abortion rights. Standing outside Saint Patrick's with one of these counter-demonstrations. It was frightening. This mass of people waving wire hangers in the air and screaming 'You are the murderers!' into the church. And there was Barry screaming away, and not only waving his wire hanger but wearing a sandwich board with this poster of a woman sprawled out and bleeding in some alley, and I mean this poster was seriously graphic, and I'm standing there trying to talk to him while he's wearing this thing. I mean, I tried to slip by, but he saw me and quit screaming to say hello, and then he started trying to convince me to get on his side of the barricade. And I'm like, Barry, I'm with you on this one, but I really don't think so. So he gets this look on his face, and he says, 'See this?' And he points to the mangled woman on his chest. 'You killed her.' And I'm like, Barry, take it easy. 'You are a murderer!' And I'm like, Barry, I think it's time for me to go now. So then he starts screaming down the street at me while I'm walking away! 'You killed this woman, Peter. You killed this woman!' And I'm like, Barry, Barry, can't we try a little discretion here?"

The story was a great success. It drew peals of laughter, and Annette said, "Oh, that's priceless, Peter. That's priceless!" After which Glickstein reported that he'd spoken to Frazier Black, and that the bakery Frazier had talked about opening for five years had failed within two months. The details of the failure amused everyone, and, in the communal spirit of ecstasy, Glickstein, too, got his moments of appreciation.

* * *

Gradually, though, the drug wore off, and it was as his head cleared into a thick, sluggish, yet still pleasant state that Peter walked down the hallway toward the back of the apartment. Someone was in the front bathroom, and he was going to use Michael's.

Of course, he did this with none of the trepidation he'd felt two years ago, when he'd ended up meeting Michael for the first time. Now his friend's apartment was practically his own. He felt that comfortable here. Entering through the marble-tiled vestibule, sitting beneath the living room's high, sculpted ceiling, standing on the balcony overlooking Central Park, he felt a grace that gave him the sensation of being observed, of being admired, envied. Even when there was no one around except Michael to see him, and even when there was no one at all, he felt watched in this way. Sitting on the couch—watched. Putting a record on the stereo—watched. Getting himself a beer and going back to the bar for an opener—watched. His body seemed both to swell and rest, and he felt utterly comfortable within it. "Peter, how do you work this VCR?" someone might ask, or "Does he have any shot glasses?" and as he explained or went to help, his voice or the way he pulled himself off the couch would have a sensual nonchalance.

Now, with this grace, he walked down the blue-carpeted hallway. He turned into the empty bedroom. A table lamp had been left on. The stereo blared loudly. He stepped past the low Danish bureau with the photographs of Michael and his father, Michael and his father and mother, Michael and various cousins, and by the low platform bed with the simple blue comforter. The bathroom door was shut. He knocked. No answer. He knocked again, harder. Nothing. But the music was loud. He turned the knob and opened the door only an inch, just in case. There was no one inside.

He pulled the door closed behind him and was alone. Taking his piss, and afterward, he was mesmerized by surfaces. Perhaps it was the lingering effect of the drug or the effect of coming down off it. Perhaps it was the sudden solitude away from the party. Anyway, he stared and thought almost nothing. He focused on the patterns in the wallpaper, on the crisscrossing slats of a wooden basket jammed with magazines, and, as he leaned back against the door, on his own face in the mirror above the sink. His features might have formed some soothing grid, a visual mantra. They evoked no reaction. He just stared.

Several minutes went by before he turned to leave, and he'd taken two steps into the bedroom before he saw Michael on the bed. It was as if the volume of the stereo obscured Peter's vision—even as he noticed Michael he didn't really see him; his friend's body seemed to be on another plane, merely another surface. There was an instant when he could have walked right past it. But then it registered—Michael's bare shoulders, a corner of his face—and the next thing he glimpsed, or that hit him consciously, was peripheral—the gold buttons of Lee's jacket on the carpet nearby. These were followed by her breast in his mouth, half her face, her head twisting, her breast pushed upward by his lips and hand, the base of her throat, her mouth open, tense, her jaw tight. . . . And neither of them knew he was there.

So many times he'd imagined this, catching them cold like this or finding out they'd been like this, and for every scene of betrayal he'd conjured he'd pictured a dozen times that many versions and repetitions of the violence that followed—his taking a swing with a length of lead pipe into Michael's teeth; his grabbing a fistful of Michael's hair and ramming his forehead into the mantel above the living-room fireplace; his slipping a finger quickly into Michael's mouth and jamming it down into the soft tender tissue beneath his tongue; Michael saying "You're not really going to try and fight me, are you?" and his saying "Maybe you should have thought this through" or "No, Michael, a fight involves two people and this is going to be over too quickly to involve you" and then lifting the pipe from where he'd held it hidden behind him; his thrusting Michael's face through a pane of glass; his gripping Michael's hair at the base of his skull and pounding his forehead into the hard ridgy white marble edge of the mantel above the fireplace; his pressing his finger deep into that sensitive tissue beneath Michael's tongue until he nearly passed out, then removing the finger and taking one clean uppercut snapping Michael's jaw; his swinging the pipe before Michael could react, cracking half his teeth, then walking out, one single harshly punitive swing.

Where had he been as he pictured these batterings? In his office at Walker, Gottlieb, in his carrel in the law school library, in bed when he couldn't sleep, long ago with his guitar when he couldn't write, anyplace where he'd imagined the possibility of Michael with Lee, even in something less than full-on sex, just kissing deeply. . . . He didn't know how he would deal with Lee, and he never thought much about it, but about what he would do to Michael he could dwell a solid hour and could have gone on endlessly if he hadn't stopped himself.

Here in the bedroom, though, glimpsing them together and standing maybe ten feet from them, no such assault entered his mind. His one thought of stopping them was that Michael still wasn't inside her, that they were still half clothed, that saying anything, doing anything, making them aware of him in any way would cut this off before they went further. The thought was lucid and swift. It was like the sudden idea of hitting Kurina that had come to him before he'd actually done it, and that no internal voice had rushed in to contravene. But the recognition that he could make them quit led to nothing. It brought an instant of utter paralysis. He stepped out of the bedroom and walked straight to the apartment's front door.

"Peter, where are you going?" Annette called.

He didn't answer.

He didn't know where he was going. But he went home. And an hour or two later, Lee followed. She found him on the bed, motionless, his hands resting low on his chest, the fingers overlapping. He glanced over and their eyes met. She said nothing. At the foot of the bed, with deliberation, she dropped her jacket with the gold buttons on the floor.

Her gaze steady, she reached beneath her silk blouse. She unsnapped her bra and slid out of its straps. She smiled politely. The silk sloped to her nipples before falling as abruptly as a tablecloth. She unlaced his sneakers and pulled off his socks. She licked along his insteps and ankles. Catching her dangling forelock of blond hair along the curve between forefinger and thumb, she dragged it back.

She worked her way up, with hands and mouth, to his crotch, and had his pants crumpled across his thighs, and it would be impossible to describe how badly he wanted to grab beneath her arms and pull her body over him, knees to knees, chest to chest, all her weight directly on him, her tongue fully, unflickingly, ungracefully against his. Or to hold her breasts, her nipples lightly at the centers of his palms. He did neither. He couldn't force his hands to move.

"I just want you to know," she said softly, "that was the only time that's happened."

And again he saw the gold buttons on the carpet in Michael's bedroom, again Michael plying her breast, her knee lifted as if to fence Michael in, keep him there, her lips apart, her throat long, her chin turning and tipping back.

She resumed kissing Peter's testicles and the base of his

cock, and she might have been dangling a slight yet uncrossable distance above him. She seemed out of reach.

Then she stood and turned toward the bureau at the foot of the bed. She lifted her skirt—pantyhose, nothing under them—and, facing him again, she held a pair of nail scissors, small, silver, curving.

"Lee, what—?"

She was going to stab through her belly, stab through her—

She didn't seem to hear. Her skirt pinned up against her elbow, she plucked the gauze of her pantyhose between her fingers and jabbed through with the point of the scissors. She cut a narrow revelatory strip in the fabric. Finished, she smiled, as if to say, What did you think I was going to do?

She replaced the scissors on the bureau and slowly shifted over him, kneeling and straddling him. She bent him toward her and pressed him a half inch in. She was too constricted to take him deeper. For a minute she fucked just that much of him; she pushed down further by stages. And in this way, suspended above him, their noncontact tangible and excruciating, she brought him carefully toward coming. Nearing it, and in the throes of it, and after it, he was in total eclipse.

Twenty

IT WAS KARINA WHO HELPED SAVE HIM, SPARE HIM, AS IF BY releasing a trap door. She abetted his escape, let him do what he needed.

Not that he ever saw Karina again. Not that they ever spoke. Rather, it was his recollection of her, the fact of her in his past, that gave him license. He needed to love Lee.

And when, the morning after Michael's party, and during the days that followed, Lee stunned Peter with the violence with which she begged his forgiveness (for there were moments when he felt ready to leave, and she believed he would), he was able, by stages, to give it. At one point, she jabbed her forehead repeatedly against the molding of the bedroom door, as if to obliterate emotion with physical pain. Beneath the dull pounding, he imagined hearing, not quite the sound of her skull cracking, but a shifting, a relenting, of bone. He rushed out of bed to stop her. And perhaps, even as he held her, his hand over her forehead as if to protect or heal it, coaxing, "Lee

Lee Lee Lee Lee. Okay . . . it's okay," perhaps even then he doubted her reasons. Certainly he had doubted them before. He had questioned them to himself only hours ago. Why was she so afraid of his leaving? Now that she'd slept with Michael, why didn't she just go after him completely? Wasn't it because she knew Michael wasn't interested, that she didn't mean much to him, that Peter, close to Michael as he was, was the nearest she could get? Hadn't it always been about that? That Peter was the best she could do? From that first night at P.S. 5. Wasn't that it?

But no. No, it wasn't. Not all of it. For as Peter stood, palm and fingers pressing against her forehead, he felt she was crying for a confusion of things she could never communicate clearly, things she herself could no longer comprehend but only felt; she seemed to be sobbing for the very fact that there were things they didn't and would never understand about each other, and hearing and watching and touching her, he, too, ached for the impossibility of understanding. And the space of incomplete knowledge between them affected his body like a warning, but also as something poignant. The aching of inevitable distance struck him as a kind of love.

And maybe, in fact, it was.

In any case, the time he'd spent with Karina helped him to stay with Lee. Because hadn't he, too, been unfaithful? When at last he declared his infidelity (which he'd resisted doing, not wanting to diminish the memory by confessing it), Lee seemed to realize that he wouldn't leave her after all. At first, she was staggered, even disbelieving (she pressed him for details—most of which he would not give—as if to prove he'd made it up), then worried and jealous, but soon she grew giddy with relief. "You had an affair," she said, bewildered. And thankful.

Later, she asked what he would do about Michael.

"I don't know," he said, but tersely, harshly.

* * *

And indeed he was harsh with his friend, and Michael was bitterly, almost cruelly, hard on himself. They met in the park, and as they walked Michael was in an agony of self-accusation. He called himself all kinds of damning things, and expressed worse with his eyes, and bluntly Peter agreed with him, impassively Peter said it was all true. Once, Michael tried to slide out from the blame he'd covered himself with, and which Peter refused to lift from him. Michael said he hadn't known what he was doing, and that neither had Lee; he blamed it on the ecstasy they'd taken. But Peter said no. He stood in front of Michael and half-seethed, half-wailed it, struggling to stay calm, to keep his dignity. "No!"

And Michael backed away, returned, severely, to self-condemnation.

Eventually, though, it was Peter who did the final backing off. "Michael," he said sharply, wanting to take things much, much further, to point out that what had happened with Lee was only one of his friend's insidious failures, to peel away the self-delusions. Michael gazed at him with eyes as diffuse as the dusk air. He seemed utterly helpless. He seemed to have placed his life in Peter's hand; and how could Peter crush it?

Peter told him to stop, to just stop talking, and they left the park in silence.

But of course, it wasn't only a rush of sympathy that kept him from thoroughly attacking his friend. For though Peter didn't understand them at that moment, weren't there other reasons for maintaining Michael as he was? And didn't Peter feel a hint of them even now, at this angriest of times, as they turned onto Central Park West? For people walked by them on the wide, lantern-lit sidewalk, and wasn't he walking with Michael Marr? And wasn't that something, even if, in his mind, he denied it meant much at all? Didn't he *feel* it? Like a warm collar turned up around his neck? Didn't it suffuse his shoulders and loosen his hands? Didn't it enter his lungs with the air he breathed, and fill them secretly, exquisitely? And didn't it seem to change the actual weather, to alter the edges of the autumn wind, as if early May, not late November, were next in line?

Oh, yes, it was something, something beautiful, in a way, and didn't it make him feel blessed?

Two weeks later, Peter stood behind the press crew in the ballroom of the Sheraton Hotel. "A quarter century ago," Michael said, quietly, humbly, gravely from the stage of the hushed ballroom, "my father was elected President. He was never able to serve the country that had given him its confidence." Michael's voice rose. "He was never able to help us realize our vast promise as a nation. He was never able to help us fulfill our vast potential as people. He was never able to help us toward goodness of heart and greatness of achievement. But today"—he paused—"I hope to do my small part to make up for our shared loss. Today I hope to make all of our lives easier, and harder, in the way my father intended. Easier because we will lend each other our support. And harder because we will not turn away from the challenges we meet. Today I am asking for your confidence. Because a year from now, when Roy Kramer retires from the seat in which he has so admirably served, I hope to represent our district in the Congress of our United States. . . ."

And the following Saturday, in Lee's church on Fifth Avenue, Peter was married. He was still very much in law school. At least, he was in it the way he'd always been, going to a minimum of classes, doing a minimum of work. He would get by. He was smart enough, and his classmates were helpful enough. His grades would be around the middle of his class, good enough to be hired back by Walker, Gottlieb, or, if not, to get an offer from one of the city's other large firms.

As for his music, well, one of his acoustic guitars had a fairly prominent place in his and Lee's living room. It rested on a stand beside a small bookshelf. The stand was of the type used on concert stages. So it might have seemed the guitar was constantly being played. In fact, it had the look of an ornament. It had recently been polished, and it was tilted at a few very particular degrees, and it was turned at a certain angle to the bookshelf and the wall, like a sculpture carefully positioned within the decor of the room.

His other guitars were wedged onto the top shelf of a closet.

He'd never called Garavelli.

And so he stood at the altar in the Fifth Avenue church, between Lee, his bride, and Michael, his best man.